HEY, ROOMIE!

The Fractured Soul Saga: Book Two

Ametra S. Rayford

Cover typography and layout by Arrayed Formats™

This book is a work of fiction. Names, characters, places, and incidents are either products of the author's imagination or are inspired by actual events and used fictitiously. Any resemblance to actual persons, living or dead, is intentional and presented as fictionalized for the purposes of this story.

ISBN: 978-1-7370148-4-3

Published by Arrayed Formats™

DEDICATION

To the masters of mayhem, the architects of chaos, and the virtuosos of villainy whose real-life antics inspired this tale: Thanks for the material, you unwitting muses. May your deeds remain confined to these pages.

PROLOGUE

Reality

Michael Cavanaugh set the tumbler of bourbon down on the sleek marble table, his fingers lingering on the cool glass. The quiet drone of the heating vents filled the luxury suite, a low hum beneath the sound of snow tapping against the balcony's glass doors.

The suite was a haven of modern abundance. Textured walls in muted gray and taupe framed the space, anchored by a king-sized bed dressed in crisp white linens and furniture that radiated understated opulence. A wall of windows reaching the ceiling stretched across one side, showcasing a breathtaking view of the snow-covered city. The balcony extended just beyond, its frosted railings faintly visible through the glass. A grand piano occupied one corner, its polished surface reflecting the soft glow of the minimalist chandelier above.

On another night, the setting might have felt like a refuge. But tonight, it only made the room feel colder, shrinking with every passing moment.

He rubbed his temples, his dark hair falling over his fingers. His phone, sitting on the nightstand, buzzed for the third time in as many minutes. Chelsia. He didn't have to check the screen to know. The warmth of her earlier messages echoed in his mind—reminders of the meal she'd been planning for weeks, a surprise she'd hinted at without fully revealing. Tomorrow marked their one-year anniversary. A year that, despite his usual pattern, had been a good one.

Yet tonight, Chelsia wasn't the one sitting across from him.

With legs crossed, his guest reclined in the armchair, her raven hair framing her pale face like ink on paper. Her eyes—piercing, as if charged with an otherworldly light—were fixed on him, unblinking, relentless. She was the storm within this room, a cold pressure that threatened to break him.

"You've hardly said a word," she remarked with an edge to her tone. "Am I supposed to apologize for wanting to see you?"

Michael's jaw clenched. "You followed me here. You flew across the country without telling me and then just popped up out of nowhere. What did you expect me to say?"

She shrugged, her long black trench coat shifting with the movement. "I wanted to surprise you. I thought you'd be happy."

"Happy?" He let out a dry laugh and got up, pacing toward the window. Outside, the streets were eerily quiet, the snow muffling the usual chaos of downtown Portland. "How am I supposed to be happy about this? This is an ambush. You know... you know what tomorrow is."

The woman's lips curved into a smile, though it lacked warmth.

"Chelsia's big anniversary dinner?" she asked, her voice dripping with mock sweetness. "Don't pretend that's important, Michael. We both know she's just... a phase."

Michael turned to face her, his blue eyes narrowing. "Don't. Don't do that."

"What? Tell the truth?" She stood, approaching slowly. Her presence filled the room like a shadow, refusing to fade. "Look, maybe I've made mistakes. I'm here now, though. I'm ready. I want us—*us*—to work."

He shook his head, stepping away from her. "You don't get to just show up and say that. After everything—"

"After everything," she interrupted, her voice sharp now, "we deserve a real shot. No more casual flings. I want forever with you."

Her words hung in the air, suspended and fragile. Michael's chest tightened. Memories of their volatile past—the hiding, the fights, the passion, the apologies that never quite stuck—flashed in his mind. He thought of Chelsia's laughter, her unshakable optimism, and the way she'd carefully planned their anniversary, down to the wine pairing and a dessert she'd been perfecting for weeks. And yet... the presence of the woman in his suite stirred something deep and complicated inside him, a pull he couldn't deny.

She stepped closer, her trench coat shifting to reveal the bodice of a simple black dress. She reached for the belt, loosening it in a fluid motion before letting the coat fall to the floor. Beneath the dress, which clung to her skin, a shimmer of lace hinted at something calculated.

"I'm done waiting for you to figure this out," she breathed, her voice a dangerous mixture of vulnerability and seduction. "We both know you can't resist me. You never could."

"Look—" Michael started, his voice hoarse. She silenced him with a single finger pressed to his lips.

"Stop fighting it," she whispered. "Stop fighting me."

Her hand moved to his collar, brushing against his neck, and Michael froze. It was as if the cold seeped into his skin, battling with the heat of her touch. His breathing quickened, his resolve weakening under the weight of her proximity.

For a moment—just a moment—he let his eyes close, the memory of their past colliding with the reality of the present. Her scent, her presence, the intensity of her focus—it was intoxicating. He hated her for it. He hated himself more.

When he opened his eyes, she was closer than ever, her lips a breath away from his.

The phone buzzed again, as if louder this time, demanding his attention. Michael jerked back, stepping away from her and toward the nightstand. His heart pounded as he grabbed the phone, not even looking at the screen.

"Answer it," the woman said, her voice laced with quiet triumph, "and tell her you're with me."

Reflection

Though the morning started with the promise of sunny skies, the horizon had shifted beneath menacing dark clouds that made it appear to be much later in the day than it was.

The foreboding sky seemed a fitting backdrop for the somber occasion as Michael, renowned violinist and one-third of the group Tourists of Dreams, played softly with his group—Devin Early on the piano and Joran Talbert on the cello—as the unseasonable rain pounded against the windows. Even the heavens seemed to grieve the loss of the woman they had all come to pay their respects to.

A pang of guilt plagued Michael as he played. He didn't know Lavinia Blake. He hadn't even heard of her until Joran told the group about the request made by Lavinia's husband, Edmund. The Blakes were, apparently, great fans of the group and intended to see several of their shows during their current tour when Mrs. Blake suddenly fell ill.

Edmund Blake had come to Joran personally, likely because he was the leader of Tourists of Dreams, to ask that the group play at the memorial. Joran was only too happy to agree for whatever reason. It surely couldn't have been because of the rather hefty sum of money that Blake offered, especially since Joran didn't take a cent. Instead, he divided it between Michael and Devin.

That Joran could be a weird one.

Michael shook his head, trying to clear his mind. This was not the time or place to be thinking of money. He needed to focus on the music, on honoring the memory of the woman who had touched so many lives.

As the notes of the mournful piece drifted through the church, Michael's mind wandered yet again. He'd been hiding something from the rest of the group for months and wondered whether it could end up blowing up in his face. Michael wanted to tell them. He especially wanted to talk with Joran about it; however, he could never quite muster the courage to do so.

At first, Michael thought it was because Joran was still so invested... so affected by the recent disintegration of his marriage. Though he and Katherine hadn't been married for very long, theirs was a very passionate coupling. Katherine was six foot one inch of wavy raven hair, skin with a lustrous pearlescent sheen, and colorless eyes that made her seem almost otherworldly.

At six-foot four, Joran Talbert was lanky yet strong, with golden blond curls and green eyes.

Together, they were visually stunning. Emotionally, they were a mismatched disaster. By the time Katherine walked out on him, the change in Joran was clear. Physically, his once-toned frame withered beneath the weight of grief. The vibrancy in those green eyes, previously a reflection of shared dreams, dimmed to a haunted emptiness. His shoulders, formerly squared with confidence, now stooped under the burden of fractured vows.

For weeks, he was a shell of the man they once knew. Neither Michael nor Devin knew how he'd survive the tour that he'd insisted they undertake. Music had always provided an escape for one or another of them over time, so they went with it. The money they stood to make also helped.

To the combined surprise and relief of both Michael and Devin, Joran gradually rebounded in spectacular fashion. The slump in his shoulders straightened, as if the heaviness of the past had lifted, and his gait carried the confident cadence of renewed hope. He was a portrait of joy reborn, not just the Joran that they once knew—somehow stronger and more energetic.

The spark in Joran's eyes, dulled by past disappointments, reignited with a flame of passion and connection, and one day he finally confided in both Devin and Michael the reason... and the name of the woman responsible.

Michael stirred in his sleep, a thin line of sweat on his brow as he frowned. He remained in the clutches of the dream, and he could still see himself playing at the funeral of Lavinia Blake all those months ago. Michael couldn't remember the name of the woman with whom Joran had found love. He couldn't remember what she looked like, even though he'd stolen several glimpses of her as she sat at the back of the church in a lovely black dress and then later, when the service had ended and Joran took a moment to talk with her. Michael knew with everything in him, she was breathtaking. Trying to recall any aspect of her visage seemed impossible.

As Michael Cavanaugh struggled in slumber, he could only remember two things.

He remembered how desperate he was to figure out when it would be a good time to tell Joran what had gone on behind his back... and that, before he could do so, Joran Talbert left Tourists of Dreams and disappeared.

Return

"I guess I'll have to tell her myself."

Michael looked into the wide, deeply set eyes of the beauty that lay beside him in the plush king-sized bed. She was long and lean, her body chiseled in some places and deliciously curved in others. Her hair, despite being mussed and slightly damp from recent exertions, framed her oval face in dark, silky waves as she gazed at him through resplendent eyes.

He reached over to caress her cheek as the gravity of their conversation took shape.

"No," he said firmly. "I told you I'd take care of it."

"Really?" she replied, her eyes flashing with an intensity that made Michael catch his breath. Despite the tension in their conversation, the energy between them stirred something primal within him. He snaked an arm around her waist to pull her closer. She briefly surrendered to his nuzzling before extracting herself from his grip. "When? How much longer am I supposed to wait?"

"Come on, Katherine," Michael said, smoothing back a lock of her dark hair. "Why the sudden change of heart, hmm? This is how it's been for ages. I wanted only you from the beginning! You said that it would look suspicious to Joran if I was never with anyone, so I started seeing other people."

"That hardly matters now," she interrupted with a roll of those glorious eyes. "Joran Talbert is old news, so he shouldn't be living rent-free in your head anymore." Katherine chuckled, though there was no mirth in it. "He tucked tail and scurried out of town, leaving you and Devin to pick up the pieces of the group while he dawdled in regret and self-pity."

Michael said nothing. There was nothing to gain by arguing, and Katherine seemed to relish the idea of Joran in decline. His thoughts wandered back to the dream he'd had during the night and the months leading up to Joran's abrupt departure from their lives.

It was true that Joran initially dangled on the precipice of despair after Katherine left him. Michael never shared with her how Joran had rebounded, finding solace and joy in someone else. He'd always known that detail would wound her pride more deeply than any betrayal ever could.

References to Joran's mysterious new love crept into conversations during the last days of Tourists of Dreams, though Joran never divulged much.

What little Michael had seen of her—mostly from a distance—had been enough to make an impression, even if her face remained frustratingly elusive in his memories. It was clear from Joran's demeanor that his adoration of the mystery woman had surpassed anything he'd ever experienced with Katherine, something Michael knew Katherine would find offensive.

Thoughts of Joran and his enigmatic paramour haunted Michael, unsettling him in ways he struggled to articulate. Even now, with Joran long gone and the group functioning as a duo, those memories lingered.

"Are you even listening to me?" Katherine's voice broke through his reverie, snapping him back to the present.

"What?" Michael blinked, focusing on her.

"We're not done talking about that little girl you need to dump," she said, her tone icy.

"She's not a little girl," Michael shot back. He exhaled, closing his eyes briefly. "This hasn't been easy. I wasn't... I wasn't expecting this to happen. She knows something is wrong. I keep telling her it's only about the tour, but..."

Katherine arched a perfect brow. "But nothing. Fix it, Michael. I mean it. I don't care how you do it. It just needs to be done."

"And if it's not?" he asked, his voice low, almost defiant.

Katherine leaned closer, her eyes glowing with an unsettling mix of satisfaction and menace.

"The last thing you want is for the three of us to end up in the same room together. It wouldn't end well... I can promise you that."

ASHES

CHAPTER ONE

November's icy breath coated the streets of Portland, Oregon, with frost, snowflakes dancing and disappearing as the morning sun rose. The chill seeped into every crack and crevice, forcing those who braved the outdoors to bundle up against it.

Inside the cozy pharmacy on Hawthorne and 12th Street, the frigid weather had no power. Warm air swirled through the space, carrying the scent of antiseptic and the rustle of paper bags being filled with prescription orders.

Chelsia Toussaint stood behind the counter, her fingers flying over the keyboard as she worked. Her deep chocolate eyes flicked up to survey the area, taking in the neatly stocked shelves and the drone of the refrigerator storing temperature-sensitive items.

She noticed her coworker, Moira Bevins, efficiently packing medication into small white bags for pickup. When Gillian Falconeri's voice interrupted her concentration, she snapped to attention.

"Chelsia, can you check our inventory for Mr. Crawford's medication? I forgot to make sure we have enough for his appointment tomorrow, and if we need more, I want to know now," Gillian said in her soft yet commanding tone.

"Absolutely, Gillian," Chelsia responded with a smile.

Gillian, owner of Falconeri's Apothecary, had been a fixture in the neighborhood for decades, her presence as colorful as the pharmacy itself. Beneath a crisp white lab coat, she sported a floral scarf in vivid magentas and greens, which clashed spectacularly with the oversized bow perched atop her bleached-blonde hair. Her fashion sense—a garish hybrid of Aunt Pittypat's

Southern charm and Baby Jane Hudson's theatrical eccentricity—always made an impression. Her flushed cheeks and carmine lipstick completed the look.

Behind the lace, colorful petticoats, and oversized bows, Gillian Falconeri was one of the most skilled pharmacists in town.

Falconeri's Apothecary had been a staple in the Hawthorne district for over a century, with a reputation for personalized care, fair prices, and a wide selection of homeopathic remedies. Despite its weekday-only hours, the community valued it, often preferring it to larger chain pharmacies.

The pharmacy's brick exterior stood proudly on the corner, with its vibrant green door welcoming customers seeking refuge from the cold. Within, it was a welcoming haven rather than a store. Antique shelves lined the walls, displaying an array of carefully labeled tinctures and ointments beside more well-known and commercially made products. Potted plants added a touch of warmth to the space as they sat on windowsills, filtering the harsh winter light that poured through the glass.

Chelsia moved into the storage room, where the cluttered rows of shelving formed a labyrinth of mismatched containers, half-empty boxes, and bottles strewn without rhyme or reason. Finding what she needed always took a little longer than it should, but she had long since accepted that organization wasn't a priority here.

Scanning each label, she found what she was looking for. Retrieving the bottle, she moved to one of the counting tables and reached for nitrile gloves, snapping them on before opening it.

Counting the stock, her mind drifted briefly to Michael. Tomorrow marked their one-year anniversary, and a flicker of warmth settled in her chest. An entire year. It felt like something worth celebrating—something steady, something certain. She exhaled, snapped the bottle shut, and tucked it under her arm, letting the quiet hum of the storage room settle her nerves before she returned to the counter.

"We've got plenty of the medication, Gillian," Chelsia announced as she returned to the counter, tossing the gloves into the trash. Her eyes met Moira's before both women looked away.

"Thank you, Chelsia," Gillian replied with a kind smile, her soft blue eyes crinkling at the corners. "I knew I could count on you."

Chelsia couldn't help returning Gillian's smile as she reflected on the incredible things yet to come. Tomorrow would be wonderful—it had to be. But somewhere in the back of her mind, a thought stirred, as fleeting and sharp as an icy wind through a cracked window. She pushed it aside and focused on the warmth of the moment instead.

CHAPTER TWO

Chelsia sat at the break room table, her thoughts drifting as she looked through the small window overlooking the alley. The frost on the glass sparkled in the winter light.

A pang of nostalgia washed over her, drawing her to the day she first arrived in the city. She hadn't planned to stay long when she stepped off the bus outside Union Station on that overcast April afternoon. Life, she thought, would continue as it always had, with no family, no close friends, just the occasional temp job and a room rented week by week. Within a month, however, what was temporary had quietly turned into something more.

Portland had a way of pulling her in. Maybe it was the quiet rhythm of the city, the way the mist settled over the Willamette River each morning, or the unassuming charm of its neighborhoods. Or simply that work was steady enough and the modest paychecks felt like a step toward stability.

One morning, the temp agency sent her to Falconeri's Apothecary as an inventory clerk and occasional cashier. She told herself she'd leave once she saved enough. Fate had other plans.

Surviving one day at a time made it easier to stay than to leave. Starting over somewhere else felt daunting, even with her savings slowly growing. In Portland, she wasn't happy, though she wasn't failing either. For now, that seemed to be enough.

Days turned to weeks, and Gillian offered her a full-time position. More unexpectedly, she found a connection with Moira. They had started as strangers—Chelsia, the new girl in town, and Moira, the reliable presence at the pharmacy's front counter. Between shared lunches and quiet conversations over coffee, they found something in each other neither had expected.

When Moira suggested Chelsia move into her sprawling, inherited house, it had been a kindness Chelsia hadn't seen coming.

"It's not like I've never been alone before," Moira had said, her voice tinged with sadness. "It's just... I've never carried a burden of silence in a place that's supposed to feel like home, you know?"

The words struck a chord with Chelsia, who had been searching for something she couldn't name. Moving in together made sense, and for a time, it worked.

One afternoon, Moira surprised Chelsia with tickets to see Tourists of Dreams perform at the Crystal Ballroom, complete with a meet-and-greet after the show. Known for their hauntingly beautiful sound, a fusion of orchestral and rock elements, the band's original compositions had earned them a devoted following.

Central to their success was Joran Talbert, a brilliant yet enigmatic composer whose eventual departure left fans reeling. Rumors of personal struggles and his mysterious disappearance only deepened the band's mystique. In his absence, Michael Cavanaugh, the band's violinist, stepped into a leadership role, guiding them forward while preserving their legacy. The performance that evening was part of a limited tour—a statement of resilience under Michael's direction, a bridge between what the band had been and what it was becoming.

At the meet-and-greet, Moira was star-struck, her attention fixed entirely on Devin Early, the band's pianist. Meanwhile, Chelsia drifted away from the crowd and found herself in Michael's line of sight. His piercing blue eyes met hers, and for a moment, the chaos of the room seemed to dissolve. Their conversation was brief yet charged with energy—a connection that changed her life.

Within weeks, Chelsia had moved into Michael's sleek, modern loft, leaving behind the cluttered comfort of Moira's home, and, unintentionally, the friendship they'd built. Though Moira tried to hide her hurt, it seeped into their interactions, coloring even the simplest conversations with resentment.

"Hey, what are you thinking about?" Moira asked, breaking through her thoughts as she entered the break room.

"Nothing," Chelsia lied. Admitting she had just finished eulogizing their friendship would do no good. She sighed and looked away from the window. "Just excited about Michael's visit."

Moira rested against the counter, her red hair catching the light like a fiery halo. "Right," she said flatly. "The famous musician is gracing you with his presence. Ring the alarm bells."

"Subtle as always, Moira."

Moira shrugged, turning to reach for the coffeepot on the counter. "I call it like I see it, and I don't see how you can truly know someone when you're miles apart most of the time."

"Which might have made sense at the start, but we've been together for a year, Moira! A year!"

"A year of him coming out here maybe half a dozen times and you going out to see him—how many? None." Moira poured herself a cup of coffee, the clink of ceramic breaking the quiet.

Chelsia's brow furrowed. Before she could fire back, Moira spoke again, her voice low.

"I get it. He's charming, successful, talented. A real catch. Sometimes people aren't who they seem, though, Chelsia... even when they're standing right in front of you."

The words settled in the air, thin and cold, like the edge of a blade. Chelsia's hand stilled briefly around her mug, her breath catching before she forced down a retort with a sip of tea. *Michael.* She had to mean Michael.

Her lips twitched into a small, polite smile, just a little too controlled around the edges.

"What's that supposed to mean, Moira?"

Moira shrugged one shoulder, her eyes flicking briefly to her coffee cup. "Just an observation. Hey, what do I know? Maybe you and Michael are the exception."

The remark slid past Chelsia like a needle under the skin—thin, almost imperceptible, but impossible to ignore. She forced herself to look away, her attention dropping to the steam curling from her tea. It rose in slow, lazy tendrils, fading into nothing.

Chelsia's lips drew into a thin line, her voice brittle as glass when she finally spoke.

"I should get back to work."

Moira turned away without replying, her focus on the coffeepot as though the conversation had already dissolved into steam and silence.

But as Chelsia rose from her seat and walked out of the break room, a thought settled somewhere deep in her chest. Moira's words clung to the air, like a ghost brushing against the edges of her mind. And though she shoved them away, locking them behind the same doors where she kept her other unwelcome thoughts, the chill remained.

CHAPTER THREE

Standing at the front counter, Chelsia watched bundled-up pedestrians drift by outside. The familiar rhythm of the pharmacy—customers trickling in, the rustle of paper bags, and the occasional buzz of the phone—helped steady her mind after the recent exchange with Moira.

"Chelsia, can you grab some 50,000 IU vitamin D capsules for the Yambao order while I put the rest of her stuff together?" Moira's voice was polite yet distant.

"Sure thing," Chelsia replied, forcing a friendly smile as she went to the storage room, though Moira's words from earlier clung to her like static.

She found the bottle easily, carrying it back to the front before handing it over. Moira only nodded curtly in thanks, her attention already back on the order.

"Another busy day, huh?" Gillian remarked as she joined them behind the counter, her voice warm and light. She glanced at the clock, then at the small stack of remaining orders. "We're almost there."

"Definitely," Chelsia replied. She glanced over at Moira, her tone deliberately bright. "We make a great team, don't we?"

"Yeah, I suppose we do," Moira said, so carefully that it almost felt rehearsed. Her hands stilled briefly on the prescription bag before she continued packing the order without looking up.

Gillian's eyebrow rose, her silent scrutiny moving between the two women.

"Well, I certainly couldn't keep this place running without you both," she said finally.

A grateful smile touched Chelsia's lips, but she felt the weight of Moira's animosity—a subtle hum only she could feel.

Even with the pharmacy's unchanging routine, an unspoken awkwardness persisted between Chelsia and Moira. At one point, Moira brushed past her to grab a prescription bag. She gritted her teeth, willing herself not to react. It was Gillian who eventually broke the simmering silence.

"Chelsia," she called out from behind the pharmacist's counter, where she was signing off on orders, "you can cut out early. I know you're excited about tomorrow, and I'm sure you'd much rather be home putting final touches on things."

"Are you sure, Gillian?" Chelsia asked, trying to keep the excitement out of her voice even as she caught Moira's wide-eyed look out of the corner of her eye. "I've already got tomorrow off, and I have no problem staying."

"Of course!" Gillian said. "There are only a couple hours 'til closing, anyway. Moira and I can manage."

"Thank you so much!" Chelsia said, slipping out of the short white lab coat.

She hurried to the back, securing the garment on one hook while grabbing her coat from another. In her hurry to zip her coat, the fringe at the end of her scarf caught between the zipper's teeth.

"And, Chelsia," Gillian said, noticing the snag and choosing to leave it be, "once Michael's trip is done and things return to normal, we really should talk about whether you intend to apply for that pharm tech license. You'd be amazing at it, and it would keep me from having to hire a tech through the agency."

"I'm still thinking about it, Gillian," Chelsia promised as she finished bundling up, careful to avoid looking over at Moira.

Moira had applied for her own pharmacy technician's license months prior and was denied. The criminal background check required as part of the application process uncovered a multitude of transgressions. A series of shoplifting offenses in her mid and late teens was part of the reason Moira was sent to Beaverton, Oregon, to live with her grandparents. Heaven forbid anyone back home found out that Moira Bevins, the only child of the 'country club' Bevins of Atherton, California, was a thief.

"All right, I'm heading out!" Chelsia announced, her voice filled with anticipation.

"Have fun with your rockstar boyfriend," Moira said as she packed the next prescription bag with unnecessary force. Her voice was light, almost sing-song, but it failed to hide the brittle edge underneath.

"Thanks, Moira, I will!" Chelsia answered with a smile so dazzling it seemed to be made of sunshine.

Moira turned away sharply, her shoulders stiff, her face hidden as she busied herself with the order.

"Enjoy your time together, Chelsia," Gillian said genuinely, placing a reassuring hand on the younger woman's shoulder. "You've earned this break."

"Thank you, Gillian," Chelsia said. "I'll see you both on Monday."

With gratitude, she left the pharmacy, her heart full of anticipation for the days ahead. Her footsteps lightly crunched against the snowy pavement as she headed home, ready to embrace whatever the long weekend had in store.

CHAPTER FOUR

Chelsia stood by the window, her breath fogging the glass as she gazed at the delicate snowflakes fluttering down from the sky. They drifted gently, their silent descent matching the pulse of her anticipation. A small smile tugged at her lips, her heart swelling as she thought of Michael. Tomorrow, he would finally be here.

"Everything needs to be perfect," she whispered to herself, pulling away from the chilled pane.

The apartment was perfect, yet she felt the need to examine every detail again. She moved through the living room like a conductor, fine-tuning her orchestra. The throw pillows were fluffed and aligned just so. Picture frames, already straight, received a final, almost ceremonial adjustment.

One frame held her attention, her fingertips softly tracing the glass. The photograph captured her and Michael during one of their rare vacations—a sunlit beach, their faces aglow with laughter and happiness. Her crown of natural curls, usually carefully coiled, was voluminous on that day, tumbling around her face in dynamic spirals that complemented the glow of her smooth chocolate skin. Her dark eyes sparkled in the photo, reflecting the easy joy of the moment as her full lips stretched into an effortless smile.

For a moment, Chelsia lost herself in the memory, warmth blooming in her chest. This was the life they were building together, one cherished moment at a time. This was the life she'd only dreamed of when she arrived in Portland on that dreary day in April.

With a satisfied nod, she continued into the kitchen. A thick cookbook lay open on the counter, its well-loved pages marked with sticky notes. A photo of creamy mushroom risotto, which she planned as the main course, stared back at her. Chelsia's menu was a labor of love: pan-seared scallops for the appetizer, the risotto as the entrée, and a decadent chocolate soufflé to end the evening. To balance the richness of the meal, she planned to make a vibrant spinach and berry salad. On the counter sat two bottles of red wine, their labels elegant, promising undeniable indulgence.

"Only the best for him," she murmured, smoothing the corner of the cookbook's page.

She transformed the usually quiet dining room into an intimate space. Fine china gleamed in the soft glow of the overhead light, flanked by crystal glasses that caught the fading sunlight like prisms. A small vase of red roses graced the center of the table, their buds just beginning to open. Unlit candles nestled in silver candlesticks stood ready to illuminate the night with their soft glow.

Her excitement bubbled like champagne, effervescent and impossible to contain. Tomorrow, Michael would see the effort she had poured into every detail, from the table settings to the menu. She could already imagine his smile, the way his eyes would light up when he tasted her cooking.

"Tomorrow," Chelsia whispered, her voice imbued with hope and happiness. "Finally."

The evening sun dipped below the horizon, casting the apartment in a golden glow before retreating into twilight. Chelsia sank into the plush cushions of the couch, clutching her phone. Her heart raced with anticipation as she dialed Michael's number, the sound of ringing on the other end seeming to echo in her chest.

"Hey, Chelsia!" His voice, warm and familiar, immediately soothed her nerves.

"Michael, hi!" she replied, the excitement in her voice spilling out like an unguarded secret. "How was your day? Are you all packed? Are you sure you don't want me to meet you at the airport?"

He chuckled, a low, comforting sound. "You know you don't have a car, right? Don't worry about it. I'll be just fine. Besides, I've got... a few errands to run between the airport and the loft."

Chelsia hesitated, curiosity sparking at his mention of errands, though she decided not to press. "All right," she mumbled. "Just promise me you'll call when you're close."

"Of course. I can't wait to see you either, Chels. Goodnight."

"Goodnight, Michael."

As the call disconnected, Chelsia set the phone down and reclined against the cushions, her thoughts a kaleidoscope of joy and anticipation. Tomorrow would be perfect.

The city lights twinkled through the floor-to-ceiling windows, casting reflections across the sleek surfaces of the hotel suite. Michael sat on the edge of the leather armchair, his phone resting on the glass-topped table beside him. He exhaled slowly, rubbing his temples as the pressure in his chest refused to ease.

"You said you'd break things off with her." Katherine's voice sliced through the quiet.

"Katherine, please," Michael replied, his tone strained. He glanced at her, his brow furrowed with frustration. "Just stop. I don't need you drilling this into my head on repeat. It'll get taken care of."

Katherine, seated with casual elegance on the couch across from him, regarded him coolly. The room's light glinted off the deep maroon silk of her blouse as she crossed her legs. Her stare was unrelenting, her posture poised and formidable.

"It had better," she said impatiently.

With his elbows resting on his knees, Michael peered intently at the floor, seeking answers. A suffocating stillness hung in the air between them. Outside, the snow fell silently, a stark contrast to the storm brewing in the room.

CHAPTER FIVE

The shrill ring of a phone shattered the stillness of the early morning. Chelsia groaned as she rolled over, fumbling for her phone on the bedside table. Squinting at the screen, she saw Gillian's name. Her stomach dropped.

"Hello?" she croaked, her voice thick with sleep.

"Chelsia, I'm so sorry to bother you on your day off," Gillian began, her tone filled with regret. "You see, Moira called in sick, and... well, I need you to come into work today."

"What?" Chelsia was suddenly wide awake. Her pulse quickened, tension tightening in her chest. "Gillian, you know what today is and why I'm scheduled off. Can't you find someone else? Maybe from the temp agency?"

"Believe me, I've tried," Gillian replied, sounding genuinely apologetic. "No one is available on such short notice. The agency said they'd try. I've been waitlisted, and there's no guarantee, especially with this weather. Deliveries are coming in today... you know how Fridays can be. I swear I'll make it up to you. It's just that, right now, I really need your help."

Chelsia sighed, frustration prickling at her. "Fine," she said flatly. "I'll be there."

"Thank you, Chelsia. And again, I'm so sorry."

The call ended, leaving Chelsia staring blankly at her phone. Her thoughts raced—Michael, their plans, the sheer unfairness of it all. A nagging suspicion crept in, one she couldn't shake. Had Moira done this on purpose?

Taking a deep breath, Chelsia dialed Michael's number. When it went to voicemail, she hesitated, then began typing a text instead.

"Hey babe, bad news... Moira called in sick, and I have to go into work today. I'm so sorry! I'll try to get off as soon as I can. Please understand. I'll make it up to you, I promise. Let me know when you land, okay? Please."

She pressed send and stared at the screen, hoping for an immediate response. None came. With a sigh, she got ready for work, the excitement of the day replaced by a dull ache of disappointment.

Though Chelsia typically found the low buzz of the pharmacy's activity soothing, today it bothered her. She moved mechanically, greeting customers warmly even as her thoughts drifted. She rang up purchases, answered questions, and smiled through her frustration, knowing that it was a mask.

"Hey, there's a bit of a line forming," a customer mentioned, snapping Chelsia back to the moment.

"Sorry about that!" she said, flashing an apologetic smile. With renewed focus, she worked quickly to catch up, despite the anxiety gnawing at her.

In between customers, she checked her phone obsessively, hoping for a response from Michael. The silence was deafening. She reminded herself that he was likely busy, first on his flight and then running the errands he'd mentioned, but the lack of communication was concerning.

"Chelsia, is everything okay?" one of their regulars, Mrs. Mead, asked kindly as Chelsia handed her a bag of purchases.

"Yes, of course," Chelsia said, forcing a brighter smile. "Thanks for asking."

After the morning rush cleared, Chelsia stole another glance at the clock, wishing for a miracle.

"Chelsia," Gillian said softly, approaching from the consultation area. Her hands were clasped, her blue eyes filled with sympathy. "I just wanted to say I'm sorry about all this. I know it's not fair to you."

"Thanks, Gillian," Chelsia replied with a tired smile. "It's just... not exactly how I thought this morning would go, you know?"

"Believe me, I understand," Gillian said, wringing her hands. "If there was any other option, I wouldn't have asked. Moira's absence really put us in a bind."

"Is she really sick?" Chelsia asked, finally voicing the thought that had nagged her since the phone call.

"She swore she was, and Moira's never lied to me before," Gillian said, her voice softening slightly as she glanced toward the window, her hand fidgeting with the frilled cuff of her sleeve. "I don't know what else to tell you... I promise we'll figure this out."

Chelsia silently nodded, her thoughts too muddled to sort through.

By late morning, Chelsia had stopped checking her phone and thrown herself into her tasks. Sitting at the back counter, she labeled prescription bottles with efficiency, setting each one aside for Gillian's final review. The repetitive action was almost comforting, yet the ache in her chest remained.

"Chelsia," Gillian said gently as she approached, "you don't live far from here, so how about taking a longer break?"

"Really?" Chelsia's eyes widened in surprise.

"Of course," Gillian said with a small smile. "Michael should be in by now, right?"

"For a few hours already," Chelsia admitted.

Gillian nodded. "You can go see him for a bit and come back afterward."

"Thank you," Chelsia whispered, her voice trembling. "This means more to me than you know."

"Go on, then," Gillian urged, her smile encouraging. "I'll manage here for a little while."

Chelsia hurried to change into her coat, already imagining the warmth of Michael's embrace and the sound of his voice. She stepped out through the pharmacy's rear exit and into the brisk air, her breath curling in the cold as she walked down the alley.

Not long after, Gillian frowned as she spotted Chelsia in the stockroom, surrounded by the morning delivery. Pill bottles and boxes covered the shelves in various stages of unpacking, chaos Chelsia navigated easily.

"Chelsia?" Gillian asked, confused. "What are you doing here? I thought you went home."

Chelsia hesitated, her hands pausing mid-motion before she picked up a bottle of blood pressure medication. She glanced at Gillian and bit her lip.

"I couldn't do it," she admitted quietly. She set the bottle aside with a sigh. "A few minutes wouldn't be enough. Things will keep until after my shift."

Gillian's eyes softened. "I get it," she said after a pause. "If you change your mind—"

"I'm fine," Chelsia interrupted. "Really. Thank you."

Gillian hesitated, her blue eyes searching Chelsia's face before she finally nodded. "All right. Please tell me if there's anything you need."

As Gillian's footsteps retreated to the front of the pharmacy, Chelsia reached for another box, tearing open the cardboard seam. The turmoil of her thoughts matched the disarray of the stockroom, though she placed each bottle carefully on the shelf. The name of the medication on the bottle's label briefly blurred, but she blinked it back into focus, her vision sharpening along with her resolve as she continued to work.

CHAPTER SIX

Mrs. Hargrove shuffled into her kitchen, her cane tapping softly against the polished hardwood floors. The cold had seeped into her bones, leaving her joints stiff and uncooperative. The delicate porcelain teapot on the counter, steeping chamomile, offered a small reprieve from the season's relentless chill.

She reached for the silver sugar bowl, the clink of a spoon against its rim, the only sound breaking the quiet. As she began preparing the tea, an unfamiliar scent stopped her mid-motion.

Mrs. Hargrove sniffed the air, her brow furrowing.

It wasn't the chamomile. This was sharper, heavier, with an unsettling edge. At first, it reminded her of the time her late neighbor, Mr. Pellegrini, had burned sulfur in his fireplace to "clear negative energy" after a streak of bad luck. She had humored his eccentricities despite finding the acrid smell unbearable. Now, that same sense of discomfort crept over her, though this odor was less pungent and more insidious.

"Odd," she murmured, setting the spoon down with care.

The scent trailed her as she moved into the living room, her cane tapping rhythmically against the floor. Soft light from an alabaster lamp diffused through the room, creating a warm and inviting ambiance. A sleek gas fireplace stood silent against the far wall, framed by smooth marble that shimmered. It was a centerpiece she rarely used, though its modern elegance always drew the eye.

A handwoven rug of muted blues and creams stretched across the floor, its fibers cushioning her cautious steps. Neither warmth nor beauty could divert her attention. The smell was stronger here, its presence undeniable.

Mrs. Hargrove stopped, her weight resting heavily on her cane. Her eyes swept the room, scanning for the culprit. Nothing was out of place: the bookshelves were orderly, the spines of the books neatly aligned. The windows were latched securely, keeping the biting cold at bay. Yet the scent clung to the air, stubborn and pervasive.

She stepped closer to the fireplace, her stomach clenching with worry. Carefully, she bent down, one hand gripping her cane for balance while the other hovered near the seam where the floor met the wall.

For a moment, she stilled, her breath caught in her throat as she focused all her attention on the faintest hints of her surroundings. Then it came again—stronger now.

Gas.

Her stomach clenched as she straightened abruptly, her free hand trembling as she moved to the nearby end table, her fingers brushing the cold glass surface as she wrestled with the sudden surge of fear.

The room was eerily silent, save for the ticking of the brass clock on the mantel. There was no hiss, no audible confirmation of her growing dread. The acrid tang in the air was enough to make her pulse race.

"I can't ignore this," she muttered, her voice barely more than a whisper.

Her hand found the phone, and she dialed quickly, each press of a button feeling slower than the last. Bringing the receiver to her ear, she waited, the seconds stretching unbearably.

"This is Mrs. Marguerite Hargrove in 7B," she said when the line connected, her voice unwavering despite the flutter of nerves in her chest. Her eyes shifted uneasily to the floor, as though expecting the smell to take form. "You need to come right away."

CHAPTER SEVEN

Afternoon light filtered softly through the pharmacy's windows, in contrast to the crisp morning clarity. The morning rush had subsided, leaving behind a calmer pace of customers and deliveries. The stockroom had been cleared of empty boxes, but piles of inventory still needed to be sorted.

"Chelsia," Gillian began, her voice gentle as she approached the younger woman in the pharmacy's stockroom, "I want to apologize. I've been unfair to you. Moira called out sick, and that's not your fault. I should have managed the pharmacy on my own rather than revoking your scheduled time off."

Chelsia's breath hitched. Her brow furrowed as her dark brown eyes shone.

"Thank you, Gillian," she whispered, her voice cracking with conflicting emotions.

"Go home," Gillian urged, resting a supportive hand on Chelsia's shoulder. "Be with Michael. Enjoy your anniversary. I'll manage here without you."

Chelsia nodded, unable to find the words to express how she felt as she stepped away from the cluttered shelves.

The heavy wooden door of the pharmacy closed behind Chelsia with a resounding thud, sealing her off from its warmth and security. On the sidewalk, she tugged her coat tighter against the biting cold, her breath forming clouds in the crisp air.

The weak winter sun hung low in the sky, casting a gentle light over the quiet street. Bare branches clawed toward the heavens like skeletal fingers, and the occasional car passed with tires whispering against the frosty pavement. The crackle of her boots through the thin layer of snow was the only sound to break the silence.

Chelsia slipped a hand into her pocket, lightly toying with her phone, before deciding not to bother removing it.

She'd be home soon enough.

Turning onto her street, she froze.

Flashes of red and blue reflected off the snow, their rhythmic pattern painting the scene in bursts of color. Police cruisers and a duo of ambulances lined the curb in front of her building, while a small crowd of onlookers murmured among themselves.

"Such a shame," a woman muttered, shaking her head.

"You'd never expect something like this here," a man replied, his hands buried deep in his coat pockets.

Chelsia's heart pounded in her chest. Dread settled like a stone in her stomach. She scanned the faces in the crowd, her eyes locking on the tall figure of Alan, the building's doorman. His usually pristine uniform looked rumpled, and his gloved hands twitched at his sides as he spoke to an officer.

Moving mechanically, Chelsia approached the building's entrance. A uniformed officer stepped forward, blocking her path.

"Sorry, miss. You can't go inside," he said firmly.

Chelsia blinked, her throat tightening. "I live here."

The officer's brows furrowed. Tall, with closely cropped salt-and-pepper hair, he carried himself with a kind, professional air. His badge identified him as Officer Raymond Carter.

"What's your apartment number?" he asked.

"8B," she replied after a pause, her voice quieter than she intended.

"And your name?"

"Chelsia Toussaint."

Carter turned toward Alan, who stood nearby, having finished speaking with the other officer. His dark brown skin appeared mottled under the flashing lights. Alan met Chelsia's eyes briefly before looking away, his focus dropping to the snowy pavement between them. His hands shifted at his sides again before he clasped them together, fingers curling tightly within the soft leather of his gloves. His shoulders rose slightly, stiff and squared, like someone bracing for impact.

"She's... she's a frequent guest of Mr. Cavanaugh," Alan said slowly.

For a heartbeat, his attention flicked toward the building's glass doors, his lips parting slightly as if to add something else. But then, without another word, he stepped back, turning slightly away from her, leaving only silence in his wake.

Carter's posture changed subtly as he placed a comforting hand on Chelsia's shoulder.

"Miss Toussaint, can I have a word with you over here?" he asked, steering her away from the murmuring crowd.

"What's going on?" she demanded, her voice unsteady as her mind raced.

He waited until they were a few steps out of earshot before speaking. "You live in 8B, correct? You know Mr. Cavanaugh?"

"Yes," she replied, the knot in her stomach deepening. "Michael's my boyfriend. Is he okay?"

Carter exhaled slowly. "Maintenance responded to a call about a smell in the building. It led them to Mr. Cavanaugh's apartment." He hesitated. "When they entered, they found him."

"What do you mean, found him?"

His voice dropped further, as if trying to shield her from the impact of his words. "I'm sorry to tell you this... He's passed away."

The world tilted, her breath catching in her throat as she stumbled back a step. "No," she whispered, her head shaking in disbelief. "No, that's not—he was fine. I talked to him yesterday. There must be some mistake."

"Miss Toussaint..."

"What do you mean, passed away? Passed away how?"

"As I was saying, your neighbor in 7B reported what turned out to be a gas leak..."

"No, that's not right!" she demanded, her voice rising. "That's not it at all!"

The double doors swung open, diverting their attention before he could respond. Two EMTs emerged, each guiding a stretcher draped in white sheets. The figures below lay eerily still.

Chelsia's pulse roared in her ears. Her eyes flitted between the stretchers and Officer Carter as she searched for understanding.

"Wait," she said, her voice trembling. "You said you found Michael. There are two stretchers... Who... who is the other person?"

CHAPTER EIGHT

Chelsia stood on the icy sidewalk, her breath curling in misty plumes. The apartment building that had once been her sanctuary now loomed before her, its familiar façade marred by garish yellow tape fluttering weakly in the breeze.

The surrounding chaos was surreal: police officers moved with brisk determination, their radios crackling faintly; onlookers whispered in hushed tones, their voices blending with the distant bustle of traffic. Alan, the doorman, stood near the steps, his usual calm replaced with quiet anxiety. He gestured toward a food truck vendor who was unloading cups of steaming coffee and tea to distribute among those present.

The aroma barely registered in Chelsia's mind. Her world had narrowed to a single, unbearable truth. Michael, her beloved Michael, was gone. And the question gnawed at her with icy fangs: *Who was the other person?*

"Who is the other person?" she demanded, louder this time, her voice trembling as she turned to Officer Carter.

His expression hardened, the lines around his mouth becoming more pronounced.

"Miss Toussaint," he began carefully, his tone measured, "I understand you want answers. Right now, we're still looking into things and collecting information. Details can't be shared just yet."

"I'm not asking for details!" she snapped, her voice rising. "What I'm asking is for you to tell me who you found in my apartment with my boyfriend!"

Carter's posture remained stiff, though discomfort flickered briefly across his face. He gestured toward the food truck nearby.

"Can I get you something? Coffee? Tea? It's going to be a while before we have updates."

"You can get me some answers," she said, her voice taut with frustration, "not tea!"

Her hands balled into fists, and for a moment, she felt the onlookers' stares. As she glanced over her shoulder, she saw Alan looking at her. It was there in his eyes again—pity. Or was it something else? Chelsia swallowed hard and turned back to Carter.

"Please. Just tell me what you know."

Carter sighed, his shoulders sagging. "Look," he said gently, "we're still sorting everything out. Residents should be able to return to their apartments soon. For now, we're just asking for patience."

Patience. The word grated on her. She managed a brittle, "Do you think I care about going inside?"

Carter hesitated, his eyes narrowing as though debating how much to say. Then his voice softened. "Is there someone you can call? A friend or family member who can be with you right now?"

"No," she admitted after a long pause. "There's no one."

In the background, the EMTs wheeled the stretchers toward their respective ambulances. Chelsia's eyes settled on one of them—the stark white sheet unmistakably outlining Michael's body beneath. Her stomach churned, and she looked away as bile rose in her throat.

Carter coughed gently, pulling her attention back. "Do you know how we can get in touch with Mr. Cavanaugh's next of kin?" he asked. "We'll need someone to confirm his identity as part of the investigation."

Chelsia bristled, swallowing hard. "Why can't I identify him?"

His brief pause spoke volumes. "I wasn't sure you'd want to do that," he said.

The words cut deep, as if the validity of her connection to Michael was being challenged. She crossed her arms.

"If not me, then who?" she said evenly.

"We'll track down his family," Carter said. "We'll make sure they're notified and..." His voice faded, and his eyes fell.

"I never met his family," she admitted. "It just... didn't happen. All I know is that they're somewhere in Nashville." Her lips curled into a sardonic smile. "Belle Meade. He used to tease me because at first I'd make the mistake of saying that he was from Belle Reve—like in *A Streetcar Named Desire*." Her voice cracked. Tears threatened as she added, "God, he would laugh at me every time."

The rising murmurs of the crowd silenced Carter before he could respond.

Chelsia turned, her breath catching as she spotted the commotion near one ambulance. The stretcher was motionless; EMTs surrounded it in a crouch. The hydraulic lift had jammed, preventing the stretcher from being loaded.

Her heart thudded painfully in her chest. The delay drew unwanted attention, whispers rising among the crowd. Chelsia's pulse quickened, and she trembled as the sight of the stretcher became unbearable.

"No," she murmured, her voice shaking. "No more waiting."

"Miss Toussaint—" Carter said.

Chelsia ignored him, already moving. She marched toward the stretcher, her steps uneven, breaths shallow.

Gasps erupted from the crowd, and Alan called out a startled, "Miss Chelsia!" as her trembling fingers found the edge of the sheet.

"Miss Toussaint!" Carter repeated firmly.

With a quick tug, she pulled the sheet back.

The sight before her made her knees buckle. Michael's face was ashen, his lips tinged with a bluish-gray hue. His eyes were closed, and redness rimmed his nostrils, as though something unseen had suffocated him. His once-vibrant features were eerily still, the man she knew reduced to this unrecognizable figure.

Her vision blurred around the edges. The last thing she registered was the growing murmur of the crowd and the sting of the cold pavement as darkness claimed her.

CHAPTER NINE

Chelsia's vision swam under the harsh fluorescent lights overhead as she blinked slowly. The murmur of machinery mingled with the pungent aroma of antiseptic, grounding her in the unfamiliar hospital room. A steady beeping nearby matched the rhythm of her heartbeat.

A dull ache in her temple made it difficult to lift her head. Her fingertips skimmed her scalp, pausing at the tenderness just above her left ear. The hospital bed beneath her was narrow and strange, her legs tucked beneath a scratchy blanket.

Fragments of memory flashed in her mind: the chaos outside her building, the stretchers, Michael's lifeless face beneath the sheet. Pain constricted her chest, drawing a soft groan that grated against her parched throat.

"Hello?" she rasped, her voice barely carrying over the din of hospital activity.

The door creaked open, and a petite nurse stepped in. Her eyes, framed by thin glasses, softened with concern as she approached. The hospital badge dangling from the lanyard around her neck read Tamara Holmes, RN, beneath a faded photo and the logo of Providence Portland Medical Center.

"You're awake," Tamara said with a gentle smile. She placed a hand on Chelsia's shoulder, stopping her from trying to sit up further. "Take it easy. Let's not make it worse."

"What happened?" Chelsia croaked. "Why am I here?"

Tamara adjusted the IV line, her tone soothing. "You fainted and hit your head. You were brought in for an evaluation. We ran a CT scan and some other tests—nothing serious. You've got a mild concussion, though, and you're dehydrated, so we're giving you fluids."

Chelsia pressed her fingers to the tender spot, wincing. "I... I need to go home."

Tamara crouched, her gaze meeting Chelsia's. "Not just yet," she said. "The doctor wants to keep you overnight for observation. Concussions can be tricky, and you don't want to end up back here if you leave too soon."

Chelsia shook her head weakly, regret flooding in as the room spun and nausea rolled over her.

"I don't care about that," she said after clearing her throat. "Please, I can't just sit here. I need to find out what's going on."

Tamara hesitated, her expression shifting briefly. "Miss Toussaint... there's an officer who wanted to talk to you. He'll likely come back tomorrow with the answers you're looking for. Right now, you need rest. You've been through a lot."

Chelsia felt the weight of her words on her chest. Before she could respond, a figure appeared in the doorway.

He was tall and broad-shouldered, his short blond hair streaked with white. A badge clipped to his belt loop caught the light as he stepped inside, his intense blue eyes scanning the room before settling on her.

"Miss Toussaint," he said, his voice low and even, "I'm Detective Ryan Bennett. How are you feeling?"

Tamara cut Chelsia off before she could respond. "Detective, Miss Toussaint isn't well enough for questions. Doctor's orders."

Bennett raised his hands in mock surrender, his mouth twitching into a smirk.

"Fair enough," he said simply. He turned toward the door, then paused. "Oh, right—almost forgot." Reaching into his pocket, he pulled out a phone. "This fell out of your coat pocket during transport. I kept it safe."

Chelsia's eyes narrowed as she took the phone from his outstretched hand.

"Kept it safe?" she repeated.

Bennett smirked again, almost teasing. "I'll be back first thing in the morning." His tone turned serious. "Get some rest."

Chelsia gripped the phone. "What do you need to talk to me about?"

Bennett paused, tilting his head slightly.

"Tomorrow," he said, before disappearing down the hall.

Tamara placed a hand on Chelsia's arm, her touch reassuring. "Try to rest. I'll be right down the hall if you need anything."

Chelsia nodded, unsure she could form a coherent response as the door clicked softly shut behind the nurse.

CHAPTER TEN

A low vibration from the medical equipment filled the still room. Clutching her phone, she double-tapped the screen, casting soft light across her face as she unlocked it.

Her thumbs flew across the smooth glass, tapping out a frantic search. The first results were vague, offering little clarity. Then, one headline stood out:

INCIDENT AT DOWNTOWN APARTMENT COMPLEX

Her breath caught as she clicked the link.

"A gas leak was reported at Marlowe House in the Pearl District earlier today, leading to a response from authorities. Residents were evacuated for several hours before being allowed to return. Two bodies were removed from one of the units, though the identities of the deceased are not yet known. Anonymous sources suggest the gas leak may have caused the deaths, though officials have declined to comment, citing an ongoing investigation."

As Chelsia reread the article, her chest tightened. It remained maddeningly sparse, feeding her growing fear.

"Two bodies..." she whispered. "Who was the other person?"

Her hands fell to her sides, still clutching the phone as the screen dimmed. The silence in the room bore down on her.

Her stomach churned, the anxiety swirling uncontrollably. The monitor beeped faster, each tone more insistent. Chelsia gagged, retched, and just made it over the side of the bed before vomiting. The burn clawed at her throat, leaving her gasping. Tears streamed down her face as she choked back sobs.

Her body trembled as the monitor's beeping slowed. She slumped back onto the bed, clutching the blanket. The glow of the machines offered no comfort, a cruel contrast to the chaos in her mind.

"Tomorrow," she murmured hoarsely, her vision swimming as tears spilled freely. "What am I supposed to do tomorrow?"

CHAPTER ELEVEN

The weak morning sun cast patterns across the room through the slightly open blinds. Chelsia stirred, wincing at the tug of the IV line taped to her arm, her body still aching from the events she could barely recall.

A nurse bustled in, her sneakers squeaking against the tiled floor. She was a tall, slender woman in her forties with auburn hair tied back in a low ponytail. Her badge read Jenna Clarke, RN, and her warm smile barely masked the professional detachment beneath it.

"How are we feeling this morning, Miss Toussaint?" Jenna asked as she adjusted the IV drip.

"Tired," Chelsia murmured. "Sore."

"That's to be expected," Jenna said, removing a pad and pen from her pocket to jot a note. "We'll do some more tests later today to monitor your progress."

The absence of a discharge plan registered, but she was too tired to question it. Instead, her eyes fell upon the neatly wound phone charger on the nightstand—a temporary loan from the unit's lost and found. Her phone was tethered to it like she was to her IV.

The device buzzed occasionally, a soft glow revealing notifications she had no energy to address. Gillian's texts, glimpsed earlier in the morning, flashed in her mind:

"Hey, just checking in! How did things go with Michael?"

"Haven't heard from you. Call me when you can."

"Chelsia, I'm getting worried. Please let me know you're okay."

Chelsia couldn't bring herself to respond. What could she say? That Michael was dead, and her entire life had unraveled in a single moment?

Jenna finished adjusting the IV and patted Chelsia's arm. "I'll leave you to rest now," she said kindly. "Buzz if you need anything." She slipped out of the room, leaving Chelsia alone with her thoughts.

A knock at the door broke the silence. Chelsia looked up as Detective Bennett entered, his tall frame filling the doorway. Though his rumpled suit spoke of long hours, his blue eyes softened when they met hers.

"Morning, Miss Toussaint," he said, closing the door quietly behind him. "How are you holding up?"

Uncomfortable under his stare, Chelsia shifted, her usually radiant brown skin looking dull in the harsh fluorescent light. She met his eyes briefly before looking away.

"I've been better," she murmured.

"I can imagine." Bennett pulled a chair closer to the bed and sat down, resting a worn notebook on his knee. "I wanted to check in. How's recovery going?"

Chelsia frowned, a lump forming in her throat as her discomfort grew. "Is this a wellness visit, or are you here to ask about...?" She trailed off, her voice catching.

Bennett gave a knowing nod. "Michael Cavanaugh," he finished for her. "We'll get to that. First, I need to ask: what are your plans for when you're discharged?"

The question brought no comfort.

"You're talking like I can't go back home," she said carefully, watching his face.

Bennett hesitated. "Miss Toussaint, I reviewed Officer Carter's report. It mentioned that you told him you lived in 8B. Alan Stanton, the building's doorman, said something different."

She swallowed hard. "Different how?" she demanded. "I live there!"

"No one's saying otherwise," Bennett said gently, holding up a hand. "We had to check, though. Legally, nothing ties you to the apartment. The lease was solely in Mr. Cavanaugh's name."

The words hit her like a physical blow. "That means nothing," she said, her voice rising. "Alan can tell you how often I was there—"

"He did," Bennett said, interrupting. "He said you were a 'frequent presence.' That's all."

Chelsia's shoulders slumped as reality sank in. "So what are you saying?" she asked, her tone bitter. "Spit it out."

Bennett sighed. "Look, this doesn't have anything to do with the investigation itself, though it presents something of a loose end. Without being on the lease, you can only collect your belongings."

The finality in his voice stung. She looked away, her jaw clenched. "I could take over the lease," she muttered.

Bennett's expression turned sympathetic. "Miss Toussaint, the rent for that loft is over $5,000 a month. Not to be insensitive, but... can you afford that on your own?"

Her head snapped back to face him, the fight draining from her. "No, Detective Bennett," she said bitterly. "Even with my savings, rent and utilities would wipe me out in six months." She slumped back against the pillows, the heart monitor beeping slower now. "So that's why no one's talking about discharge. I'm the only idiot who didn't realize I no longer have a home."

Bennett let the silence linger before clearing his throat. "Miss Toussaint... I need to ask you a few more questions."

She stiffened, nodding. "Go ahead."

"There was a gas leak," he began, his voice measured. "A malfunctioning valve in the fireplace. That's what caused..." He hesitated. "Well, it caused what happened."

Chelsia stared at him. "The fireplace?" she repeated. "How? We didn't even use it that much. It's mostly just for looks."

"How often did you use it?" Bennett pressed.

"Rarely," she said. "We had central heating. The fireplace was just... ambiance."

Bennett scribbled a note, then looked up. "What about yesterday? Was it on?"

Chelsia blinked, the question catching her off guard. "No," she answered. "I didn't use it..." Her voice faltered as tears welled in her eyes. "Yesterday was our anniversary," she whispered. "Michael might have turned it on later... for me... for me to come home to."

Bennett's pen stilled, his blue eyes sharp. "Your anniversary?" he asked, his voice carefully neutral.

Chelsia nodded, tears spilling onto her cheeks as the room blurred around her. "We were supposed to celebrate... and now..."

Silence stretched for several minutes before Bennett cleared his throat and spoke again, shifting uneasily in the chair. "We've been in touch with his family. They're flying in later today."

Chelsia's stomach twisted. "I've never met them," she said. "It feels strange to do so now."

Bennett nodded as the furrow in his brow deepened.

"From the information we received, they were aware that Mr. Cavanaugh was in a relationship," he said carefully. "They didn't know it was with you."

Chelsia's eyes widened in disbelief.

"Well, who did they think it was with?" she asked as her voice rose. When the detective didn't answer right away, her next words came out softly, tinged with resignation. "We've circled this drain for long enough, Detective Bennett. I think you should tell me about the woman found in my apartment with Michael."

Bennett briefly hesitated.

"Her name was Katherine Elise Talbert."

Chelsia's dark eyes widened as the monitor beside her quickened.

"Katherine," she whispered. "Katherine Talbert?"

"You know her," Bennett said quietly, his pen poised.

Chelsia's grip on the blanket tightened.

"I... I recognize the name. She was married to Joran Talbert, the former leader of Tourists of Dreams."

CHAPTER TWELVE

In the silence, the click of Detective Bennett's pen against his notebook was unnervingly loud. He looked at Chelsia, his expression balanced between professionalism and something softer—sympathy, maybe, or caution.

"You already knew," Chelsia whispered. It wasn't a question.

"Found out during the night," he admitted with a nod.

The name hung in her mind like a ghost: *Katherine Talbert*. A chill spread up her spine as the implications churned through her mind. Her knuckles cracked as her fingers gripped the blanket.

"Am I a suspect in this?" Her question, unintentionally harsh, sliced through the quiet like a whip. His slight shrug irritated her.

"We're just gathering all the details," he said, deflecting. "Do you think anyone meant Mr. Cavanaugh harm?"

Her lips parted with a retort before she paused, forcing herself to think. She pictured Michael's amiable smile, the way he'd always pulled her close. The memories cut through her, intrusive and unwelcome. She exhaled through her nose, shaking her head slowly.

"No," she said finally. "I can't imagine why anyone would."

Bennett's blue eyes searched her face. He wrote nothing down.

"And Katherine Talbert?" he asked.

Chelsia flinched. "How could I possibly know?" she snapped, anger flaring before she could rein it in. "I didn't even know her name until now!"

The echo of her raised voice filled the room as her eyes drifted to the ominously gray sky outside. Her nails pressed into the fabric of the blanket as she fought to regain control. Bennett let the silence stretch, his deliberate calm only irritating her more. Slowly, he closed his notebook, slipping the pen into his jacket pocket.

"There's nothing more to ask at this point," he said. "The investigation will likely wrap up within a few days."

Chelsia's head snapped toward him. "What about Joran?" she demanded, her voice laced with frustration. "He was married to Katherine, wasn't he? Maybe he has something to say about Michael carrying on with his ex."

Bennett sighed, almost imperceptibly. "We considered that after her identity came to light," he admitted. "Their divorce was finalized a while back. From what we've gathered, the former Mrs. Talbert was the initiating party, and it was uncontested."

"So, he's off the hook just like that?" Chelsia's tone was accusatory.

"Mr. Talbert's remaining involvement with anyone in the band was financial," Bennett said, glancing briefly at his notes. "He set it up so that Mr. Cavanaugh and Devin Early could keep benefiting as the remaining members of Tourists of Dreams after he stepped away. Mr. Cavanaugh's percentage of the royalties will go to his parents, and what percentage Katherine Talbert received in the divorce is negligible when compared with Joran Talbert's overall share. There's no monetary motive here."

"What about something other than money?" Chelsia asked. "You just said that Katherine was the one wanting the divorce."

"And, I also said it was uncontested," Bennett shrugged. "We got enough info from Devin Early to make us feel satisfied that Joran Talbert had moved on with his life. His former wife wasn't even an afterthought anymore."

Chelsia settled back against the pillows, frustration coiling in her chest. "So why ask me all these questions?" she demanded. "Why are you really here?"

Bennett straightened his posture. "It's a formality," he said simply. "Tying up loose ends."

"Loose ends," she repeated, her voice trembling. "My whole life is a loose end now! You can sit there, writing in your little book, dotting your i's and crossing your t's, but what's supposed to happen to me?"

"Family or friends?" he suggested carefully, his eyes softening. "Maybe you could be with them?"

Chelsia let out a hollow laugh. "All I had was Michael," she said.

Eyes fixed on the blanket, she squeezed it tightly, fighting back her emotions. Before Bennett could respond, the buzz of her phone broke the tension, the sound grating against her frayed nerves as the device vibrated atop the tray beside her bed. Chelsia glanced at it without answering.

Bennett shifted awkwardly in his chair. "I'll check back in later," he said, standing.

Chelsia shot him a withering look. "Don't bother," she muttered. "Dot the i on me, too. Case closed."

Bennett paused at the door, his tall frame backlit by the dim hallway lights. He looked at her for a moment, as though debating whether to say more. Finally, he stepped closer again, his tone gentle.

"Look, I know this is a lot to process," he began carefully. "It's a terrible tragedy. And considering the circumstances... I can't imagine the duality of this betrayal—losing Michael, and then discovering the truth about Katherine like this."

Chelsia remained silent.

"Miss Toussaint," Bennett continued, "try to remember that this could have been so much worse. You could have lost your life, too."

Her head shot up as she glared. "What are you talking about?"

"Think about what might have happened had you been home," he said firmly. "Or, if you were there when the gas leak occurred. Worse, what if Mrs. Hargrove hadn't smelled it? An explosion could've leveled the building, and maybe the surrounding ones, too."

Her phone stopped buzzing abruptly, leaving the room heavy with silence.

Chelsia snorted. "I don't feel like playing guessing games, Detective," she said flatly. "What-ifs won't change anything."

Bennett looked ready to argue, then thought better of it. He adjusted his jacket and tucked his notebook away.

"I'm just trying to help."

"You can't," Chelsia replied, her voice trembling. "No one can. I'm alone—again. With nothing—again."

Bennett hesitated for a moment longer before turning and stepping out of the room. The door clicked shut behind him, leaving Chelsia alone. She clenched her fists beneath the blanket, her nails digging into her palms as her chest rose and fell with uneven breaths.

"Get it together, Chelsia," she muttered to herself. "Figure this out."

In the dim light filtering through the window, her thoughts churned with frustration and grief. Anger burned hot beneath the surface, mingling with the cold weight of fear.

"Damn it, Michael," she whispered. "Why? You were supposed to be different."

CHAPTER THIRTEEN

The hours in the hospital blurred together. Morning brought with it the dim light of a clouded sky filtering through the window. Snowflakes drifted lazily past the glass, the city outside blanketed in white, though the pristine view only emphasized the room's chill.

Despite being served a breakfast of oatmeal, orange juice, and a banana, Chelsia showed little interest. The smell of the food turned her stomach, and she left the tray untouched.

By mid-morning, the doctor appeared, explaining that her vitals were stable before ordering the disconnection of the heart monitor and IV. Chelsia nodded vaguely, barely processing his words. The nurse who followed carefully unhooked the wires and tubing, leaving Chelsia feeling both light and lost.

"Your discharge papers will be ready later today," the nurse said with a smile. "We'll let you know when it's time."

Lunch came and went—a tray of grilled chicken, green beans, and a roll—joining breakfast as another ignored offering. Chelsia sat silently, staring out the window as her phone buzzed intermittently beside her. The persistent vibrations were harsh reminders of the world outside, and she ignored them all.

Early afternoon brought a nurse carrying a plastic hospital bag.

"Here's everything you'll need for discharge," she said, placing it gently on the bed.

Chelsia glanced at its contents with little interest: her discharge papers, the banana from breakfast, and an unexpected pair of blue hospital socks with slip-proof grips on the bottoms.

Her thoughts spiraled, returning to Detective Bennett's words, his talk of close calls and what-ifs. She felt the crushing aftermath of Michael's death, a burden compounded by Katherine's presence and the pain of betrayal. While the city outside was hushed under a relentless snowfall, her mind raced for answers.

The buzzing of her phone cut through the silence again, pulling her out of her thoughts. This time, she reached for it. The screen glowed with an incoming call, the name **Gillian** illuminated.

"Hey, Gillian," Chelsia said, her voice strained.

"Chelsia! How was your anniversary? I can't wait to hear all about it!" Gillian chirped, her voice bright and oblivious. "Oh, and I wanted to let you know I found someone from the temp agency to cover you for Monday. You deserve a day off after having to work for part of Friday when Moira called out sick. Don't worry if she's still under the weather; we're covered."

Chelsia's breath caught in her throat. The words refused to come. Tears welled in her eyes, threatening to spill over. She bit her lip, fighting for composure.

"Gillian... Michael is dead."

There was a sudden intake of breath on the other end. "What? Oh my God, Chelsia... I—I don't even know what to say." Gillian's voice cracked, raw with shock. "How did this happen? When? Why didn't you call me?"

"I didn't know who to call or what to do," Chelsia admitted, her voice trembling. She couldn't bring herself to tell Gillian everything, not yet.

"Can I do anything? Do you want me to come over?" Gillian asked urgently.

"No," Chelsia said quickly, glancing at the quiet machines around her. She was relieved the heart monitor was gone. It would have betrayed her location instantly. "I just... I need some time to process everything."

"Of course," Gillian said. "You shouldn't be alone, though."

I've always been alone.

"It's fine," Chelsia insisted. "Right now, I just... Like I said, I need time."

"You let me know if there is anything I can do, okay?" Gillian continued.

"Thank you," Chelsia said before she ended the call. She set the phone back on the table, her hands trembling.

By early evening, the nurse's assistant arrived with a wheelchair. He was a young man with short, spiked hair and a friendly demeanor, dressed in light blue scrubs with a badge that read **Kevin**.

"I'll take you downstairs," he said with a polite smile.

Chelsia nodded, clutching the hospital bag in her lap as Kevin wheeled her into the elevator. Her hat, a simple knit cap she'd removed from the pocket of her coat, now rested on her head, shielding her thick coils from view. The ride to the ground floor was quiet except for the ding marking each floor. Outside, the snow was still falling, the flakes illuminated by the dim streetlights in the gathering dusk.

The waiting Lyft was warm, though the contrast made the chill in her hands more apparent. A middle-aged driver with kind eyes helped her into the car, carefully placing the hospital bag beside her in the back seat before pulling away.

At a nearby bank, the Lyft came to a stop. Chelsia stepped out, the snow crunching loudly beneath her boots in the stillness of the parking lot. Sliding a debit card into the ATM, she entered the familiar PIN and waited. Her finger hesitated over the keypad before selecting a withdrawal amount. Moments later, the screen flashed: **Card Retained. Contact Your Bank.**

Her stomach dropped as the machine swallowed the card. Another door closed in her already unraveling life.

Turning back toward the parking lot, she noticed a car parked across the street. Its driver was barely visible behind the windshield, and the silhouette inside left her unnerved.

Chelsia's breath caught. Someone was watching her.

She glared at the vehicle before climbing back into the Lyft.

The car rolled to a stop in front of a two-story motel. Its faded sign read, **'Cedar Shade Inn,'** the neon letters flickering faintly. Grime streaked the building's beige exterior, and snow collected in uneven patches on the sagging roof. Near the motel entrance, a group chatted, their laughter and cigarette smoke combining with the cold, damp air as slush coated the cracked pavement.

With a sinking heart, Chelsia stared at the building after exiting the Lyft. Nothing had changed. She left this motel more than a year ago, after Moira had invited her to move in. She'd thought it was a turning point toward a positive outcome. Standing in the biting cold, clutching a plastic hospital bag reminded her once again of how quickly things could change—or revert.

The Lyft pulled away, leaving her standing alone. She slung the hospital bag over her shoulder and approached the motel's entrance. The glass door was cloudy, its metal frame scratched and dented. She pulled it open reluctantly, pausing just inside to glance back.

Across the street was the same car she saw near the bank, the figure behind the wheel unmoving. Chelsia turned away, biting her lip. The door slammed behind her, the sound echoing in the dim hallway.

Seconds passed before she stepped back outside, the cold air biting at her skin. The bag from the hospital hung over one shoulder, its weight oddly comforting as she scanned the street, deciding.

Crossing the cracked parking lot with determination, she approached the car parked across the street. She'd already suspected who was inside, and her certainty solidified when the driver's window rolled down as she neared.

"What the hell do you want?" Chelsia demanded, her breath clouding in the freezing air. "Why are you following me?"

Detective Bennett looked momentarily surprised, as if he hadn't expected her to confront him so directly. He recovered quickly, his expression settling into calm.

"Something's been bothering me," he said candidly, "since I saw you last."

She crossed her arms, the hospital bag bumping against her hip. "You mean since the interrogation?"

Bennett raised an eyebrow. "I didn't interrogate you because you aren't a suspect. I just had to—"

"Dot your i's and cross your t's. Yeah, I know." Her tone was biting as she cut him off mid-sentence. "You still haven't said why you're following me."

"I'm not following you," he said evenly.

She arched a skeptical brow.

He sighed. "I just wanted to make sure you landed somewhere safe."

Chelsia let out a bitter laugh, the sound harsh against the quiet snowfall. "Safe? Here? In a place I never hoped to see again?" She gestured toward the motel behind her. "You weren't trying to make sure I was safe. You wanted to make sure I didn't go back to the loft."

Bennett's lips pressed into a thin line, though his eyes never left hers.

"Why did you come to this place? Did you have trouble at the bank?"

Her temper flared again, her hands curling at her sides as she didn't answer.

"Look," he said, his voice gentler now. "It's cold out here. Why don't you get in the car? At least warm up a little."

Chelsia shook her head. "No thanks. I'm fine."

Though hesitant, Bennett let it be. "Michael's parents are in town," he said, switching tactics. "They're taking care of things up at the apartment. Probably clearing out his stuff as we speak."

Her heart clenched, and she looked away, the snowflakes melting against her heated cheeks.

"Everyone gets to wrap things up in a nice little bow except for me," she said bitterly.

"I got the Cavanaughs to agree to let you come back tomorrow morning for your belongings," he said after a moment. "With a police escort."

Chelsia glanced back at him. "I guess that would be you?"

"It was my case," Bennett said simply. He glanced at the motel, fidgeting. This time, he didn't bother hiding his distaste. "Do you have to stay here?"

She stiffened. "Where the hell else am I supposed to go?"

"It can't be about money," Bennett said. "You mentioned having savings. So, what happened? Trouble at the bank?"

Chelsia hesitated, the wind causing her eyes to water as the snow continued to fall. Finally, she spoke.

"I went to the bank because, early in our relationship, Michael gave me a debit card from his account."

"His account?" he repeated, emphasizing the pronoun.

"It was for emergencies," she admitted, her voice clipped. "I'd sometimes use it for things I didn't want to spend my money on."

Bennett tilted his head as if fitting the pieces together. "So, you went to withdraw funds, and there was a problem with the account?"

Chelsia's lips twisted into a wry smile. "Michael's parents crossed that 't' faster than expected."

"Whatever was in that account didn't belong to you," he said, regarding her carefully.

Her face hardened, and she bit back her reply. The silence between them stretched, broken only by the sound of a passing car.

"You don't have to stay here," he said finally. "Look, it's not much, but the department has resources for situations like this. I can get you a room at a decent hotel for the night. Somewhere warm and safe. No strings attached."

Chelsia blinked, surprised by the offer. "Why?"

"You shouldn't have to stay here," Bennett said simply.

She hesitated, her mind racing. She didn't want to accept help from him, didn't want to feel like a charity case. What she wanted, more than anything, was to disappear again—to put as much distance as possible between herself, Portland, and this nightmare. Too bad the ATM had claimed her ticket to do so.

The wind picked up, tugging at the hem of her coat and slipping beneath the knit hat covering her hair as the biting cold found its way to her scalp. With a nod, she acknowledged Bennett's steady gaze.

"Fine," she said. "One night."

Bennett gave a small nod of acknowledgment. "Get in. I'll make the call."

Chelsia briefly hesitated before crossing around to the passenger side of the car. The door handle was cold beneath her fingers as she opened it, and she slid into the seat, her hospital bag resting on her lap. The warmth of the interior hit her immediately, making her aware of just how long she'd been standing outside. She said nothing as she settled in, though her shoulders relaxed as the tension loosened.

Bennett reached for his phone, already dialing as he glanced at her briefly.

"This won't take long," he said.

Chelsia didn't respond. Instead, she looked out the window, the snow continuing to fall gently in the glow of the streetlights. She pressed her lips together, her thoughts as clouded as the frosted glass separating her from the outside world.

CHAPTER FOURTEEN

Chelsia spent the following morning seated by the window in her hotel room, watching the gray, quiet skyline. A cold cup of coffee rested on the table in front of her, the once fragrant brew now dulled by neglect. The cream had settled into an unappetizing swirl, and she hadn't taken more than a sip.

The room felt brighter than the weather deserved. Warm-toned walls and vividly patterned curtains framed the window, softening the gray light filtering in. A queen-sized bed with crisp white sheets sat against one wall, its pillows propped neatly against a dark wooden headboard. The covers were pulled back on one side, leaving an impression where she had slept. On the bedside table, a chrome lamp stood next to an alarm clock and her phone, which remained silent.

Though the room offered thoughtful amenities—a microwave, coffeemaker, and a stocked mini-fridge—she barely noticed. Chelsia's short twist-out framed her face in soft spirals, the defined coils offering a striking contrast to the exhaustion etched into her features.

The long, hot shower had been a welcome relief, washing away some of the past couple of days. She was equally grateful for the quick stop at a nearby discount store, where she'd picked up toiletries, a few basic clothing items, and the phone charger Bennett had insisted on buying for her, as if trying to soften the blow of her circumstances.

She glanced at her phone. Since Gillian's call the day before, there had been no further activity. Not even from Moira. Chelsia frowned, thinking of her friend's silence. For a moment, bitterness rose in her chest, and she shook her head, choosing not to dwell on it.

Her thoughts returned instead to Michael, replaying their last few phone conversations. Something in her instincts had told her something was off, but Michael had brushed her concerns aside with his usual charm. He'd assured her he was only stressed about the upcoming tour, worried about whether the shift in leadership would help or hurt the group. He'd even expressed gratitude for Joran's efforts to ensure Michael and Devin could continue without legal entanglements.

Michael had promised, though, that everything was okay.

"The only thing that matters is you, Chelsia," he'd said. "After our anniversary, we'll sit down and figure out what's next."

What role did Katherine play in what was supposed to come next? Chelsia thought.

A knock at the door pulled her from her thoughts. As she crossed the room, a knot formed in her stomach. She opened the door to find Detective Bennett standing there, a large brown bag in his hands.

"Good morning," he said, his tone lighter than she expected.

Chelsia sighed, stepping aside to let him in. "You have a knack for showing up unannounced."

"Glad you let me in anyway," he replied good-naturedly, setting the bag on the table as the door closed behind him. "Figured you'd be awake."

She folded her arms, leaning against the wall.

"Not exactly a hard guess. Who could sleep?"

He looked at her sympathetically. Instead of addressing the issue, he simply gestured to the bag.

"I brought breakfast. You should eat something."

She raised an eyebrow. "You have no idea what I like."

Bennett smirked. "I covered all the bases. Lactose-free options, gluten-free options, vegan-friendly, and food for the rare normal person in Portland."

She chuckled despite herself. "Impressive. You've outdone yourself dotting your i's this time."

Walking over to the table, she opened the bag and peered inside. The assortment included a plain bagel and cream cheese, fruit cups, oatmeal, yogurt, and a foil-wrapped breakfast sandwich. She chose the sandwich and returned to her chair, unwrapping it carefully.

He pulled out a chair and sat, leaving the food untouched.

"How are you doing?" he asked, his voice soft. "I mean, did you really not sleep at all?"

Chelsia took a small bite of the sandwich, chewing thoughtfully. "I napped off and on," she admitted. "Not exactly quality rest. Nothing to do with the bed, though. The room's fine." She glanced at him. "Thanks again. For this."

Bennett nodded. "You're welcome." He hesitated before continuing. "Have you thought about where you'll go next? The precinct will pay for another night here, but that's likely as far as they'll go. The case is closed. It'd be different if we had a reason to keep you on our radar and needed you to stay put."

She sipped from a bottle of orange juice taken from the bag.

"I'm not sure," she mumbled. "I still have my job. So, I'm not totally down and out."

"You also still have your own money," he reminded her. "And there are better places than the goddamned Cedar Shade Inn." He leaned forward, his tone cautious. "We're going to the apartment today. You'll need somewhere to put your things."

Chelsia stiffened, her appetite fading. "I can't just sign a lease at any old place."

"Why not?" Bennett asked. When she didn't respond, he frowned. "What other options do you have?"

She slammed the bottle onto the table, her temper flaring. "Stop treating me like a loose end, Detective. I'll figure it out because I always do."

His expression grew taut. "You'd better figure it out fast. The Cavanaughs are giving you thirty minutes to gather your things. Any longer, and they'll consider it trespassing, which is why they insisted on a police escort." He sighed, running a hand through his hair as his features softened. "They also caught wind of what you tried to do at the ATM last night. I... managed to talk them out of pressing charges, arguing there might have been a mix-up since you'd just been discharged from the hospital. But... I wouldn't push your luck any further."

Chelsia stared intently at Bennett, her dark eyes unwavering. The set of her jaw and flare of her nostrils spoke volumes of the frustration and anger bubbling within her. Slowly, she pushed the sandwich away, stood, and walked to the bathroom. She closed the door behind her, and moments later, Bennett heard the unmistakable sounds of her being sick.

CHAPTER FIFTEEN

A biting morning chill followed Chelsia and Detective Bennett into the pristine lobby of Marlowe House. Faint classical music played from above, blending with the scents of wood and citrus cleaner. She found comfort in the building's warmth, though her anxiety remained.

Behind the concierge desk stood a man she didn't recognize. He wore the crisp Marlowe House uniform: tailored black blazer, gold-trimmed name badge, polished shoes. It wasn't Alan, the doorman who'd greeted her countless times before.

"Good morning," the concierge said smoothly. "You must be Miss Toussaint and Detective Bennett."

She arched a brow. "Where's Alan?"

"Alan is on leave," the concierge said simply, offering no further details. There was something unsettling about his response, and the way the detective averted his eyes. She let it go as the man turned to retrieve a key from a small lockbox. "I'll need both of you to sign for this," he added, sliding a clipboard across the counter.

Chelsia frowned as she picked up the pen. "I already have a key," she muttered.

Her hand froze briefly as she caught a glance between Bennett and the concierge. It was subtle, almost unnoticeable, yet it spoke volumes.

They changed the locks. Of course. Probably at the request of the Cavanaughs.

Clenching her jaw, she signed the clipboard and stepped aside to let Bennett do the same. Moments later, the concierge handed the key to Bennett with a smile.

The elevator ride up was suffocatingly silent, save for the ding of passing floors. Bennett stood with his hands in his pockets, his calm demeanor unshaken. Chelsia, however, couldn't hold back.

"It's ridiculous!" she blurted. "Changing the locks? What do they think I'm going to do, steal something?"

He turned his head slightly, giving her a look. "Miss Toussaint..."

"No, really," she pressed. "They're treating me like some kind of thief."

"Miss Toussaint," Bennett repeated gently, "weren't you trying to access Michael's bank account the other night?"

"Whose side are you on?" she snapped, her cheeks flushed with anger.

His face remained unchanged. "Do you think I'd side with someone about to commit a crime?"

The elevator dinged again, announcing their arrival as the doors opened. Bennett stepped out first, his pace steady, leaving her to seethe as she followed. The hallway was quiet, the plush carpet muffling their footsteps. They stopped in front of the door to 8B, where Bennett slid the key into the lock. He pushed the door open wide and stepped aside, motioning for her to enter first. She hesitated, staring into the space she'd once called home.

"Miss Toussaint," Bennett said softly.

She forced herself to take a shuddering breath. Focus. There was no time to waste. She had thirty minutes to pack what was left of her life.

Chelsia entered the room with heavy steps, her eyes scanning the space. The bare walls showed the conspicuous absence of the artwork and photographs that had once adorned them. Faint furniture imprints remained in the dust on the floor. While the blinds remained on the windows, the soft, flowing drapes that had framed them were gone.

Her eyes fell on the gas fireplace in the corner. Once a source of comfort and warmth, it now stood as a grim reminder of Michael's death. Her breath hitched as she kept moving.

Behind her, the door closed with a gentle click. She didn't need to turn around to know that Bennett had stepped inside.

Her voice was barely above a whisper when she spoke.

"The first time I came here, it was as Michael's guest."

Bennett stayed quiet, letting her continue.

"I knew he was from Nashville," she said, her steps slow as she wandered through the space. "So, when he sent a car to pick me up, I thought I'd meet him at a hotel like always. I didn't expect the car to bring me to Marlowe House, or that Michael would be waiting for me in the lobby."

Her eyes glazed over, and she paused. "He had a bouquet of roses and orchids. Beautiful, expensive. I couldn't believe it."

She ran her fingers along the wall as she walked past, her voice softening further as they traced the faint outline where a picture frame had once been.

"He held me close in the elevator, his arms around me like he didn't want to let go. When we got here, the loft was..." She paused, a bitter smile touching her lips. "It was perfect. Candles, soft music, and the works. He'd cooked this amazing dinner. He always said he wasn't much of a chef, but that night he could've fooled me."

As she neared the bedroom door, her pace slowed. "When it was time for dessert, he brought over this little covered dish. Said it was something extra special he'd made just for me. I lifted the lid, and there were keys underneath."

Chelsia's fingers brushed the doorframe as she stepped inside. The bedroom was just as stripped as the rest of the loft. All that remained were a few plastic storage totes and a large wardrobe box overflowing with her clothes.

She stared at it for a moment, then turned to Bennett. Her dark brown eyes shimmered with unshed tears, though her lips curved into a smirk.

"Well," she said dryly, "at least they didn't set fire to it."

Bennett nodded, his gaze pensive, though he didn't smile.

CHAPTER SIXTEEN

Chelsia sat in the passenger seat of Bennett's car, holding her phone to her ear. Outside the window, the gray skies hung heavy, threatening another snowfall as the car idled near the curb.

"Oh, Chelsia, I've been so worried about you," Gillian's warm, motherly voice came through the line. "I didn't want to pry, but then I saw the news: the gas leak, Michael..." Her voice faltered briefly. "And now they're saying someone was found with him?"

"I'm okay, Gillian," she said, her tone guarded, ignoring the question.

"What matters right now is you. I just... I can't believe it. Michael always seemed so kind, so devoted to you. And now, to hear this speculation?" Gillian let out a soft sigh. "It makes little sense."

Chelsia's gaze dropped to her free hand, betraying her inner conflict. "It actually makes no sense," she murmured.

"None of that changes the fact that you've lost someone you love," Gillian said firmly. "I know how much you love him, and that's all I'm worried about. Have you been eating? Sleeping? Where are you staying?"

"I'm not at the apartment," she said cautiously.

There was a pause on Gillian's end. "I get that. It would be too hard, I imagine. But where are you? I'll come to you if you need me."

"You don't have to do that," Chelsia replied quickly. "I'm all right, Gillian."

"Sweetheart, it's okay not to be fine right now. You've been through so much. Please, let me help you, even if it's just bringing you something to help you rest."

"I'll manage."

A quiet beat settled between them before Gillian spoke again, her voice softer. "Do you know when the services are?"

"His parents are handling everything," Chelsia said after a moment. "I think it's happening back in Nashville."

"That makes sense. Do you need a ride to the airport?"

Chelsia hesitated as she studied her reflection in the glass. The words sat heavy in her mouth.

"I don't know yet."

"Well, whatever you decide, don't even think about work," Gillian said gently. "I'll put you on bereavement leave for two weeks. If you need more time, just let me know. Promise me you'll take care of yourself."

"I will."

"And if you need anything at all, even if it's just something to help you sleep, you know how to reach me."

"I'll let you know," Chelsia murmured, her voice barely above a whisper.

"Promise me?"

"I promise."

"All right, sweetheart. Goodbye."

"Bye, Gillian."

Chelsia ended the call and placed the phone on her lap just as Bennett opened the driver's side door and slid into the seat. He handed her a small key on a plastic tag.

"All set," he said simply as he buckled in.

"I could have paid for that," she said, glancing at the key.

"But you didn't," he replied, starting the car. "And it was the least I could do." He cast her a sidelong glance. "Besides, I only paid for a month. I expect you to figure your life out well before then, Miss Toussaint."

Chelsia chuckled dryly, shaking her head. "You might as well call me Chelsia. I owe you that much."

Bennett smirked, keeping his eyes on the road. "I'll think about it... Miss Toussaint."

The murmur of the car engine filled the space between them. Bennett broke the silence after a moment. "I've got the overnight shift tonight. I'll need to catch some sleep at some point, which will be much easier if I know what you're going to do."

Chelsia leaned back against the seat, her fingers curling loosely around the phone in her lap.

"Gillian put me on bereavement leave. Two weeks." She left out the part about Gillian's offer of medication.

"That's plenty of time to figure things out," Bennett replied with a nod.

Chelsia stared out the window. "It's plenty of time for a lot of things. I'm just... still not sure."

Bennett glanced at her briefly. "And you still won't say why?"

She didn't answer, her attention fixed on the passing streets.

Bennett sighed. "I'll take you back to the hotel. Tomorrow's Monday. There'll be plenty of places open, apartment complexes you can check out since you'll have time."

Chelsia gave a slight nod, her eyes still on the window. Something shifted in her expression, and she turned back toward him.

"What happened to Alan?"

Bennett's hands tightened slightly on the wheel.

"What do you mean?"

"The guy at the desk earlier said that he was on leave."

"Well, he's half-right."

"They fired him?"

The detective's shrug was noncommittal, his focus never leaving the road.

"For failing to get Katherine Talbert's signature in the guest register when Michael brought her in," he explained. "She didn't have a bag or anything with her, and you already know Marlowe House requires an I.D. for every visitor so that they can add it to the log when they sign in.

"Michael... talked Alan into letting it slide, so her name was missing from the registry. Not knowing who she was at first added a bit of time to the investigation, and Michael's parents got wind of it. They were... looking for someone to blame, even though their reasoning makes no sense."

He paused briefly, his voice softer.

"Good guy, Alan. Just made the wrong call at the worst time."

Chelsia's lips barely parted as she replied.

"Ah."

Her gaze drifted back outside, the faint blur of streetlights catching in her distant stare. The silence returned, heavy and final.

The car turned into the drive-through of a fast-food restaurant. Bennett turned to Chelsia.

"You need to eat something. What'll it be?"

After a moment's hesitation, she relented, ordering something simple to take back with her. The smell of food filled the car as they continued to the familiar building where she'd spent the night.

He parked and got out, retrieving the airplane carry-on-sized bag Chelsia had hastily packed with some clothing and personal items before they dropped the remaining items off at the storage facility. As they walked into the hotel, the thought of clean clothes felt almost luxurious.

The clerk at the front desk greeted them with a polite smile, and Bennett handled the transaction with his usual efficiency, paying for another night's stay, this time on his own dime. He carried her bag up to the room, placing it neatly on the floor by the bed before turning to her.

Though he wanted to say something more, he checked himself and remained silent. Instead, he handed her a card with his contact information.

"Do the sensible thing," he said.

Chelsia took the card, tucking it into her pocket. "Thanks, Detective."

Bennett walked to the door, pausing with his hand on the handle. He glanced back at her, a smile tugging at the corners of his mouth.

"Goodnight, Chelsia," he said before letting himself out.

She exhaled slowly, settling into the quiet, already looking forward to a fresh change of clothes and a moment's peace.

CHAPTER SEVENTEEN

The two weeks that followed blurred together in a haze of desperation and unspoken grief. Snow clung stubbornly to the curbs and rooftops, melting into slush that left the streets damp and gray. The cold air continued to seep through Portland, a constant, biting reminder of the season.

Inside the small hotel room she was now paying for, Chelsia moved through her days in a restless cycle of searching, waiting, and hoping. Craigslist became her lifeline, a digital thread of potential places to start over, though every lead seemed to unravel into another dead end.

Instead of a traditional bank account, she'd always made use of a reloadable debit card. Her funds dwindled with each Lyft ride, takeout meal, and hotel extension, the balance ticking steadily downward despite the paid bereavement leave. The app's interface glared at her from the screen as she checked the balance, knowing that she was running out of time.

The MAX train rattled softly as it sped along the tracks. Chelsia stood near the doors, one hand gripping a pole for balance, the other holding her phone. She scanned the latest Craigslist listing, the small font swimming in front of her tired eyes. The air in the train car smelled faintly of damp wool and old coffee, the sounds of murmured conversations and occasional coughs filling the space.

Chelsia tugged her scarf tighter around her neck as she checked the address again. It wasn't far, another two stops. She tucked her phone back into her coat pocket, her fingers brushing against a dwindling stash of cash. Days of unrelenting strain had left her shoulders rigid, her body in a state of constant readiness.

North Portland held the first house, a modest bungalow. As she drew closer, the frost-covered grass shimmered subtly in the weak winter sun. The man who greeted her at the door wore a polite smile, his eyes darting briefly over her shoulder before meeting hers.

"Come on in," he said, stepping aside.

The room was in the basement, clean and claustrophobic, with a single window very high on the wall. It offered a meager view of the outside world: a patch of snow-dusted dirt pressed against glass, with low light filtering through the cold earth above. The window felt less like a connection to the outside and more like a taunting illusion of freedom.

Chelsia asked the usual questions about utilities and quiet hours, her voice even despite the sinking sensation in her chest. There was something in the way he'd looked at her, a rapid transition of surprise, disappointment, and concern that he hadn't concealed quickly enough. When the tour ended, the man stood by the door, his hands stuffed into the pockets of his flannel jacket.

"I've got a few more interviews to complete," he said, his tone hesitant. "Um... ultimately, I think we're looking for someone who's a better fit."

Chelsia's nod was brief, and she didn't bother to ask what he meant. She felt the walk back to the MAX stop drag on, burdened by the rejection she'd just faced.

Chelsia's next appointment was in Southeast Portland, a duplex that promised "quiet and convenience." The man at the door offered a polite yet guarded welcome.

"You're... Chelsia?" he asked, his tone almost curious.

"That's me," she said evenly.

The room was serviceable, its beige walls bereft of decoration. She asked about the shared spaces, the rent schedule, and the neighbors. His responses grew increasingly clipped, his posture stiff. The tour's end found him at the door, a strained smile on his face.

"I'll be in touch," he said. "But... I don't think this is the right fit."

Chelsia nodded once, her jaw clenched. He didn't need to say more. The ambiguity of her name had fooled him; the reality of her presence was sobering.

The third rejection came via email immediately after she left the viewing in Lake Oswego. She hadn't even made it back to the bus stop before she received it:

"We've moved forward with another applicant."

Gillian called every few days, a balm against the cold reality of Chelsia's existence.

"Chelsia, sweetheart, how are you holding up?" Gillian asked during one such call. "I just want to make sure you're eating, sleeping... you know, surviving."

Chelsia adjusted the strap of her crossbody bag as she stepped off the train. "I'm fine, Gillian," she replied, her voice carefully neutral.

"'Fine' isn't good enough," Gillian countered. "What about a proper meal? I can come over, or we can meet somewhere—my treat."

She hesitated, glancing down at the cracked sidewalk beneath her feet. She didn't want to lie, yet the truth was too complex.

"I appreciate it. I'm handling things, though."

Gillian sighed softly, her disappointment palpable. "You know I'm here for you, don't you? I don't want to overstep, and I hope you realize you don't have to go through this alone."

"I know."

"Good," Gillian said, her tone brightening. "And please don't hesitate to ask for anything you need. Even if it's just to talk. Or if you need something to help you rest."

Her lips twitched in a smile. The offer was unspoken, though clear—Gillian would provide prescription medication if necessary.

"I'll be okay," Chelsia said carefully.

"Promise me," Gillian pressed.

"I promise."

"Take care of yourself, sweetheart. I'll check in again soon."

As the call ended, Chelsia tucked her phone into her bag and stepped onto the street. Gillian's concern did little to loosen the knot in her chest.

Back at the hotel, Chelsia sank onto the bed as her phone buzzed with another notification. She arched a brow at the sender: Detective Bennett. She hesitated before opening the email, which contained a brief message and a single link. Her breath caught as she clicked it, the screen filling with Michael's death announcement on the website of *The Tennessean*.

"It is with great sadness that we announce the passing of Michael Cavanaugh, a gifted musician, and beloved son of Henry and Patricia Cavanaugh. Michael passed away unexpectedly while on business in Portland, Oregon, leaving behind a legacy of talent and passion.

"As a founding member of the acclaimed group Tourists of Dreams, Michael's artistry and dedication touched countless lives, earning him admiration from fans and peers alike. His vibrant spirit was reflected in his music, and his contributions to the band are unforgettable.

"Michael's devoted parents, Henry and Patricia, and his cherished friend and bandmate, Devin Early, survive him. They find comfort in their memories of him and the journey they shared. His absence leaves an immeasurable void in the hearts of those who loved him.

"Michael's family requests privacy during this difficult time and invites all who knew him to remember his life through the music he so passionately created."

"Business!?" Chelsia said angrily as she threw the phone.

Bitterness twisted tighter as she realized her exclusion from every detail, her grief pushed aside for a narrative that didn't include her.

CHAPTER EIGHTEEN

By Sunday afternoon, Chelsia felt overwhelmed by the last two weeks. She sat at the small table in her hotel room, staring out at the slushy streets below, holding a mug of tea. The question lingered at the back of her mind, surfacing whenever she paused long enough to think: *Why stay?*

When she'd first arrived in Portland, it had been little more than a stopgap, a place to land while she figured out her next move. The months, though, had passed quickly, and the temporary arrangements became more permanent than she'd ever intended. The odd jobs led to something steady, and soon enough, the city's quiet pace felt like something she could live with, if not call home.

Now, with everything upended, it seemed logical to leave. No family. No real friends, not anymore. Just the growing uncertainty of what came next. Yet the thought of leaving was as unmanageable as staying. Portland had become familiar: the misted mornings, the unassuming streets, the rhythm of it all. It wasn't home, though it was a space she could navigate, and in some ways, that was enough.

Besides, leaving would mean starting over. Again. Packing what little she had and heading into the unknown with no clear destination, no plan. It was like trying to rebuild from rubble before the dust had even settled.

For now, staying made more sense. It was practical. She could survive here. The city's streets, buses, and rhythm were familiar. Leaving it behind wasn't something she was ready for yet.

Her suitcase sat in the corner, half-packed. Her clothing, though clean, seemed like an afterthought—practical and unremarkable. She sighed, her fingers tracing the rim of the mug.

Tomorrow, she would return to work. Tomorrow, she would face her coworkers, her responsibilities, and the questions she wasn't ready to answer.

She still wasn't any closer to finding a suitable place to live, and the app on her phone mocked her with its dwindling balance.

CHAPTER NINETEEN

The bell over the door chimed as Chelsia stepped into Falconeri's Apothecary. The familiar scent of lavender and eucalyptus wrapped around her in a reluctant embrace, but something was... different. She paused for a moment, clutching her umbrella, rain dripping from its edges onto the welcome mat.

"Chelsia!" Gillian's voice, warm and tentative, drew her attention. Behind the counter, her blue eyes softened with relief. "Welcome back. How are you holding up?"

"I'm managing," Chelsia replied, forcing a small smile. It was the best answer she could muster.

Gillian smiled, studying her for a beat longer than Chelsia was comfortable with. "We've missed you," she said finally, her voice quiet.

"Thanks," Chelsia murmured, her eyes drifting around the store.

At first glance, it looked much the same, though minor changes caught her eye. The counter was neatly organized, the rows of herbal remedies perfectly aligned. The door of the stockroom, usually kept open, was closed.

As she moved toward the back to drop off her things, the door to the stockroom opened and Moira emerged, a box of supplies balanced on one hip. Her eyes met Chelsia's briefly before darting away.

"Oh. Morning," she said curtly.

"Morning."

Chelsia stood still as Moira walked past, her gaze fixed on the spot where her friend—no, former friend—had been. There was something unsettling in the way Moira avoided her, in the brusque tone of her greeting, with no hint of sympathy for what had happened to her. Surely she knew about Michael, but had remained detached and unresponsive.

Questions circled in Chelsia's mind, twisting and darkening with each passing second. Her jaw tightened as she continued to the break room, forcing herself not to look back. Moira's indifference hung in the air, impossible to ignore.

Chelsia would not forget it.

The day began with a consistent stream of customers, each offering a mix of condolences and cautious small talk. Chelsia forced herself to stay composed, grateful for the distraction of ringing up orders and answering routine questions. Still, the strain between her and the rest was undeniable. Gillian offered only a brief glance, and her conversation, though polite, felt impersonal. Moira avoided eye contact altogether as she stocked shelves and handled the inventory.

It wasn't until the lull of late afternoon that Chelsia began noticing more substantial changes. The stockroom, once chaotic and cramped, was immaculate. She found each shelf clearly labeled and its contents precisely arranged. The break room smelled of citrus from a recent cleaning.

Chelsia glanced at Gillian, who was organizing paperwork at the counter. "Did you do all this?"

She knew better than to ask whether Moira had. Moira was, after all, born into wealth and had never met a vacuum that she liked.

A flicker of apprehension crossed Gillian's face as she paused.

"No, no," she said, quickly returning her focus to the papers in front of her.

Chelsia frowned and dropped it.

That evening, Chelsia returned to the Cedar Shade Inn, having checked out of the hotel the day before, the rain-soaked streets glistening under the dim glow of streetlights. Her shoes squelched against the cracked linoleum as she stepped into her motel room, her shoulders drooping as the weight of the day settled over her. She tossed her umbrella into the corner, water pooling beneath it, and let her bag slide off her shoulder onto the sagging bed.

She had stopped by a nearby convenience store to grab a few essentials: microwavable bowls of soup, crackers, a few cups of instant oatmeal, and a bottle of water. It wasn't much, but it would have to do.

Peeling off her damp jacket, she hung it over the back of the lone chair in the room, its legs wobbling slightly under the added weight, before she explored the bag's contents and selected a container of tomato soup.

Chelsia glanced around the dingy space as she removed the lid to the bowl of soup. She pulled at the corner of the plastic seal, the sound of its release sharp in the quiet room. The smell of broth drifted upward, yet it failed to awaken her nonexistent appetite.

Sliding the bowl into the microwave, another expense, since microwaves weren't an amenity at the Cedar Shade Inn, she closed the door and pressed the start button. With the muffled popping from inside the microwave breaking the silence, Michael's face surfaced in her mind again. She tried to push the vision away. It clung, insistent.

She could almost hear his voice, the low timbre that always calmed her nerves during their late-night phone calls. Then the memories shifted, darkening with the truth she now knew. Michael had always claimed to be nervous about leading Tourists of Dreams, with the pressure of stepping into a spotlight he wasn't sure he deserved. "Imposter syndrome," he'd called it. Chelsia had believed him. She'd believed every explanation for the distracted smiles during video chats, and the sudden moments of silence on the phone.

Now, she couldn't help wondering. Had Katherine been there all along? From the beginning? The thought clawed at Chelsia, relentless and cruel. Were all the tender moments between her and Michael false? How many quiet evenings and whispered promises were spent thinking of someone else?

Were there times when Katherine was just outside the frame of the screen during Chelsia's video calls with Michael? Had Michael's distractions been guilt, or simply indifference?

Realization swept over Chelsia like a gust of chilled wind: Had *she* been the affair?

The question hung in the air, suffocating her. Her hands trembled as the timer sounded and she opened the microwave to retrieve the bowl. Michael had been hers for a year. Exactly one. And on their anniversary, he'd died naked in bed with another woman.

Chelsia closed her eyes, exhaling shakily. The soup's aroma did nothing to soothe her nausea. Outside, the rain turned heavier, a low rumble of thunder rolling in the distance. December had arrived, though the earlier cold snap had lifted, leaving the city in its familiar damp grayness. Portland seemed to wear melancholy like a second skin, a reflection of her own state of mind.

CHAPTER TWENTY

The rest of the week at Falconeri's only deepened Chelsia's concerns. Customers occasionally commented on her previous absence, their words often punctuated with surprise.

"I thought Becky was staying on," an older woman remarked to Moira one afternoon, her voice carrying over the quiet murmur of the store.

Chelsia glanced up from the register, her heart skipping a beat. Before Moira could respond, Gillian stepped in smoothly.

"Becky was filling in," she said, shooting a quick glance at Chelsia.

Moira smirked, saying nothing.

The tension in the air became unbearable by Friday. As the day wound to a close, Chelsia lingered, waiting until the last customer left and Moira had gathered her things to leave.

"See you Monday," Moira said, staring just long enough for the words to feel pointed.

When the door closed behind her, Chelsia turned to Gillian, her pulse quickening.

"Gillian, what's going on?"

Gillian blinked, startled. "What do you mean?"

Chelsia stepped closer. "Don't think I haven't noticed—the stockroom, customers asking about someone else... Moira's stupid little looks. If I've done something—"

"You haven't," Gillian interrupted, her tone defensive. She sighed, setting down the stack of receipts she'd been sorting. "Chelsia, it's not that. I just thought you might need space after everything, so I've been trying not to smother you."

Arms crossed, Chelsia stared at her. "Okay, then who's Becky?"

Gillian's hesitation spoke volumes. Finally, she relented. "She's a pharmacy technician. She filled in while you were on bereavement leave."

Chelsia shifted uneasily. "And?"

"And she helped us implement a few changes," Gillian admitted. "She reorganized the stockroom, cleaned the break room, and streamlined some processes. It made a big difference."

Chelsia's voice dropped. "Am I being replaced?"

"No," Gillian said quickly, her blue eyes widening with alarm. "Absolutely not. Chelsia, I've been encouraging you to get your pharmacy technician's license for a reason. I don't have room for two clerks."

The words hit harder than Chelsia expected. She leaned against a nearby counter, her mind spinning.

"I don't want to lose you," Gillian added gently. "If it's about the cost of the application, I'll cover it. But I need someone who can take on more responsibility here."

Unable to look at Gillian, Chelsia nodded. The conversation felt too much like the closing of a door that Chelsia wasn't ready for.

The frosty night air stung Chelsia's cheeks as she walked, her thoughts a whirlwind. Without realizing it, she found herself in front of Marlowe House. The building loomed above her, its glowing windows a stark contrast to the dark emptiness inside.

The doorman approached—still not Alan—when the realization struck that this was no longer her home.

"Chelsia!"

The sound of her name froze her in place. As she turned, she noticed Detective Bennett's worried, exasperated face peering from his car window.

"You just don't listen, do you?"

CHAPTER TWENTY-ONE

The smell of freshly brewed coffee and crispy bacon filled the air at Elmer's Restaurant, the buzz of conversation and the clinking of plates forming a cozy backdrop. Chelsia sat across from Detective Bennett at a corner booth near the window. The rain outside dripped steadily against the glass, the gray skies mirroring her mood.

Bennett, as always, seemed unbothered by the weather or her surly silence. He was halfway through a massive German pancake, its golden-brown surface blanketed with glistening strawberries and powdered sugar. Across the table, her Crabacado omelet, an enticing swirl of flavors that included crab, avocado, and cheese, sat nearly untouched.

"You know," he said around a mouthful of pancake, his amusement unhidden, "if you don't start eating, you're going to waste away. You're already little enough."

Chelsia shot him an arch look without responding. With a sigh, she finally picked up her fork and sliced into the omelet. She couldn't help but smile as the warmth of the egg and creaminess of the filling touched her tongue. Bennett said nothing. His eyes flicked to her face, his smirk softening into satisfaction as he switched to the plate of hash browns, breakfast meats, and fruit the server had just set down.

They sat in silence for a few minutes, the din of the restaurant filling the space between them. Bennett finished a strip of bacon before glancing at her with a raised brow.

"Why are you back living in that dump?"

Chelsia paused mid-chew, glaring at him.

"You know, the Cedar Shade Inn," he pressed, cutting into his sausage. "I thought you were going to find an apartment."

She carefully swallowed and set her fork down with a soft clink. "How did you even know?" she retorted. "Why are you following me? The investigation is over. Michael's death, Katherine's—it's all wrapped up. Shouldn't your interest in me be over too?" Her tone was accusatory, yet her eyes flashed with something that wasn't quite anger.

"Because I'm a detective," Bennett said simply, "and I don't like leaving things unsolved."

Chelsia's lips twitched in annoyance as she resumed eating, more out of stubbornness than hunger.

"I tried finding a place," she said after a moment, her tone biting. "More than a few times, actually. It didn't work out."

Bennett set his knife down and regarded her seriously.

"You can't stay at that motel."

"It might not matter after a while anyway," she said, cutting into her omelet with a little too much force. "Seems like everything in this city is working against me staying in it."

"What does that mean?" Bennett asked, his tone measured.

Chelsia exhaled sharply. "Michael's dead. The only friend I thought I had won't look me in the eye anymore. And now, some bitch waltzes in while I'm on bereavement and takes my job."

Bennett frowned. "What do you mean, took your job?"

She waved her fork absently. "Gillian, my boss, keeps pushing me to become a pharmacy technician because Moira, the other clerk, can't get licensed." She stabbed another piece of her omelet. "And now Becky, this temp pharmacy tech from the agency Gillian uses, shows up while I'm out and does such an amazing job that Gillian suddenly realizes how much easier her life could be if she had an actual tech working for her full-time."

Bennett studied her carefully. "So, get the license." Chelsia blinked at him in surprise. "It's not that complicated," he continued, shrugging. "You need a place to stay? Get an apartment. You're worried about your job? Get the license. Problems solved."

Chelsia rolled her eyes. "This again?"

"Yes, again," he said firmly. "Until you tell me something that'll convince me to drop it."

Chelsia stared at him for a long moment before looking away.

"I'm stuck," she admitted finally, her voice quieter.

He didn't interrupt as he waited for her to continue.

"It makes sense to leave," she said after a moment, her gaze fixed on the rain streaking the window. "But I can't seem to do it. I don't want to start over, even though nothing here feels the same anymore. Everything's pointing me toward the exit, and I just... can't." She hesitated, her voice dropping further. "If I was going to leave, it was supposed to be with Michael."

His look softened. "You can't base your life on what was supposed to be," he said. "You need to deal with what's in front of you."

Chelsia managed a weak smirk as she looked at him. "The only thing in front of me right now is a meddling cop."

Bennett chuckled, the tension easing for a moment. "I'm serious," he said. "If you keep dangling in limbo without making a move, things are going to get worse before they get better. And at some point, the decision will be out of your hands."

She glanced down at her plate, her appetite waning again.

"Look," he said, leaning forward with his elbows on the table. "I get feeling stuck. I do. But not when the options are this clear. Get the license. Find a place to stay. It doesn't even have to be long term. A tech license would give you stability and probably a decent pay bump. Plenty of places offer six-month leases. And six months? That's plenty of time to make something happen."

Chelsia didn't respond, her mind turning over his words.

The server approached their table with a bright smile. "Can I get you anything else? Ready for the check?"

Bennett glanced at Chelsia, then back at the server. "Actually, can we see the menu again? She'll need something to take home."

Chelsia's eyes followed the server as he hurried off. Bennett smirked at her across the table.

"You know I'm right," he said in a teasing tone.

She rolled her eyes and picked up her glass of water, taking a long sip instead of answering.

CHAPTER TWENTY-TWO

A low, gray sky hung over Portland as Chelsia exited the bus by the storage unit Bennett had taken her to weeks before. The cold, impersonal building with its rows of beige units came into view as she approached, the air thick with the scent of wet pavement and evergreens. Pulling her scarf tighter against the chill, Chelsia approached the office.

The clerk behind the counter was a grizzled man in his late sixties, with a face creased like worn leather. He barely glanced up as she handed over the cash, his fingers tapping the keys of his computer.

"Another month," he muttered, sliding her receipt across the counter.

Chelsia nodded, slipping the paper into her coat pocket before heading toward her unit. Her boots echoed on the concrete path, the sound muffled by the damp air. Unlocking the unit, she stepped inside, shivering slightly as the stale air greeted her.

The space was mostly empty, containing only the plastic totes and the large wardrobe box she'd taken from her old apartment. She scanned the contents blankly, her mind elsewhere as she removed a small, folded duffel bag from her other pocket, shook it open, and filled it with a few more clothing items.

The bus ride back to the Cedar Shade Inn passed in a blur. Her thoughts were weighty, looping without resolution. She wanted to move forward, but every step seemed to lead her deeper into a mire of uncertainty. Later, she barely noticed when her stop came into view, rising mechanically and stepping off the bus.

Once inside her motel room, Chelsia set the duffel bag on the chair and dropped onto the edge of the bed. She opened Craigslist on her phone, scrolling through the familiar list of rooms for rent. Her thumb hovered over a listing she recognized, a place she had visited weeks ago. An additional note in the description caught her eye:

Applicants must know the neighborhood and be mindful of potential conflicts before applying.

She stared at the words, her stomach twisting as the implication soured her mood further. *They might as well have said, 'Applicants must know they're going to be denied if they don't look the part,'* she thought.

She tossed the phone aside with a sigh, then fell back, staring at the water-stained ceiling.

CHAPTER TWENTY-THREE

The week dragged by in a dreary monotony. Each morning began with microwave oatmeal; each evening, with reheated soup—always the same. The only reprieve came during workday lunches, when Chelsia ventured to a nearby deli for something fresh.

At the pharmacy, the atmosphere was thick with unspoken tension. Gillian's blue eyes carried a quiet concern whenever she looked at Chelsia, though she no longer broached the subject of the pharmacy tech license. Moira maintained a strained silence, speaking to Chelsia only when work demanded it. However, Chelsia noticed Moira observing her, Moira's expression shifting between apathy, sorrow, and self-satisfaction.

She told herself that she'd confront Moira eventually, just not yet. The time would come, and when it did, she'd be ready. For now, she remained focused. Chelsia's work was impeccable, a silent statement of her competence. Even Moira seemed to notice, muttering a rare compliment one afternoon. Chelsia ignored her entirely.

On Friday, she returned from lunch earlier than usual. As she stepped through the door, she nearly bumped into a young woman on her way out.

"Oh! Sorry about that," the woman said brightly, her face lighting up with a smile.

Chelsia murmured a polite, "No problem," stepping aside to let her pass.

The woman, beaming, practically skipped out of the pharmacy, leaving behind a trace of floral perfume. Inside, Chelsia noted the silence, expected from Moira and slightly odd from Gillian, as she hung up her jacket in the back room.

As closing time approached, Chelsia noticed Moira leave in a hurry. It was normal, yet the air crackled with something strange and palpable. Gillian secured the front door and then slowly turned to Chelsia, a hesitant look on her face.

"Can I speak with you in my office?" Gillian asked softly.

Chelsia blinked in surprise. Gillian rarely used her office, preferring the open space of the pharmacy floor for discussions. The formal setting set her on edge, but she nodded as she followed.

The office was cozy, with shelves lined with pharmaceutical reference books and framed photos of family and friends on the desk. Chelsia hesitated before sitting in the chair opposite Gillian.

Gillian's demeanor was subdued, her hands clasped on the desk. Her serious demeanor stood in almost laughable contrast to the garish ensemble beneath the lab coat. Gillian hesitated, her eyes shining with emotion Chelsia couldn't quite place.

"Chelsia, there's something I need to tell you." Chelsia's stomach sank. "That young woman who was leaving earlier when you came back in from lunch was Becky. She'll be rejoining Falconeri's in two weeks."

Chelsia stared at her, the words settling in like stones. "I thought you said there wasn't room for three employees."

"There isn't," Gillian admitted, her voice tinged with regret. "Becky is taking your place."

"What? How?" she demanded.

"You know how, Chelsia, and why. You don't have a pharm tech license."

"Moira doesn't have a license, either! Why am I the one being let go?"

"I don't have a reason to let Moira go," Gillian said softly, her expression pained.

"You don't have a reason to let me go, either!" she shot back, her voice cracking.

"Moira has tenure," Gillian said, her tone desperate. "I needed a technician, Chelsia! That's why I kept pushing you to apply, because I didn't want it to come to this. It was purely by chance that Becky was the one they sent while you were..." Her voice trailed off, the implication of Chelsia's bereavement leave hanging between them.

Chelsia's grip on the chair's arm tightened. "I've worked hard here, Gillian. I've shown up on time, taken on extra tasks, and I've done everything you asked me to do. Why does that count for nothing?"

"It counts for a lot, Chelsia," Gillian replied firmly. "You've always done great work—that's why I hired you on full-time. I've been patient because I saw potential in you. But this is a pharmacy, and I need someone who can handle technician duties, not just someone who's good with customers or can unpack a box of peppermint oil."

Chelsia shook her head, frustration bubbling beneath the surface. "You could've given me more time to figure this out. You could've warned me it would come to this. Instead, you just—" She stopped herself, biting back harsher words.

"I *did* warn you," Gillian said brusquely. "I've been talking with you about getting your license. You haven't and won't share why. What was I supposed to do? The state has regulations, and we're not exempt from them." She looked down, pausing briefly. "Even Moira said it'd be nice to have someone like Becky around all the time."

Chelsia froze, her brow furrowing. "Moira said that?"

Gillian winced, as if realizing she'd said too much.

"That's not the point. The point is that I can't keep pushing you to do something you're obviously not ready for." She took a breath. "The fact is that this is Oregon, an at-will employment state. I don't have to justify this. I'm trying to explain it to you because I do care about you. Please don't make this harder than it already is."

When Chelsia didn't respond after a moment, Gillian raised her hands in a small, pleading gesture.

"Am I wrong? Tell me you're ready to apply for your license, then! I'll cut the check for the fees and call Becky back tonight—right now! I'll make something up. I don't care! If you're ready to do this, that's all I need. Are you?"

The silence that followed spoke volumes. Gillian sighed, her blue eyes glistening.

"I'm sorry, Chelsia. I truly am."

Chelsia got up and left without another word, absently gathering her things. Gillian called after her, asking that she think about it over the weekend. She didn't respond.

The weekend passed in a haze of regret and self-recrimination. By Monday morning, a hardened resolve had taken root. Chelsia entered the pharmacy with an intense demeanor, moving with crisp, purposeful actions. Moira noticed immediately, the habitual smugness on her face melting into uncertainty. Though Gillian tried to engage her, Chelsia remained polite and professional, setting quiet boundaries between herself and the others.

The pharmacy buzzed with a steady hum, punctuated by the occasional ringing of the bell above the door and quiet chatter at the counter. Chelsia focused on her tasks, her attention fixed on the work in front of her.

"Chelsia," Gillian said softly as she approached the counter where Chelsia was checking inventory. Her tone was hesitant, as though testing the waters.

She looked up briefly. "Yes?"

"I—never mind," Gillian said quickly, her blue eyes darting away. She straightened items on a nearby shelf, a needless act that only highlighted Becky's attention to detail.

Chelsia let the matter drop. She had no interest in opening the door to a conversation that would lead to an undesired place. Instead, she resumed her work, carefully ticking off items on the inventory sheet.

On Wednesday, the rain returned with a vengeance, hammering against the pharmacy windows as customers trickled in and out. Chelsia's morning routine had been as predictable as ever: oatmeal, a half-hearted attempt to read the news on her phone, and a long ride on the bus through streets gleaming with puddles.

Midway through her shift, Moira brushed past on the way to the stockroom, their shoulders nearly touching. Restocking coins, Chelsia remained stiff and avoided looking up from the register.

"You're awfully quiet," Moira said, her tone carrying an edge Chelsia couldn't quite place at first.

Then it clicked. Moira was probably fuming that Chelsia didn't seem to care about being largely ignored over the past several weeks, or about being subtly squeezed out of her job.

"That's because I have nothing to say," Chelsia replied, not looking up.

Moira dawdled for a moment, as though debating whether to respond. Finally, she shrugged and walked away, her footsteps fading as she departed.

By Thursday morning, the rain had tapered off, leaving the streets slick and gleaming. The pharmacy was quiet as Chelsia walked in. After putting her jacket away, she set about her tasks with the same meticulous focus she had maintained all week.

Moira, uncharacteristically hushed, spent most of the morning in the stockroom. Gillian moved through the store absently, her mind clearly elsewhere.

On Friday afternoon, Chelsia stepped outside at the end of her shift, clutching her bag. Rain threatened overhead, the air thick with the promise of a storm.

Detective Bennett leaned against his car, brows raised. "Came to see if the rain had washed you away yet," he said, his attempt at humor fading when he caught the look on her face.

Chelsia didn't respond, her silence stretching long enough for Bennett to open the passenger door.

"Come on," he said.

Without a word, she got in.

CHAPTER TWENTY-FOUR

The car ride passed in silence, broken only by the purr of the engine and the rhythmic swish of the windshield wipers against the glass. From the passenger seat, Chelsia's eyes followed the rain-washed streets, her hands resting in her lap.

Bennett stole glances at her, his brow furrowed with concern. She hadn't spoken since she got in, and he wasn't used to this kind of quiet from her. It was like the rain had dampened her usual fire.

"You want to tell me what's going on?" he asked finally.

Chelsia hesitated, her lips pressing into a thin line. She stared through the window for a moment longer before speaking.

"I'm done at the apothecary," she said flatly. "Next Friday is my last day."

Bennett's hands clutched the steering wheel. "What? You quit?"

"No."

"Gillian followed through with her threat to let you go?"

"She's replacing me with Becky," Chelsia replied.

Bennett blinked, startled. "I didn't really think she'd do it. Without cause? That can't be legal."

Chelsia shook her head, faintly amused. "Haven't you heard? Oregon is an at-will employment state."

"Bullshit," he said gruffly, still gripping the wheel.

"Doesn't matter," she said with a shrug. "Falconeri's has been a neighborhood staple for decades. Even if I filed a complaint or sued, the court of public opinion would crush me. It's not worth it."

Bennett frowned, his mind working through the implications. "That's still wrong."

Briefly glancing at him, Chelsia gave a small shrug and returned her attention to the wet streets.

"If anything," she began, "it just proves what I've been saying all along. It's time for me to go. I've wasted weeks fighting what's clearly inevitable."

They fell silent again, the weight of her words settling over them.

"Is there any part of you that wants to stay?" he asked after a time.

"At Falconeri's?"

"In Portland."

She hesitated, then let out a quiet chuckle, surprising him. "Only the part of me that hates being told what to do."

A corner of Bennett's mouth quirked upward, but the humor didn't reach his eyes. "That sounds about right."

The silence between them was more comfortable now, and when Bennett finally pulled into the lot of a fast-food restaurant, Chelsia raised an eyebrow.

"You're eating," he said simply as he parked.

Fifteen minutes later, they were back in the car, a warm bag of takeout sitting on her lap. As they pulled up to the Cedar Shade Inn, she looked over at him.

"Not going to comment on taking me back to 'the dump'?"

His eyes momentarily rested on her. "Not tonight," he said, his tone unusually subdued.

When Chelsia got out of the car, he waited until she was safely inside before driving away.

Chelsia's last week as an employee of Falconeri's Apothecary crept forward with a heaviness that seemed to settle into every corner of her life. Monday had come and gone, and Tuesday stretched long and uneventful, the minutes blending into each other as she moved through her shift with mechanical precision.

Thursday afternoon ushered in the return of Becky to complete her paperwork. She was warm and friendly, her auburn hair tied back in a loose ponytail, her smile bright. She greeted Moira like an old friend, their brief conversation betraying a camaraderie formed during Chelsia's absence. When she turned to Chelsia, her smile became guarded.

"Well, hello!" Becky said, holding out her hand.

Chelsia took in Becky's appearance with a quick, sweeping glance: clean-cut and professional in her tailored slacks and silken green blouse. With a polite, inscrutable smile, she shook Becky's hand.

"Welcome to Falconeri's," she said simply.

Inside, though, her thoughts clashed as she wondered when the Universe found her so easily replaceable in spaces that belonged to her: first with Michael and now at the pharmacy.

Friday arrived with little fanfare. Pausing outside the pharmacy, Chelsia read the brightly colored note on the door. It announced that Falconeri's would close early, at 2 p.m., and thanked customers for their understanding.

Stepping inside, she immediately headed for the back so she could hang up her coat. The sight of the break room stopped her in her tracks. Balloons, streamers, and an enormous banner that read, "Thank You, Chelsia!" greeted her. She stared for a moment, her emotions cycling through anger, sadness, and resignation before she forced herself to move on.

The day went smoothly, her impeccable work a final, silent statement. At 2:12 p.m., Gillian called her and Moira into the break room, where a small bakery cake sat on the table next to a punch bowl and a stack of plastic red cups.

After helping themselves to some of the punch, Gillian, her voice thick with emotion, gave a tearful speech, recounting Chelsia's contributions and remarking on her work ethic.

"You'll always be a part of the Falconeri's family," she said, raising her cup in a toast.

Moira sipped her punch without a word. Chelsia's face went blank as she raised her cup.

"Thank you, Gillian. My time here has been unlike anything I've ever experienced... and I promise to never forget it, or either of you."

After the party, Chelsia unpinned her name tag and placed it atop the counter before walking to the front door. Gillian hovered uncertainly, as though waiting for a hug. Chelsia simply waved with her free hand, the other holding the plastic bag containing a few wrapped slices of the celebratory confection.

She stepped outside the pharmacy into the muted gray light of the late afternoon, the familiar chill of the air biting at her cheeks. She clutched the bag of carefully packaged cake slices from her farewell party in one hand and gripped the strap of her shoulder bag with the other. The memory of brightly colored balloons and kind words from Gillian seemed like an afterthought, a story she no longer belonged to.

As she saw Bennett casually propped against his car, her pace slowed. Seeing him was no surprise to her. What surprised her was the woman standing beside him.

She was striking. Thick, dark hair pulled back in a practical ponytail framed a face that hinted at a stunning beauty she must have had in her youth. Her green eyes gleamed even in the dull light, as lively as a spring meadow. She wore a dark blue and green plaid flannel coat over a black turtleneck and jeans, her sturdy work boots showing the wear from long days.

Chelsia hesitated, her instinctive distrust flickering to life. She stopped several feet away, studying the woman as Bennett straightened and gave her a nod.

"Chelsia, this is Bellamy Porter. She's an old friend of mine."

Bellamy extended a hand. Her grip was firm when Chelsia accepted it.

"Nice to meet you," Bellamy said warmly.

Chelsia's polite smile didn't quite reach her eyes.

"Same."

Bennett gestured toward his car. "Come on, let's talk somewhere else."

She hesitated. While she'd grown used to being ambushed by Detective Bennett, she didn't know Bellamy. Still, the idea of a quiet place away from Falconeri's to decompress was tempting. After a moment, she nodded.

Chelsia sat in the back seat, her eyes flicking between the rain-speckled windows and the subtle exchanges between Bennett and Bellamy. Bennett, ever the gentleman, had opened the passenger door for Bellamy and the back door for Chelsia before sliding into the driver's seat.

The coffee shop, on the outskirts of town, had a cozy, farmhouse-style vibe. The scent of fresh-brewed coffee and baked goods greeted them as they stepped inside, and the warmth of the space was a welcome reprieve from the damp chill outside. Bennett ordered for them, insisting that Chelsia get something more substantial than coffee.

At a corner table, Bellamy sat across from Chelsia, cautiously observant. Bennett took the chair beside Bellamy, settling in with the quiet confidence of someone who was orchestrating something.

"Ryan tells me you're looking for something new," Bellamy began, her tone conversational.

"Ryan?" Chelsia blurted.

Bellamy smiled faintly. "Bennett," she clarified. "Old habit."

Chelsia glanced at him, wondering how old the habit was, but he merely gestured for Bellamy to continue.

"I've got a farm in Canby," Bellamy said. "It's manageable, and in great working order. I can always use an extra set of hands, though, someone to help with the basics: feeding the animals, cleaning stalls, taking supplies from one place to another. Nothing too complicated, and I'd make sure that you learn everything you need to know and that you're comfortable tackling anything on your own."

Chelsia raised an eyebrow. "On a farm?"

Bellamy nodded. "It's honest work, and I can offer you a fully furnished room in my house. Private, with plenty of space, and I pay well."

Chelsia blinked, surprised by the straightforwardness of the offer.

"I will not micromanage you," Bellamy continued. "I'm much too busy for that. As long as I can trust that the work gets done, you'll have autonomy. And if you're not sure about staying long term, that's fine. Ryan mentioned that was likely the case."

Again, Chelsia's eyes flickered to Bennett.

"I just thought you could use a soft landing before figuring out your next steps," Bellamy added. "I'd rather have someone who's honest about their intentions than someone pretending to be all in."

Bennett leaned forward, his tone gentle. "I'm not trying to tell you what to do, Chelsia. I just want you to know you have options. You've been through a lot, and it feels like everything's been working against you. This could be the chance to get back on solid ground, if you want it."

Chelsia hesitated, her fingers tightening around her coffee mug. She looked between the two of them, weighing her options. On the surface, Bellamy seemed genuine, but something about her put Chelsia on edge. Perhaps it was her overly warm smile, or maybe her excessive eagerness to assist, though the latter might be explained by Bennett's influence.

Then again, it could just be her own defenses kicking in after weeks of bad luck and betrayal.

Finally, she exhaled. "Okay," she said. "I appreciate the offer. I'll give it a shot."

Bellamy's smile widened, the edges of her green eyes crinkling with something that felt—despite Chelsia's guardedness—real.

"Well, then," Bellamy said, her tone light and teasing as she reached for her coffee cup. "Looks like we'll be seeing a lot more of each other." She raised her mug slightly in a toast. "Hey, roomie!"

EMBERS

CHAPTER TWENTY-FIVE

Detective Bennett's car rumbled softly as it pulled away from the café. Chelsia sat quietly in the back seat, her hands resting on a paper bag of leftovers. The warmth from the food contrasted with the coldness of her thoughts.

A few miles down the road, parked beneath a worn wooden sign, sat a rugged Ford F-250 with a deep forest green finish. Its sturdy build and mud-splattered tires told of long miles on unpaved roads and work that didn't end at sundown.

"Thanks for the ride," Bellamy said as the car coasted to a stop. Despite her worried look, her green eyes shone in the dim light. "You sure you two will be all right getting back?"

"We're fine," Bennett replied evenly as they all stepped out. "I've driven these roads more times than I can count."

She smiled faintly. "Doesn't make 'em any less dark, Ryan."

Chelsia, after closing the door, couldn't resist glancing toward Bellamy, with gratitude and apprehension pulling in opposite directions.

"Thank you," she said finally. "For everything."

"No need to thank me yet." The warmth in Bellamy's voice softened her expression. "You haven't seen the place or met the chickens."

"Chickens?" Chelsia blinked in surprise.

"Oh, yeah." Bellamy chuckled. "I hope you're not afraid of 'em. They're opinionated, but harmless."

Bennett let out a short laugh, crossing his arms over his broad chest. "You're underselling them, Bell. Those birds have it out for anyone who gets between them and their feed."

She smirked, leaning casually against the open door of her truck. "That's fair. But I'm telling you, the chickens are the least of your worries."

Chelsia raised an eyebrow. "What's worse than feisty chickens?"

Without missing a beat, Bellamy replied, her tone almost dismissive, "The pigs. They'll eat just about anything."

"Wait, pigs?" Chelsia froze, unsure if she'd misheard.

A sly smile tugged at Bellamy's lips. "If you end up being a bust, I might have to feed you to them. Waste not, want not, right?"

Wide-eyed, Chelsia stared at her until she caught the glint of mischief in those green eyes.

Bennett snorted softly, shaking his head. "Don't let her scare you. She's bluffing. Mostly."

"Guess you'll have to wait and see." Bellamy winked before climbing into the truck. "Drive safe," she called, turning the key in the ignition. The engine roared to life.

Bennett raised a hand in a casual wave, watching as the truck backed up and disappeared down the gravel road. Its taillights faded into the darkness like embers swallowed by the night.

Only when the vehicle was out of sight did he and Chelsia return to the car, sliding into their respective seats and buckling their seatbelts.

"All right," he said. "Let's get you back."

The dashboard light glinted on the white streaks in Bennett's short blond hair as he drove intently, his posture folding slightly forward. Silence settled between them, broken only by the low hum of the engine. Meanwhile, Chelsia's curiosity itched at her, the memory of Bellamy's warm, knowing smile still fresh in her mind.

"Oh, Detective Bennett," she began, her voice teasing as she turned to glance at him. "You and Bellamy, huh?"

His jaw tensed, a blush creeping up his neck as his hands gripped the wheel.

"It's not like that," he said gruffly. "Well… not anymore."

She smirked, leaning her head back against the window. "Not anymore, huh? So, it *was* like that?"

He sighed deeply, eyes fixed on the road ahead. "Bell's just an old friend," he muttered, though the words didn't quite land.

"Uh-huh," she said, her smirk widening. "Maybe now she is…"

"Maybe always," he interrupted, though he didn't sound entirely convinced. After a pause, he added, "We were… close. High school sweethearts. College, too. Things changed after I joined the force."

She raised an eyebrow, curiosity piqued. "Why?"

His hands shifted on the steering wheel, fingers tapping lightly against the leather. "I don't know," he admitted. "She seemed… unsettled by it. Like being with a cop wasn't something she wanted."

"You never asked why?"

He glanced at her briefly, regret shadowing his blue eyes. "No. I didn't want to risk making things worse. I figured if she wanted to talk about it, she would. So, I learned to live with it."

For a moment, she studied him, noticing the way his expression softened, as if the memory still had a powerful grip on him.

"I guess you two haven't drifted apart that much," she observed. "She's still enough of a friend to do you a favor and take me in as a charity case."

His head shook firmly. "You're not a charity case," he said. "You've had a bad run of luck, that's all. Bellamy's just… Bellamy. She's always been one to help people who need it."

"What do you mean?"

"She's known for it," he explained. "Taking in people who are short on options. Gives them a roof over their heads, feeds them, hires them, and helps them get back on their feet. When the time comes, she sees them on their way. She's good people."

Chelsia turned her gaze to the dark trees bordering the road, reflecting on the strange sense of unease she'd felt when she first met Bellamy. That instinctive recoil unsettled her more than she cared to admit, but she pushed the thought aside, unwilling to dwell on it.

Her phone buzzed in her pocket, breaking the silence. She pulled it out, stomach sinking at the sight of Gillian's name flashing on the screen. Another call. Another message. She pressed the button to silence it.

"Persistent, isn't she?" he remarked, casting her a sideways glance.

She let out a bitter laugh. "You'd think she'd feel guilty enough to leave me alone."

"Any regrets?"

Her fingers tightened around the phone. "Some," she admitted reluctantly. "Doesn't mean I have to like how things turned out, though."

He nodded thoughtfully. "Forget about Gillian," he said, his voice unexpectedly gentle. "Forget about the apothecary. You've got a fresh shot now."

She snorted softly. "And what about Moira? Should I forget about her, too?"

His brow furrowed. "Do you want to?"

A pause hung in the air before she spoke, her voice quiet. "No. I won't be forgetting her anytime soon."

The car turned into the motel's parking lot. The weathered exterior sat beneath the flickering neon glow of a vacancy sign. Her stomach twisted, not in the dismay she once felt about staying there, but with a knot of emotions she couldn't quite untangle.

The Cedar Shade Inn had once loomed in her mind as a symbol of failure. It was a place she'd never imagined herself staying, let alone returning to. Now, as she took in its cracked asphalt parking lot and peeling paint, a flicker of gratitude stirred within her. It wasn't perfect. It wasn't even good. But it had given her a place to land when she needed it most.

Still, the sense of transition was undeniable. This wasn't home, and it never would be. But as doubts whispered in the back of her mind, there was also something else: a fragile spark of hope.

Bennett put the car in park and turned to face her. "I'm working the morning shift," he said. "I'll swing by after to take you to Bellamy's. Make sure you're ready."

She nodded, her fingers curling around the bag of leftovers in her lap. "Thanks," she whispered.

His expression softened into a small, reassuring smile. "You'll be all right, Chelsia. Just give it time."

She opened the door and stepped out into the chilly night air, cradling the bag. Her boots tapped against the gravel as she walked to the motel entrance. Behind her, the sound of the car pulling away faded into the quiet of the night.

CHAPTER TWENTY-SIX

The drive to Bellamy's farm stretched on, winding through miles of frost-covered fields and forested stretches. December's cold gripped the landscape, and though the roads were clear, occasional patches of ice shimmered under the weak late-afternoon sunlight. Chelsia sat silently in the passenger seat, her fingers working the hem of her coat as the car rolled steadily along.

When the final turn revealed a road bordered by neatly maintained wooden fences, she braced herself for something quaint, weathered, maybe even a little run-down. Instead, what came into view made her blink in surprise.

The property was massive, sprawling across acres of gently rolling land. Every structure looked well-maintained, painted in soft, neutral tones that gave a modern appeal while still blending seamlessly with the rural backdrop. A towering barn dominated the left side of the view, its fresh red paint gleaming against the gray sky. Smaller outbuildings—coops, pens, sheds, and storage areas—dotted the grounds, connected by well-worn pathways. Beyond them, wide paddocks housed horses, cows, and pigs, their movements creating bursts of life in the otherwise still scenery. Farther down, a greenhouse with fogged glass panels stood near rows of garden beds covered with protective tarps, bracing against winter's bite.

"Holy shit..." Chelsia murmured, stepping out of the car.

Behind them, an engine rumbled as Bellamy's truck pulled in. She climbed out, brushing a stray lock of hair from her face.

"This is all yours?" Chelsia asked, awe in her voice.

A grin spread across Bellamy's face. "Every inch. Don't let it overwhelm you—it's a lot, but it runs smoother than it looks."

From behind them, Bennett raised an eyebrow. "Smoother, huh? You mean when the chickens aren't rioting and the pigs aren't escaping their pens?"

The laugh that followed was warm and infectious. "Details, Ryan."

Chelsia's gaze swept across the farm again, lingering on a smaller building tucked toward the back. Its purpose wasn't immediately clear.

Following her line of sight, Bellamy said casually, "There are a couple of buildings we'll go over later. Nothing for you to worry about."

Chelsia nodded, unsure if the comment was meant to reassure or subtly warn. Before she could dwell on it, a sharp burst of clucking snapped her attention to the path ahead.

Three chickens darted across, their feathers ruffled and heads bobbing with purpose.

"Welcome to your first introduction," Bellamy said, her tone light with amusement.

The farmhouse was just as impressive as the rest of the property. Rocking chairs and winter greenery decorated its wide, inviting porch. Inside, the air was warm, carrying the scents of cedar and something subtly sweet, perhaps spices lingering from a recent bake. The decor was an eclectic mix: contemporary light fixtures hung alongside antique mirrors, and the furniture ranged from modern pieces to older, well-worn items with obvious sentimental value. Everything was immaculate—too immaculate—as though polished just that morning.

"This is beautiful," Chelsia said, taking in the carefully arranged details around her.

"It's home," Bellamy replied with a simple smile. "Come on, I'll show you to your room."

They climbed the staircase, the sturdy wooden banister cool beneath Chelsia's hand. The soft creak of each step was the only sound as they ascended.

The room Bellamy opened was spacious, with high ceilings and a window offering a sweeping view of the barn and paddocks. A carefully arranged quilt in complementary colors covered the dark mahogany bed. In the corner stood a small desk with an oil lamp, while a vintage armoire occupied one wall. Everything felt deliberately placed, almost like a part of a staged photograph rather than a lived-in space.

"It's perfect," Chelsia said carefully.

"You'll be up early," Bellamy said, resting her hand on the doorframe. "Chores start at dawn, and trust me, you'll sleep well after a day of work around here."

She nodded, managing a polite smile as her host disappeared down the hall.

Left alone, Chelsia stepped to the window, watching the last light of day stretch across the fields in muted gold. Her reflection in the glass caught her attention, and for a moment, she studied the face staring back at her, unsure if it belonged in this place.

Dinner was a hearty meal of roast chicken, potatoes, and winter vegetables. Chelsia ate quietly, listening as the other two fell into an easy cadence, their banter filling the room with a warm camaraderie.

"You'd never know royalty ran the farm," Bennett teased, grinning crookedly between bites.

Across the table, Bellamy groaned and set down her glass. "Oh, don't start."

"What?" he replied, feigning innocence. "She should know. Porter Meats is a big deal."

Chelsia's brows lifted with interest. "Porter Meats?"

"Porter Farms & Meats, actually," Bellamy corrected smoothly. "We produce a variety of goods using ingredients grown or raised right here on the property. Most of it goes to smaller markets."

Bennett leaned back in his chair, his voice filled with admiration. "The business has been in her family for generations—longer than most folks around here have been alive. And she makes the best sausage in Oregon. Maybe the country."

"Exaggerating, as always," she said, rolling her eyes with a playful smile before turning to Chelsia. "I do oversee everything related to the business, sausage making and all. Handling that means I need help with... well, the rest."

A chuckle rumbled from Bennett. "No sending her in to snag that recipe, huh?"

Bellamy's gaze flicked between them, a practiced smile playing at her lips.

"Oh, Ryan," she said, voice smooth with amusement. "She wouldn't even know where to begin."

CHAPTER TWENTY-SEVEN

As Chelsia stepped onto the porch, the cold air hit her, causing her breath to plume in visible clouds. Overnight, frost had coated everything in silver and white, clinging stubbornly to every surface. The return of freezing temperatures gave her pause. Hopefully, it would pass quickly; she'd grown used to the rain softening the chill with its constant mist. Rubbing her gloved hands together, she wished she'd brought a thicker pair.

From her vantage point, the farm stretched out before her, softened by the haze of morning. Horses stirred in their paddocks, breath visible as they nickered softly to one another. A few cows had already begun their slow amble toward the feeding troughs. Somewhere beyond the barn, a rooster crowed, its shrill sound splitting the quiet stillness.

"Over here, sleepyhead!" called a familiar voice.

Chelsia turned toward the sound, descending the porch steps and crunching across frost-covered gravel. At the chicken coop, Bellamy stood surrounded by a restless chorus of clucks and pecks. Green eyes sparkling, she adjusted her coat against the chill, a galvanized bucket of feed gripped in one hand while chickens swarmed eagerly at her feet.

"Morning chores wait for no one," she said, thrusting the bucket forward with a grin. "Go ahead. Toss it out. Don't worry. They won't bite."

Suspicious eyes flicked to the eager birds. "They look like they might."

Laughter rang out in the crisp morning air. "Consider it payback for the way you feasted on their kin at dinner last night."

Chelsia huffed in disbelief but stepped closer, gripping the bucket as if it might turn on her. Her boots crunched loudly with every cautious step, and the chickens surged forward, feathers ruffling as they clamored for the feed. When one particularly bold hen pecked at her boot, she flinched, earning another burst of laughter from her companion.

"You're a natural," Bellamy teased, leaning casually against the coop door. "Just wait until you meet the pigs. They're a different kind of greedy."

With an amused, skeptical look, Chelsia arched a brow. "Do I *want* to meet the pigs?"

A sly shrug. "You don't have a choice. Let's get moving."

By mid-morning, the frost on the ground glistened under the weak sunlight, hinting at a thaw that never quite arrived. Chelsia followed Bellamy past the main barn, where the last of the horses were being led into their paddocks. The rhythmic tapping of their boots against crushed stone blended with the distant sounds of animals stirring across the farm.

Inside, the barn was warmer than expected, the scent of hay and animals filling the air in a way that was grounding rather than overwhelming. A soft snort drew her attention to the nearest stall, where a chestnut mare peered over the wooden slats, ears twitching curiously.

"This is Maple," Bellamy said, stroking the mare's neck affectionately. "She's a sweetheart, most of the time. Don't let her fool you, though; she's got a stubborn streak when it suits her."

Chelsia stepped closer, hesitating only briefly before offering her hand. Maple sniffed her fingers before nudging her palm with a velvety nose.

"She's beautiful," she said, laughing softly.

"Oh, she knows it," came the smirked reply. "Come on. There's more to see."

They moved down the row of stalls, each horse earning an introduction paired with a brief story or quirk. At the end, a gelding stomped impatiently, tossing his head as they passed.

"That's Jack," Bellamy said with a chuckle. "Always thinks he's the boss. Spoiler alert—he's not."

"He's got the attitude for it, though," Chelsia replied with a grin.

Outside, the sun had risen higher, casting long shadows across the paddocks. They approached a series of pens where pigs shuffled lazily through straw, their snorts and low grunts creating a steady background noise. One particularly large sow lifted her head, dark eyes fixed on the newcomers with what seemed like suspicion.

"Pigs are smarter than they look," Bellamy said, leaning casually against the gate. "And they've got personalities to match. Don't underestimate them."

"She seems like she's sizing me up," Chelsia said cautiously.

A laugh rang out. "She probably is. They're not as easy to charm as the chickens."

Her attention drifted to smaller pens nearby, where younger pigs darted around playfully.

"They're... different than I expected."

"They grow on you," was the amused reply, though there was a glint in those green eyes that suggested she was holding back a joke. "Come on. Let's not keep the cows waiting."

The cows proved to be a calmer presence. Large, dark eyes met Chelsia's with quiet curiosity as the herd gathered near the feeding troughs. While her guide pointed out a few by name, sharing their routines and quirks, her own focus kept drifting to the synchronicity of their movements—soothing in its simplicity.

"These ladies are a little less dramatic," Bellamy said lightly. "And a lot more forgiving."

Chelsia nodded, at ease in their presence. Tentatively, she reached out to stroke the coarse fur of one cow that had wandered closer, earning a soft moo in response.

Their final stop was the greenhouse, its fogged glass panels gleaming under the winter sun. Inside, the air was humid, carrying the earthy scent of soil and herbs. Rows of pots lined the shelves, some filled with dormant plants, others boasting small, vibrant green shoots.

"This is where the magic happens," Bellamy said, her voice carrying a note of pride. "You'll get your hands dirty here eventually. It's one of my favorite parts of the farm."

Chelsia ran her fingers over the edge of a nearby shelf. "It's... a lot. You really do everything here, don't you?"

"Not everything," came the modest reply, paired with a shrug. "Just enough to keep things interesting. You'll figure it out soon enough."

By the time the sun reached its midday peak, the morning frost had melted into tiny droplets clinging to fence posts and bare branches. Chelsia wiped her hands on her jeans, casting one last glance at the greenhouse as she followed Bellamy back toward the house. Her legs ached from the unaccustomed work, but the satisfaction of completing her morning tasks softened the exhaustion.

"Not bad for your first full morning," Bellamy said over her shoulder, her tone lighter than it had been earlier. "You kept up."

A small laugh escaped. "Barely."

"Trust me, by the end of the week, you'll be moving twice as fast." They paused at the porch steps, and Bellamy brushed stray bits of hay from her coat. "Grab a drink or take five before lunch. We've earned it."

Chelsia nodded and stepped inside, heading for the kitchen. The house was quiet except for the faint creak of floorboards beneath her boots. She filled a glass with water and leaned against the counter, staring absently out the window as her thoughts drifted. The farm was massive, yet something about the work felt grounding. It kept her mind too occupied to linger on Michael, Moira, or the uncertainty of the future.

The low rumble of an engine outside broke the silence. Sunlight glinted off the polished hood of Bennett's car as it rolled up the drive. Her brow furrowed as she set down the glass and moved to the door.

On the porch, Bellamy stood with her hands on her hips, watching him climb out. "Back already?" she asked, her tone teasing, though there was something else beneath it.

His grin was easy as he shoved his hands deep into his coat pockets. "Figured I'd stop by and check in. You know, make sure you haven't scared her off yet."

She rolled her eyes and didn't respond immediately, instead glancing toward the doorway where Chelsia stepped out.

"She's still here, isn't she?"

Chelsia raised a hand in a half-wave. "Barely."

Bennett laughed, blue eyes bright. "Good to know you're hanging in there. Bell's known to be tough on new recruits."

"She's managing just fine," Bellamy said quickly, stepping forward as if reclaiming the space between them. "And we've got lunch to make, so unless you're volunteering..."

"I could be persuaded," he replied, grin widening. "Your cooking's worth it."

"I'm sure we've got it covered." She shrugged noncommittally. "But you're welcome to stick around if you're bored."

"Bored? Never."

For a moment, their eyes locked. Then she exhaled sharply and turned back toward the door. "Fine. Come in, then. But don't expect me to wait on you."

Chelsia followed them inside, catching the subtle shift in energy. As Bennett removed his coat and settled at the kitchen table, Bellamy began preparing lunch.

"So," Bennett said, glancing over at Chelsia as he broke the silence, "what's been the highlight of your first day so far?"

She smirked. "Surviving the chickens, probably."

He chuckled. "They're relentless, aren't they?"

"They're more coordinated than I expected. I'm pretty sure they're plotting something."

At the counter, Bellamy's knife moved with a little more force against the cutting board. She didn't look up as she spoke, her voice low and pointed.

"Seems they're not the only ones."

CHAPTER TWENTY-EIGHT

The sun hung lower in the sky as the afternoon waned. The air had warmed just enough to soften the ground, leaving damp earth beneath Chelsia's boots as she followed Bellamy toward the paddocks. Her limbs ached from the day's work, but there was something comforting in the steady sequence of tasks, something she hadn't expected.

They paused at the edge of a split-rail fence. Bellamy scanned the area before calling out, "Caleb! Got a minute?"

From behind one of the smaller structures, a young man emerged carrying a bale of hay. His stride was confident, shoulders broad beneath a rolled-up flannel shirt that revealed muscular forearms streaked with dust. He set the bale down with ease, brushed his hands together, and closed the distance between them.

"What's up, Bell?" he asked, curiosity sparkling in his hazel eyes.

She smiled. "Wanted you to meet Chelsia. She's new here. Figured you could show her the fence line. Chelsia, this is Caleb."

One brow lifted slightly as amusement tugged at the corners of his mouth. "The fence line? There's not much to it, but sure." He extended a hand. "Nice to meet you, Chelsia."

She accepted the handshake, noting the rough calluses and the warmth of his grip. "Nice to meet you, too."

Bellamy's smile widened as she glanced briefly toward the paddock, where Bennett had wandered closer to lean casually against the fence.

"Good. Caleb will show you around. He's been here long enough to know the ropes."

"Three months is long enough?" he teased, tone light. "Not sure I'd call myself an expert yet."

"Three months is more than long enough," she replied smoothly, flicking him a look that cut off any further protest. With a quick glance back at the paddock, she added, "Don't take all day."

A quiet chuckle escaped as he gestured for Chelsia to follow. "Come on. Let's take a walk."

They moved toward the fence line at the edge of the property, where the rails stood clean and sturdy, the maintenance clear in the farm's pristine upkeep. Caleb paused, running a hand over the smooth wood.

"There's really not much to see. The fence is in good shape, just needs a check now and then to make sure nothing's loose. Not sure why Bellamy wanted me to bring you out here."

Chelsia glanced back toward the barn, where two familiar figures stood talking.

"Me either," she said, though inwardly she guessed there was a reason, and it probably had more to do with Bennett than the fence.

Caleb leaned against a post, crossing his arms over his chest. "So, how's your first day going?"

She shrugged, smiling. "I haven't been trampled yet, so I'd call that a win."

He chuckled, a low, pleasant sound. "If you can handle the chickens, you'll do fine."

"Funny, everyone keeps saying that. I'm starting to think those birds have a reputation."

"It's warranted," he replied. "Stick around long enough, and you'll see why."

Her laugh was light, genuine. "Been pretty busy, though. That's probably the point, right?"

"Pretty much. She likes to keep people moving. Keeps your mind off things."

"Things?"

"Life. Whatever brought you here." He gestured vaguely toward the horizon. "It works, though. At least, it does for me."

Something in his tone made her pause. "What things do you need to keep your mind off of?"

For a moment, he looked out across the distant fields, his expression clouded.

"Let's just say I was in a rough situation. Hooked on some bad stuff and ended up homeless. Bellamy helped clean me up. Took me in, put me to work." A faint smile touched his lips. "She's invested in my success. I mean, she's not just trying to make me stick around here working for her. She expects me to get back on my feet and move on at some point."

"Pretty much the same here," Chelsia admitted softly. "Well, not as far as being hooked on anything. But she's left it open for me to decide how long to stay, too."

He nodded. "She's doing what she can to make sure I'm on the right track, even watching everything I eat like a hawk."

Her brows furrowed. "Watches what you eat?"

"Yeah." His smirk returned. "Bellamy's big on 'healing from within,' as she likes to call it." Hazel eyes flicked over her with an easy warmth. "Doesn't look like it's a problem for you, though."

She blinked, puzzled. "Not unless chicken, potatoes, and veggies count as healing components."

A deep, genuine laugh escaped him, and his shoulders relaxed against the fence.

"You'll get used to it, you know. The farm, the pace, Bellamy. She's intense, but she's good people."

"You sound like you've got a lot of faith in her."

"She earned it," he said simply. "I wasn't exactly an easy project when I got here, but she never gave up on me. It's not just work for her. It's personal. She really cares about the people she brings in."

Chelsia nodded thoughtfully, her gaze drifting toward the paddocks in the distance.

"She seems... complicated."

His chuckle was low. "That's one way to put it." Pushing off the fence, he brushed his hands on his jeans. "Come on, we should head back before she sends out a search party. Or worse, Bennett."

She laughed softly, falling into step beside him as they started across the field.

"What's so bad about Bennett?"

"Nothing. I wouldn't want to get between him and Bellamy, though. They've got... history."

Her steps slowed slightly as she glanced over at him, careful not to give away what little she already knew.

"History?"

"Ask her about it." His grin turned teasing. "I'm not the one to spill those beans."

By the time they returned to the barn, the sun was dipping low, bathing the buildings in the golden light of late afternoon. Near the paddocks, Bellamy and Bennett stood in quiet conversation, their voices low. Something in her stance had shifted. She seemed relaxed, or perhaps resigned.

"Made it back in one piece," Caleb called, breaking the stillness as he approached. "Fence line's still standing."

Bellamy turned, giving them both a quick once-over. "Good. You can handle the next section tomorrow." Without giving him a chance to reply, she shifted her attention. "And you—get cleaned up. Dinner's soon, and you've had enough of an introduction for one day."

Chelsia nodded without protest, catching Caleb's quick smile before he strolled off toward the barn, hands tucked into his pockets, a low whistle trailing behind him.

Once he was out of earshot, she glanced at Bellamy. "Does Caleb have a room in the house, too?"

The question seemed to catch her off guard. A smirk curved her lips as she looked toward the barn.

"No. He's got a room in one of the barns. Suits him better, I think."

Brows lifting slightly, Chelsia tilted her head. "Why's that?"

Before an answer came, Bennett spoke, his voice teasing as he absently studied his fingernails.

"You're asking a lot of questions about Caleb."

She shrugged. "Just trying to get a sense of things."

Bellamy's focus returned to the barn, her mouth tightening briefly before she spoke. "When I first met Caleb, he was a filthy transient... strung out and desperate. Tried to rob that coffee shop we went to the other night."

Chelsia's eyes widened slightly. "He... robbed the coffee shop?"

"Tried to," Bellamy repeated. "Didn't get very far before Ryan had him on the floor. Looked like he hadn't had a solid meal in weeks."

Bennett nodded, his voice quieter now. "He was in awful shape, no doubt about it. Could've gone either way for him."

Crossing her arms, Bellamy's voice softened. "Ryan convinced me to give him a shot. Suggested I take him in instead of letting the law handle it. Caleb had a choice: work here or face jail time. He chose the farm."

Chelsia looked toward the barn, her thoughts turning over everything she'd just heard. "And now?"

Bellamy followed her line of sight. "Now? He's proven me wrong. Caleb's the benchmark for anyone who ends up here. Not that I let just anyone in. I'm picky about who I give chances to."

"You make exceptions, though," Bennett said, his words carrying a quiet edge. "You wouldn't have taken Caleb in if I hadn't pushed."

Her lips pressed together briefly. "Seems to be the norm as of late."

Chelsia briefly questioned if the comment was directed toward her. She cleared her throat, focusing on the barn again. "It seems like he appreciates it."

"He does." Bellamy's voice softened further. "It's funny how you can take something rough and unpresentable and turn it into something better with the right care. Like a tough cut of meat that just needs a little tenderizing before it can become something worth serving."

A polite smile crossed Chelsia's face. "I guess that's one way to look at it."

"It's the only way," Bellamy replied. Without waiting for a response, she turned toward the house. "Come on. Let's get inside before dinner."

The farmhouse kitchen had grown cozier with the setting sun, the warm glow of the chandelier casting soft light over the table laden with dinner. A steaming pot of beef stew sat at the center, its rich aroma filling the air. Chelsia watched as Bellamy ladled the stew into bowls, the velvety broth spilling over tender chunks of beef, vibrant carrots, caramelized pearl onions, and earthy parsnips. A sprinkle of fresh parsley brightened the dish, while the scent of garlic and rosemary infused each passing bowl.

She accepted hers with a quiet "thank you," breathing in the comforting aroma before reaching for a slice of bread. The crust crackled under her fingers, golden and warm, while the herb-infused butter melted instantly, releasing hints of dill and chives. Across the table, Bennett tore into his own slice, dipping it into the stew without hesitation.

"Between lunch and this," he said between bites, "the drive out here was worth it."

Bellamy's smirk held a trace of amusement as she glanced across the table. "I'd say the company has something to do with it, too."

Chelsia ignored the weight behind the comment, focusing instead on her steaming bowl. She tore off a chunk of bread, dipped it into the rich broth, and let the bold, comforting flavors warm her from the inside out. It wasn't fancy, but it was good, simple food that felt like a hug in meal form.

The quiet stretched until Bellamy's voice broke through. "You've been awfully sociable lately, Ryan. Planning to show up for meals all the time now?"

Bennett looked up from his bowl, his smile easy even as something sharper flickered behind his eyes.

"Wouldn't want to impose. I'm just, you know, checking in."

Instead of responding, Bellamy reached for the platter of roasted asparagus, serving herself a few spears. Their lightly charred tips glistened under the sheen of oil as she arranged them on her plate.

"I'd say she's managing just fine. Haven't lost her to the chickens, have we, Chelsia?"

Chelsia glanced up, discomfited by the sudden shift in attention.

"Not yet," she replied with a small smile. "Though the day's not over."

A gentle laugh escaped across the table, though it felt oddly misplaced against the undercurrent of friction.

The rest of the meal passed in near silence, the occasional clink of silverware against plates filling the gaps between conversation. Chelsia savored each bite, her attention shifting between the tender stew and the warm light spilling in from the adjoining room.

After dinner, as Chelsia helped clear the table, Bennett caught her arm gently, guiding her toward the back hallway where shadows absorbed the warmth of the kitchen. His usual easygoing demeanor had faded, and the look he gave her carried a quiet seriousness.

"Bellamy's not wrong," he said, his voice low enough to stay between them. "I haven't been out here much lately. But that's only because there wasn't much of a reason for it. Now... there is."

She blinked, surprised by his candor. "A reason?"

"You," he said simply. "It's important to me that you're okay. This whole setup... I just want to make sure it's what you need."

Her throat felt tight, the weight of his sincerity settling over her like a blanket. "Thanks," she said softly, the word barely escaping.

A faint smile tugged at the corner of his mouth as he stepped back, giving her space.

"I'll let you finish what you were doing. Get some rest. You've had a long day."

The house was quiet as Chelsia ascended the stairs, the soft creak of the wooden steps the only sound in the stillness. Dinner had been a satisfying end to a long day, leaving her body content but her mind restless. Thoughts circled, refusing to settle. She pushed them aside as she reached her bedroom door, turned the handle, and stepped inside.

The room greeted her with the same pristine order it had when she'd first arrived; quilt on the bed undisturbed, and chair by the window exactly as she'd left it. Yet as the door clicked shut behind her, a prickle ran along her spine—a strange awareness she couldn't quite define.

The air felt... different. Not colder, not warmer, just *off*. Her eyes scanned the room, tracing over familiar details as though she expected something to be amiss. Everything appeared in its place. With a brisk rub of her hands, she dismissed the unease. It had been a long day, and exhaustion was twisting her senses.

In the ensuite bathroom, the clawfoot tub waited like an invitation. Steam curled upward as water splashed against porcelain, and the rising heat pulled the stiffness from her shoulders. She lowered herself into the bath with a sigh; the warmth wrapping around her like a cocoon. Her head tilted back, and her eyes slipped closed as the day's weight slowly melted away.

When she emerged wrapped in a towel, the feeling of unease crept in again. Nothing had changed. The room was still as orderly as before, yet something felt... unsettled.

She crossed to the door, closing it firmly and sliding the lock into place with a soft click. The sound, though quiet, carried a slight comfort. Moving through the familiar motions of drying off and changing into her bedclothes, she couldn't stop her eyes from darting briefly to the corners of the room. The sensation of being watched, or perhaps simply *not alone*, brushed against her mind, insistent yet unprovable.

The bed was warm as she slipped beneath the quilt, pulling it tightly around her. Moonlight spilled through the curtains, painting pale streaks across the floor while shadows huddled in the corners of the room.

Sleep came slowly, her thoughts circling like distant murmurs just out of reach.

CHAPTER TWENTY-NINE

The soft glow of dawn spilled through the farmhouse windows, casting beams of light across the wooden floor. Chelsia stirred groggily, limbs heavy and her mind clouded with remnants of fractured sleep. The quilt's warmth was almost enough to tempt her to stay in bed, but the distant sound of animals stirring on the farm pulled her from the haze.

Downstairs, the house was already buzzing with activity. In the kitchen, Bellamy stood at the counter, arranging a tray of golden biscuits. The rich scent of freshly brewed coffee mingled with the smokiness of the wood-burning stove, though even the inviting aromas couldn't fully chase away the fog clinging to Chelsia's thoughts.

"Morning, sleepyhead," Bellamy greeted, her voice warm yet unusually intent. For a moment, her attention lingered on Chelsia before softening. "Rough night?"

She nodded, rubbing at her temples. "Had trouble settling down."

A soft *tsk* followed. "It's the new surroundings. They'll throw you off at first." Moving to the pantry, Bellamy emerged with a small tin marked with looping, delicate handwriting. "This is an herbal tea I make myself with things grown here on the farm. Helps you settle down at night, clear your head. It'll have you sleeping like a baby."

Hesitating, Chelsia's brow knit briefly. "I don't want to trouble you."

The response came with a dismissive wave and a calm smile. "No trouble at all, or I wouldn't have offered. You're working hard. You need your rest."

She set the tin down with a decisive thud. "I'll brew some up tonight. You'll thank me in the morning."

She returned the smile, though a faint unease stirred at the back of her mind—a quiet echo of Gillian's relentless insistence about medication. *Different circumstances,* she reminded herself, shaking off the thought.

"Now," Bellamy said briskly, shifting gears, "finish waking up and get some food in you. There's coffee if you want it, or I've got tea ready if you prefer."

A simple ceramic mug was nudged forward, steam curling from the surface. The aroma was earthy, with a hint of mint and something floral she couldn't quite place. Wrapping her hands around the mug, Chelsia took a cautious sip, warmth spreading through her chest. The taste was pleasant, subtle, and soothing, unlike anything she'd had before.

"You'll need your energy, and that'll help," Bellamy added firmly. "The morning's chores don't wait for anyone, and you've got a full day ahead."

The crisp air carried the scent of earth and hay as Chelsia walked toward the barn, balancing a tray laden with Caleb's lunch. Bellamy had insisted she deliver it herself, her smirk hinting at reasons beyond simple practicality. From the tray rose the rich aroma of stew, likely leftover from the night before, though now enhanced by fresh ingredients. Sizzling slices of meat and sautéed vegetables added a livelier edge, while subtle notes of spices or garnishes she couldn't quite place gave the meal an intentional, almost personal feel.

Near the edge of the paddock, Caleb worked on a loose fence board. He straightened as she approached, wiping his hands on his jeans with an amiable smile.

"Delivery service now, huh?"

She rolled her eyes, though a small grin broke through. "Apparently. Bellamy said this was for you, and only you. Feeling special yet?"

His laugh came softly. "Always. Thanks."

He took the tray from her and settled on a nearby bench, tearing into the bread with a hunger that spoke to long hours spent outdoors. Chelsia leaned casually against the paddock rail, her arms crossed as she watched him dig in.

"You must be doing something right," she said, nodding toward the tray. "Bellamy doesn't seem like someone who hands out special treatment lightly."

Caleb dipped a piece of bread into the stew, smirking faintly. "Like I said the other day, she's got her ways of making sure people stay on the right track."

"And you're fine with that?"

For a moment, he paused, considering. "I am. Most people don't get a second chance like this. I wasn't exactly in a place to be picky when I got here." His voice softened as he looked her way. "But you're different."

"Different how?" Her brow lifted slightly.

His shoulders rose in a light shrug. "You don't seem like someone who needs a second chance. You don't have that... edge, you know? Most folks who end up here—me included—carry scars you can see."

Chelsia's fingers fidgeted with the hem of her jacket as she held his gaze briefly. "Looks can deceive," she said softly. "You don't know the half of it."

He studied her for a moment, curiosity flickering across his features, but whatever question hovered on his tongue went unspoken. Instead, he nodded toward the sprawling barns beyond the paddock.

"Bellamy's got a good setup here. Big operation, plenty of space. It's easy to get lost in it."

Her eyes followed his gesture. "It is pretty big... I was wondering if there are others. People who live here, in the barns or somewhere else."

Caleb tore off another piece of bread, chewing thoughtfully before replying. "Not really. There are workers who come and go on regular shifts, people on the payroll. But Bellamy's picky about who gets to live here. Guess she's got her reasons."

She nodded slowly, turning her attention briefly to the nearly empty tray. Those subtle details drifted through her thoughts again.

"I hope that what I told you the other day, about me and how I came here, didn't freak you out," he blurted.

Her head snapped up, surprised. "No. Why would it?"

"Druggies don't exactly have the best reputations," he said with a crooked grin. "Most people are all for rehabilitation, as long as it happens far away from them."

Shaking her head, she met his eyes directly. "I'm not one of those people."

His smile softened. "Like I said, you're different."

For a moment, neither of them spoke. Then Chelsia chuckled lightly, breaking the quiet.

"Well, enjoy the rest of your lunch. I should probably get back before Bellamy starts wondering what I've been up to."

Caleb leaned back slightly on the bench, one hand resting on the tray. "Thanks for bringing this out. You're good company, even if you're something of a mystery."

Her smirk returned as she gave a small wave and turned back toward the house.

Dinner was straightforward and satisfying: a hearty vegetable casserole paired with warm, buttered rolls. The table felt quieter than the night before, the absence of Bennett's easy banter leaving the silence more pronounced. Bellamy, however, seemed unfazed, moving through the meal with her usual composure.

"You're unusually quiet tonight," she remarked while refilling her glass of water, a small smile tugging at the corner of her mouth. "Must be missing your audience."

Startled, Chelsia looked up from her plate. "I guess I'm just tired," she said evenly. "Never quite recovered from the lack of sleep."

"Then we'll have to make sure that doesn't happen tonight." Rising from the table, Bellamy crossed to the counter and returned with the small tin of tea she'd shown earlier, her fingers tapping lightly against the lid. "You'll feel like a new woman after a mug of this."

Her fork stilled briefly over her plate. "I don't know. I rarely use sleep aids."

"It's not medication," came the smooth reply. "Do you think I'd keep something like that around with Caleb here? This tea will do more good than harm—trust me."

Reluctantly, Chelsia nodded, her polite smile concealing the discomfort stirring in her chest. Caleb's words from earlier drifted through her mind, mingling with the awareness of the farm's careful routines. Everything felt overly precise, each detail firmly in place.

After dinner, she excused herself, climbing the stairs slowly as the weight of the day pressed into her limbs. Inside her room, she closed the door and let out a quiet sigh before stepping into the bathroom. The familiar ritual of washing away the day's dust and fatigue brought a fleeting sense of normalcy.

When she emerged, her hair neatly twisted into moisturized sections and tucked beneath a silk scarf, her towel wrapped securely around her, she paused. Her attention fell to the bedside table.

A steaming mug waited there, the soft aroma of mint and lavender curling into the air. True to her word, Bellamy had delivered.

Moving cautiously, Chelsia sat on the edge of the bed, fingers brushing against the ceramic. The gentle heat pressed into her palms, offering fragile comfort in the room's stillness.

For a long moment, she studied the liquid, her thoughts circling back to her host's unerring precision, and the way every action and word carried an intent that felt impossible to ignore.

With a steadying breath, she raised the mug to her lips and took a sip.

CHAPTER THIRTY

The greenhouse air carried a damp chill, at odds with the icy sting of winter beyond the glass. Chelsia adjusted her gloves as Bellamy handed her a metal scoop, then gestured toward a burlap sack near a row of planters. Its contents were pale and powdery, fine particles clinging stubbornly to the sack's interior. An earthy scent rose from it, underscored by something sour.

"This is the fertilizer we're using today," Bellamy said briskly, already focused on tending to a row of herbs. "Sprinkle a thin layer over the soil and work it in gently. Don't overdo it."

Chelsia kneeled beside the planter, gripping the scoop carefully. The material felt rough even through the fabric of her gloves, its texture almost gritty. As she scattered it across the soil, tiny, jagged fragments caught the light filtering through the glass panes. Her hand paused mid-motion, a frown pulling at her brow.

"What's in this?" she asked, glancing briefly over her shoulder.

Bellamy turned, brushing her palms against the front of her apron. Her smile came easily, yet something about it felt hollow.

"Just a blend I've created that does wonders. It's what makes everything thrive."

For a moment, Chelsia studied hersearching, uncertain. But whatever she was looking for remained just out of reach. With a small nod, she turned back to her task.

As she worked, the texture of the fertilizer continued to catch her attention. Another sharp glint flashed under the light; a tiny fragment buried among the powder. An uneasy feeling stirred in her chest, but she shook it off and kept working.

Bellamy's confidence had a way of closing off further questions, and pressing felt pointless.

By lunchtime, the uneasiness from earlier had faded, replaced by the perpetual regularity of work. Caleb joined them at the table, freshly showered and carrying a faint trace of soap. Bellamy served plates of roasted chicken, glazed carrots, and a mixed salad.

Chelsia noticed subtle distinctions between the dishes. Caleb's salad was topped with pecans and creamy dressing, while hers carried citrus zest and fresh herbs.

"You're a quick learner," Caleb said, spearing a carrot with his fork. "Bellamy doesn't just let anyone into the greenhouse."

Chelsia glanced across the table.

"It's not about letting someone in," Bellamy said with a light laugh. "It's about who's willing to learn."

"Still," Caleb continued, shifting his focus back to Chelsia, "you've got the knack. Not everyone does. Trust me, I've seen plenty of people come and go since I got here."

She managed a small smile, uncertain how to respond.

Caleb leaned back in his chair, his tone turning playful. "By the way, I've been here for months and still haven't gotten a taste of that famous Porter Sausage."

Bellamy rolled her eyes, smirking. "That's reserved for special occasions."

"Maybe we'll get some on Christmas," Caleb whispered to Chelsia, throwing in an exaggerated wink.

Bellamy looked at him for a moment, though her smile remained unchanged. Chelsia's focus drifted back to the differences between their meals. The dishes were oddly specific, which seemed intentional, although she didn't know the reason.

Chelsia stood near the barn, brushing straw off her coat after finishing her post-lunch chores, when a familiar car rolled up the long drive. The detective stepped out, his plain shirt and slacks looking out of place against the rugged farm backdrop.

"Ryan," Bellamy greeted as she emerged from the barn, her tone clipped. She wiped her hands on her apron. "Didn't expect to see you here. Again."

"Good afternoon to you too, Bellamy," Bennett replied evenly before his attention shifted. "Miss Toussaint," he said with a hint of a smile. "How's it going?"

"Fine," she answered, tugging at her work gloves. "Getting the hang of things."

"Good to hear." He studied her briefly before turning back to Bellamy. "Can we talk?"

Jaw tight, Bellamy nodded and led him deeper into the barn. From behind a nearby tractor, Caleb emerged, one brow raised in silent question.

Chelsia shrugged, offering no answers.

As she tidied tools nearby, fragments of the conversation reached her ears despite her best efforts to seem disinterested.

"You act like you don't trust me," Bellamy said, irritation threading through her voice. "She's fine here. You don't need to keep checking on her."

"It's not that I don't trust you," Bennett replied firmly. "She's had a rough time, and I just want to make sure she's okay."

"She's exactly where she needs to be," Bellamy snapped. "You brought her here so she could get back on her feet, and I've got it handled... unless there's something else about her that you're not telling me."

There was a pause before his quieter response, the words just out of reach.

"How could you say that? That isn't what this is about."

The rest of their conversation slipped away as they moved further into the shadows of the barn.

When they reappeared, Bellamy's smile was carefully set in place, while Bennett avoided meeting Chelsia's eyes.

"Everything all right?" Caleb asked casually.

"Perfectly fine," Bellamy replied, her smile sharp at the edges. She turned to Chelsia and Caleb. "Finish checking the fence line. After that, Chelsia, you can head back to the greenhouse."

Caleb gave a mock salute, grinning as he defused the awkwardness. As they walked toward the field, he shot her a sideways glance.

"What was that about?"

"Nothing," she said with a sigh. "Just... Bellamy being Bellamy."

"And Bennett being Bennett," he added with a chuckle. After a brief pause, he nudged her lightly. "So... you and the detective?"

Chelsia froze mid-step, staring at him. "What?"

"You know," Caleb said, his tone teasing. "I couldn't help hearing the end of their chat. Is there more to it?"

A startled laugh escaped her, bright and unfiltered.

"He's old enough to be my father!"

He raised his hands in mock surrender. "All right, all right. Point taken." They resumed walking, the moment of humor fading into something quieter. "Just so you know... Even though you're pretty tight-lipped most of the time, I haven't asked Bellamy anything about you."

"I wouldn't say I'm tight-lipped," she said with a casual shrug.

"You know more about me than I do about you," he countered.

"I have no idea what you'd want to know or where to start."

"Well... Anyone waiting for you back home?"

The question hung in the air. Her shoulders stiffened slightly before she answered, her voice distant.

"I don't have a home."

"Everyone's got a home, Chelsia," Caleb said, his tone softer now. "I even have one, although I haven't been back there in years."

They walked in silence for a while, the weight of her words settling between them.

Eventually, he broke the stillness. "Fair enough. I won't pry."

"You're not prying," she said quietly. "It's just... complicated."

"I get that. Whatever happened, though, things have a way of working out."

She glanced over at him and let out a quiet chuckle. "Maybe."

The greenhouse air hung warm and dense, carrying the mingled scents of soil and herbs. Chelsia adjusted the strap of her apron, focusing on the planters in front of her. Bellamy had tasked her with transplanting seedlings into fresh soil, a repetitive process that brought a sense of calm.

Nearby, a small pile of fertilizer sat waiting, its whitish, coarse grains etched too firmly in her memory from earlier. She avoided studying it too closely; handling it was manageable as long as she didn't let her mind wander.

From the doorway, Caleb leaned casually against the frame, arms crossed and wearing a crooked grin.

"Look at you! Just a regular Poison Ivy."

Chelsia glanced up, smiling as she tucked a loose coil of hair back under her headwrap.

"I'm only following instructions."

"No," he said, stepping closer, "it's more than that. You've got an eye for this. Bellamy might not say much, but she notices."

She hesitated, unsure how to respond. Caleb chuckled, taking her silence for modesty.

"I told you that she's picky about who gets in here, and this is your second time today."

"Maybe just cautious," Chelsia said, kneeling to pat soil around a seedling.

He smirked. "Cautious? That's one way to put it."

Straightening, she brushed her hands on her apron. "What's that supposed to mean?"

His shoulders lifted in a loose shrug, the grin widening. "She's got her quirks."

"Don't we all?" she replied, her smirk earning a broader grin in return.

"What kinds of quirks could you possibly have?"

"How much time have ya got?" Chelsia shot back; her tone playful.

Before he could respond, Bellamy's voice cut through the greenhouse. She stood in the doorway, her attention shifting briefly between them.

"Caleb, the feed delivery just arrived."

"On it," he said, raising his hands in mock surrender before flashing one last smile in Chelsia's direction and disappearing into the sunlight.

Turning back to the seedlings, she focused on her task. Bellamy remained by the entrance for a few moments longer, unmoving.

The silence felt unusually intense, carrying with it an edge that made the air feel heavier.

When Bellamy finally turned and walked away, Chelsia let out a quiet breath she hadn't realized she'd been holding.

By the time Chelsia finished in the greenhouse, the late afternoon sun hung low in the sky, spilling golden light across the farm. She brushed her hands on her apron as she walked toward the farmhouse. The crisp air carried hints of fresh water from the troughs and the dusty scent of the well-worn pathways. Bellamy had insisted she take a moment to relax before dinner prep began.

Settling on the porch steps, Chelsia leaned against the railing and let the stillness settle around her. The rhythmic clucking of chickens and the distant lowing of cows blended into a calming backdrop. Her muscles ached, a satisfying reminder of the day's work.

Her attention drifted toward the horizon. Not that she had forgotten Michael, Gillian... or Moira. The physical tasks helped keep her mind from wandering too deeply.

She considered the winding path that had brought her here, not just to Portland, but to the other places she had passed through along the way. The last few years had been a series of unpredictable turns, each leaving its mark.

Footsteps approached, pulling her from her thoughts. Bellamy appeared, carrying two steaming mugs of tea.

"You're not thinking about skipping dinner, are you?"

Chelsia shook her head, managing a smile as she accepted one of them.

"Just taking a breather. Thank you."

Bellamy lowered herself onto the steps beside her. Steam rose in delicate curls from their mugs, drifting upward on the evening breeze.

"You're adjusting well," she said after a pause. "Most people take longer to settle in." A quiet sound of acknowledgment came from beside her, and Bellamy studied her over the rim of her mug. "I've noticed other things, too."

Chelsia paused, her mug hovering just below her lips. "Like?"

"You don't trust easily," Bellamy said matter-of-factly. "And you don't open up much."

Lowering the mug, Chelsia stared into its contents, feeling the conversation veer into unwelcome territory. It echoed too closely to her earlier exchange with Caleb.

"I'm the same way," Bellamy continued. "That's how I recognized it."

"Is that a bad thing?" Chelsia asked cautiously.

"No," came the response, paired with a thoughtful tilt of Bellamy's head. "It's interesting, though."

Before Chelsia could reply, Caleb's laughter rang out from the barn, followed by the rumble of an engine starting up.

Bellamy stood, brushing her hands against her thighs. "You should head inside before it gets too cold. Maybe rest in your room for a bit, if you'd like. I'll call you when dinner's ready."

As she walked away, Chelsia's attention remained on the confident stride, the way every movement seemed intentional. Despite the calm exterior, the exchange left an unsettled feeling behind, an unspoken weight clinging to the edges of the moment.

She looked down at the tea, her fingers tightening slightly around the mug. The warmth, once soothing, felt different now. It was less comfort and more something she wasn't sure she could trust.

Later that evening, the farmhouse was still when Chelsia slipped into her room, the lingering aromas of dinner soft but comforting. She closed the door gently, careful not to jostle the mug of tea in her hand, and set it on the nightstand. The small lamp spread a golden glow across the room, highlighting the rustic furniture and the quilt draped neatly over the bed. Muted tones blended with the room's simple decor, creating a sense of stillness.

She removed her headwrap, letting her coils spring free, then walked to the bathroom to wash up. Cool water splashed against her skin, clearing away the weight of the day.

Scenes from earlier replayed as she toweled off: Caleb's humor, Bellamy's careful attention, and Bennett's tension during his brief visit. His absence at dinner had been noticeable, leaving an unspoken gap at the table. He usually stayed, making casual conversation over a meal. Not today. The exchange in the barn—Bellamy's clipped responses, Bennett's quiet insistence—unfolded again in her mind, another fragment of a larger picture she couldn't yet assemble.

Settling into bed, she pulled the quilt snugly around her shoulders. The tea's herbal aroma mingled with the lavender drifting from the bedside diffuser. She took a slow sip, warmth spreading from her palms into her chest. Bellamy's words echoed back: *"You don't trust easily…"*

Scooting against the headboard, Chelsia let her thoughts drift. She hadn't always been so guarded. There was a time when trust had come naturally, maybe too naturally. Faces and places floated to the surface: cities she'd passed through, people she'd left behind, decisions she couldn't take back. Starting over had become second nature, an instinct woven into her.

Portland was supposed to be different. Michael was supposed to be different. Yet no matter how far she ran, her past always seemed to catch up. The thought settled heavily in her chest, a nagging belief that it was all some form of karma.

She reached for her phone, tapping the screen out of habit. It stayed dark, the weak signal offering no updates or connections. Setting it back on the nightstand, she let her hand rest briefly on the surface. Gillian no longer reached out, and Moira never had. The sting of that truth settled deep, though she wouldn't admit it aloud.

Her eyes shifted toward the window, where moonlight slipped through thin curtains, painting pale shapes across the floor. The farm lay quiet under the night sky, still and seemingly peaceful. But something about it felt… unsettled. The fertilizer in the greenhouse, Bellamy's carefully chosen words, Caleb's offhand comments, each detail clung stubbornly to the edges of her thoughts.

Sliding further beneath the quilt, she closed her eyes. Bennett's earlier visit lingered; his abrupt goodbye, the way he'd avoided looking directly at her. And Bellamy, with her composed confidence, her subtle control, as if every answer sat locked behind her smile.

Chelsia sighed, turning onto her side. The weight of the day settled into her limbs and sleep crept closer. Yet the questions remained, threading through her thoughts like knots in a rope: tight, tangled, and refusing to come undone.

CHAPTER THIRTY-ONE

Morning broke cold and still, frost sparkling across the barn roofs and stiff blades of grass. Chelsia stood by the kitchen window, cradling a warm mug in her hands as the sun crept above the horizon. The farmhouse remained quiet; Bellamy had yet to make an appearance, and Caleb was likely outside, already knee-deep in the day's first tasks.

When she finally stepped into the barn, the air carried the sweet scent of grain mixed with the earthy musk of animals. At the far end, Caleb stacked heavy bags of feed onto a cart.

He glanced up as she approached, a grin spreading across his face.

"Morning, Poison Ivy," he said, dusting his hands against his jeans.

Chelsia rolled her eyes, though she couldn't help smiling. "You're not letting that one go, are you?"

"Not a chance." He hefted another bag onto the pile with ease. "Bellamy said you're supposed to help me check the fence line today."

Her smile faded slightly as her brow knit together. "Sure, okay," she said with a small shrug.

This time, they walked the fence line stretching along the farm's perimeter, weaving through patches of dense trees and open fields. Frost clung stubbornly to shaded areas, crunching softly beneath their boots. Caleb carried a small toolbox, his easy stride showing no sign of discomfort from the biting cold.

"So, what exactly are we looking for?" Chelsia asked, tucking her hands into her jacket pockets. "And why does this need to be done so often?"

"Mostly damage," he replied. "Loose boards, sagging wires... anything that could let the animals wander where they shouldn't."

Her eyes scanned the fence, its construction sturdy and well-maintained. "Does that happen a lot?"

"Not really," Caleb admitted, stopping to inspect a section of wood. "Now and then, something gets snagged or knocked loose. It's rare, though. Bellamy's just... particular about keeping everything in top shape."

She raised an eyebrow. "Particular how?"

He hesitated, tapping a fence post lightly with his hammer. "She likes things in order. Might be the business side of her. On a farm this size, it'd be easy for something to slip through the cracks. She works hard to make sure that doesn't happen."

The comment settled into her thoughts as they continued along the path. The air hung still and crisp, interrupted only by the occasional chirp of a bird or the faint rustle of branches overhead.

"You've been here a while," she said after a pause. "Do you ever feel like... I don't know, something's a little off about this place?"

Caleb slowed mid-step. "Off how?"

She shrugged, keeping her voice casual. "It's just... small things. Like how Bellamy answers questions. She's always so careful, like there's something more she's not saying."

Her thoughts drifted to the peculiar fertilizer in the greenhouse and Bellamy's carefully worded explanation.

Caleb leaned an arm casually on the fence, studying her for a moment before speaking.

"You're not the first person to say that."

Her stomach tightened. "I'm not?"

"Nope." His tone remained light, but he assumed a more thoughtful look. "A lot of people are surprised that a woman runs a farm this big. Who knows how many times she's had to prove herself? Maybe being guarded is just part of how she gets by."

The distant sound of an engine cut through the quiet before she could respond. Caleb straightened, shading his eyes as he looked toward the main road.

"Delivery truck," he said. "This might be more interesting than the fence."

Shouldering his toolbox, he motioned for her to follow.

Caleb and Chelsia watched as the truck rolled to a stop near the barn. The driver stepped out, unloading a pallet and carefully stacking several crates. Bellamy was already there, clipboard in hand, her voice even as she spoke briefly with the driver.

"What's in the crates?" Caleb asked, leaning casually against the barn wall.

Bellamy glanced up, her smile distant. "Replacements for worn-out equipment. With the harvest coming up, I can't afford any delays."

Chelsia turned her attention to the stack. The smaller crates rattled softly when set down, but the largest one—vented with rows of narrow holes—remained still. The air carried a strange metallic scent, acrid and unsettling.

"All set," the driver said with a nod. "Should be everything you requested."

"Perfect," Bellamy replied, signing the form on the clipboard. "Thanks for getting this here on time."

As the driver climbed back into the truck, Caleb stepped forward, frowning at the pallet.

"I'll grab the pallet jack from the shed. Be right back."

He disappeared around the side of the barn, leaving Chelsia standing near the crates. She crouched beside the largest one, fingers tracing the rough grain of the wood. The ventilation holes caught her attention again, and another whiff of that metallic tang hit her nose, stronger this time. It hung in the cool air, clinging to her senses.

Her hand paused over a scuffed corner, where a dark stain marred the surface. It was faint, easy to miss, but the sight of it sent a shiver through her.

"Chelsia."

Bellamy's voice broke the stillness, and she jerked upright. Across the stack, Bellamy stood watching her, a small smile fixed on her face.

"Caleb won't be long," she said.

Chelsia stood quickly, brushing her hands against her jacket. Unspoken words filled the silence that followed, creating a palpable tension between them.

Moments later, Caleb reappeared, maneuvering a slightly rusted pallet jack toward them.

"Got it. This'll make things easier."

She stepped back as he slid the jack beneath the pallet. The wheels creaked softly as he lifted it, releasing another wave of the metallic scent. Caleb didn't seem to notice.

"Mind opening the doors?" he asked. "I'll stash these in the equipment corner."

Chelsia hurried to pull the barn doors open. Inside, the dim space carried the familiar mix of hay and oil mingling with the cool air. Caleb guided the load inside, his actions fluid despite the weight.

"You're quiet," he remarked as he passed. "What's on your mind?"

"Nothing," she said too quickly, stepping aside.

He smirked. "Terrible liar, aren't you?"

"Not remotely," she shot back, matching his playful tone as he unloaded the crates.

Bellamy had followed them inside, arms crossed, as she observed. Against the pale winter sky, her figure seemed larger than life.

"You're looking at those crates like they're about to sprout legs and run off," Caleb said, setting down the second box. "Relax! They're just tools."

Chelsia's attention returned to the largest crate. "For a harvest?"

"Probably," Caleb said with a shrug, hefting the last box onto the stack. "I don't ask too many questions. This is Bellamy's playground. If she says we need it, we probably do."

The crates sat neatly aligned against the barn wall, their shadows stretching across the dim interior. Caleb gave the arrangement a nod of approval.

"That's the last one."

"Nice work," Bellamy said as she moved closer. "Leave the pallet jack here. I might need to move things around later."

"I can handle that now if you'd like," Caleb offered.

"No need," she replied briskly. "It's quicker if I take care of it myself. You two should head back to the house and help yourselves to the brownies I baked. I'll finish up here." As they turned to leave, she added, "Oh, Caleb, your tea is on the counter. You missed it this morning, so I made some fresh. Don't forget again."

"Got it, Bell," he replied sheepishly, nudging Chelsia's elbow as he gestured for her to follow. She trailed after him, but something tugged at her attention.

Bellamy crouched beside the largest crate, her hand brushing over the wood as if inspecting it. The metallic scent returned, thicker than before. Or had it ever left?

"Come on," Caleb said gently, breaking her focus.

Chelsia followed, her boots scuffing lightly against the barn floor. As they stepped outside, the cold air bit at her cheeks in contrast to the warmth of the barn. She turned back once more, catching sight of Bellamy still bent closer to the crate, her head tilted slightly, as if listening for something inside.

The barn doors creaked on their hinges, groaning as they swung shut. Just before they closed completely, Bellamy looked up, her green eyes locking onto Chelsia's.

The doors thudded closed.

"Brownies sound good, don't they?" Caleb said as they walked toward the house.

"Yeah," she replied absently, her focus still on the barn as she fell out of step.

At the porch, Caleb quickened his step, reaching for the door. Chelsia hesitated, glancing back one last time. The barn loomed quiet in the fading light.

"Chelsia, you coming?" Caleb called.

She forced a smile and stepped forward. "Yeah. Coming."

CHAPTER THIRTY-TWO

The morning arrived with a biting chill, frost etching delicate patterns along the farmhouse windows. Stretching, Chelsia sat up and sighed at the wintry view. She reached for her phone on the nightstand, hoping the weather forecast might promise some reprieve from the relentless cold. Portland was supposed to be temperate, but this winter had defied expectations.

Unlocking the screen, she opened the weather app, only to be greeted by an error: *No network connection*. Frowning, she exited the app and reopened it, but the message persisted. A glance at the signal bar confirmed her suspicion: no service. Odd. She usually had at least one or two bars, regardless of where she was on the farm.

A few more attempts proved fruitless. Slowly, realization settled in. The lack of service wasn't temporary, it was permanent.

She was still on Michael's phone plan. It seemed the Cavanaughs were still crossing their t's. The phone, and its bill, had completely slipped her mind.

The thought stuck with her, casting a shadow over her morning as she set the phone aside and prepared for the day. After carefully twisting her thick coils and pinning them in place, she dressed and grabbed the phone again, slipping it into the front pocket of her flannel shirt. Maybe the issue would resolve itself.

Downstairs, the clatter of activity echoed from the kitchen, accompanied by Caleb's voice drifting in through the open window as he greeted the animals outside. Chelsia stepped into the kitchen, letting the warmth of the wood stove ease some of the tension in her shoulders. She poured herself a cup of tea, sipping it plain as she stared at the stubborn error message on the screen.

Bellamy entered suddenly, crossing the room with ease as she retrieved a pot from the stove.

"And here I was wondering if I'd need to come upstairs to wake you," she remarked. She glanced at the phone in Chelsia's hand. "Something wrong?"

Chelsia hesitated. "No. Just... no signal."

"Odd. Reception's usually pretty reliable here in the house."

"Yeah," she replied, trying for a casual shrug.

Bellamy tilted her head slightly, a teasing lilt entering her voice. "Did you forget to pay the bill?" Chelsia stiffened, and Bellamy's smile faded. "Oh," she said softly, blowing on her tea. "Is that it?"

"I didn't forget," Chelsia said, her voice clipped.

"Your boyfriend," Bellamy said quietly, more statement than question.

Chelsia looked away. "Yes."

"You didn't think to change it after...?"

"No," she admitted, her voice barely above a murmur. "Not with everything that's happened."

For a moment, Bellamy said nothing. Then she let out a quiet hum, her tone carrying a hint of sympathy.

"Understandable." Setting her mug down, she straightened. "Nothing a trip to Portland can't fix! I'll even call Ryan to tag along." Her green eyes gleamed. "Could be fun."

Chelsia parted her lips to respond, then thought better of it. Instead, she sipped her tea, the warmth doing little to ease her agitation. Bellamy didn't wait for an answer. With a glance at the clock, she pushed off the counter and carried her cup to the sink.

"Don't worry about a thing," she said cheerfully. "I'll make a quick call. We'll head out before lunch."

Chelsia nodded, her thoughts knotting as Bellamy vanished down the hall. The idea of going into Portland should have brought some relief, a chance to feel a shred of normalcy. Instead, it unsettled her, though she couldn't quite put her finger on why.

A couple of hours later, the sound of crackling gravel outside signaled Bennett's arrival. Chelsia stepped onto the porch just as his car rolled to a stop. He climbed out, weariness giving way to a smile as he looked at her.

"Chelsia," he greeted with a nod. "Heard you've had some trouble."

"A bit," she replied evenly.

"You ready to head out?"

Before she could answer, her eyes drifted toward the barn, where Caleb was hauling a bale of hay.

Bellamy emerged from the house, her boots thudding against the porch steps.

"Ryan," she said smoothly. "Thanks for coming."

"Bellamy," Bennett returned with polite restraint. "Thanks for inviting me."

She crossed her arms, her smile faint but practiced. "I was just telling Chelsia we should make it a group trip. Caleb could use a day in the city. Who knows when the chance will come again."

Bennett nodded. "Fine with me."

"Good," Bellamy said brightly before turning toward the barn. "Caleb! Grab your coat—road trip!"

At the sound of her voice, Caleb paused mid-motion, tossing the hay bale onto the pile. He brushed off his hands and grinned.

"You're the boss," he called back, jogging further into the barn.

The drive into Portland passed in near silence, the muted sounds of light traffic filling the gaps between brief attempts at conversation. Caleb's usual humor seemed subdued, his remarks sparse, while Chelsia focused on the passing scenery. Frosted branches and wreath-adorned porches hinted at the season, but the city felt cold and stark beneath an overcast sky.

In the front seat, Bellamy sat composed, her calm presence contrasting with Bennett's tense grip on the steering wheel.

When they pulled into the Eastport Plaza parking lot, Bellamy reached into her bag and withdrew two small envelopes. Turning slightly in her seat, she handed one each to Caleb and Chelsia.

"Your pay," she said brightly.

Chelsia blinked as she opened hers, catching sight of neatly folded bills. "You pay in cash?" she asked, unable to hide her surprise.

"Always," Bellamy replied. "Keeps things simple."

"Thanks, Bell," Caleb said with a grin, sliding his envelope into his jacket pocket without hesitation.

After a moment's pause, Chelsia tucked her own envelope away. The cash felt heavier than it should. It was a tangible reminder of just how much her life had changed since arriving at the farm.

Bellamy studied them briefly before nodding toward a faded Row C sign mounted on a nearby pole.

"We'll meet back here in two hours," she instructed, her voice light. Then her attention settled on Chelsia, her smile holding. "Don't get lost."

Chelsia blinked in surprise. Before she could respond, Caleb chimed in, his tone playful.

"Yes, ma'am," he said with a mock salute, as his grin returned.

Chelsia glanced at him, her surprise softening into gratitude, and gave a small nod before stepping out of the car. An icy breeze nipped at her cheeks as she walked toward the plaza, with Caleb falling into step beside her. At the plaza entrance, he gave her a wink before threading through the crowd, leaving her alone.

Inside the T-Mobile store, Chelsia wandered past the glowing magenta signs, her eyes skimming the neatly displayed phones. The prepaid options stood out immediately: simple, no contracts, no strings. Exactly what she needed.

At the register, the clerk slid a small keypad toward her. "Just follow the prompts to activate your phone number," he instructed.

Chelsia's hand hovered over the buttons, hesitating. The thought crossed her mind that she could ask to transfer her old number. For a fleeting moment, the idea felt like an anchor, something familiar to cling to. It would be easy, just a quick mention, and she'd keep a link to the life she'd left behind.

She dismissed the thought and selected the option for a new number. The phone's disconnection from her past was an opportunity for a clean slate, one she took. The clerk nodded as the activation completed, handing her a receipt with the details. Moments later, Chelsia stepped outside, clutching the bag containing her new phone and case. A quiet sense of relief trickled in, though it did little to ease the knot deep in her chest.

Chelsia returned to the meeting point with time to spare, her light shopping finished quickly and frugally. The parking lot had quieted, the distant jingling of a Salvation Army bell mixing with the occasional rush of passing cars.

Near the car, Bennett and Bellamy stood by the hood, steaming cups in hand, speaking in low tones. Chelsia slowed her steps, keeping enough distance not to intrude. Their exchange carried an edge she couldn't quite define. Bellamy's smile sat fixed in place, her shoulders squared, while Bennett's responses came short and measured, his jaw tight.

"Where's Caleb?" Bellamy asked abruptly, shifting her attention to Chelsia as she approached.

"I don't know," she answered with a shrug. "We weren't together."

"Two hours," Bellamy said coolly. "That's what I told you both."

"There's still time, Bell," Bennett replied, his voice even.

She scanned the lot, her focus moving across parked cars and scattered pedestrians. Silence stretched until a familiar figure appeared, jogging toward them. The bounce of Caleb's curls was unmistakable. He arrived slightly winded, grinning as he dug through a shopping bag.

"You should've seen the deal they had on these!" he exclaimed, pulling out a dark blue long-sleeved shirt. "I got four of them in different colors! Perfect for work. Check this out!"

He held up the shirt, the fabric soft and patterned with a faint checkered texture that caught the weak winter sunlight. The lighter stitching along the cuffs added a subtle contrast to the deep blue.

"It feels so nice!" he added, running a hand along the sleeve with visible satisfaction. As his hazel eyes shifted to Bellamy, the grin faltered and the joy on his face faded. "What's up?"

"You're late," Bellamy said, her words clipped. "For a moment, I thought you might have run off."

Caleb winced as if slapped, his shoulders slumping as he stuffed the shirt back into the bag.

"I went into a few places and lost track of time," he said softly. "I'm sorry." His eyes moved briefly to Chelsia before dropping to the pavement, embarrassment shadowing his face.

Bellamy didn't respond. Instead, she turned toward the car, her tone firm.

"We'd better head back."

She climbed inside without waiting for a reply.

The drive back to the farm was eerily silent. Bellamy sat poised, her composure unshaken, while Caleb stared out the window, teeth worrying his bottom lip. Beside him, Chelsia remained silent, her thoughts tangled with the friction from earlier and the weight of Bellamy's cutting words.

When they arrived, Caleb stayed near the car, clutching his shopping bag. Bellamy and Bennett disappeared into the farmhouse without a word. Chelsia hesitated before stepping closer to him.

"You okay?" she asked softly.

Caleb let out a deep sigh, his shoulders sagging.

"What a way to find out that after everything—all the time I've spent here, all the work I've done—she still doesn't trust me."

"Maybe she was just worried," Chelsia offered gently.

"Worried?" His voice edged higher, frustration seeping through. "She gave us two hours, and I wasn't even late, Chelsia! She went off for no reason! Does that sound like worry to you? I haven't messed up once since I got here... not once. I've done everything she's asked, and more."

He paused, his jaw tightening before he spoke again.

"I let her feed me teas and special meals without saying a word, even when it's... strange. And then she looks at me like I've shown up with a needle in my arm." His voice wavered, the hurt clear. "I didn't deserve that."

"No, you didn't," Chelsia said quietly. "I'm sorry." Hoping to ease the moment, she nodded toward the bag in his hands. "Want to show me the rest of your haul? I could trade you a look at my gloves, hat, and scarf. Total bargain. There might even be matching socks."

Caleb's lips pulled into a tired smile, but he shook his head. "Not right now, thanks."

She stepped back, giving him space. "Okay. If you change your mind, though..."

He nodded, but didn't reply. Turning away, his steps were slow as he walked toward the barn.

Chelsia stayed put, watching him disappear inside, an uncomfortable weight settling in her chest before she finally turned toward the house.

The warmth of the kitchen met her first, carrying the aroma of wood smoke and something sweet. Low voices came from the far end of the room: Bennett's calm, Bellamy's laugh stiff and distant.

Chelsia paused in the doorway, drawing a breath before stepping inside to join them.

CHAPTER THIRTY-THREE

Chelsia adjusted the straps of her work gloves as the morning light spilled across the fields, casting the barn and surrounding structures in a golden glow. Ahead of her, Caleb was already hard at work, dragging a bale of hay toward the feeding troughs with brisk, almost restless energy. She glanced back at the farmhouse. Bellamy stood on the porch, arms crossed, as she watched Caleb. Her stillness, paired with her intense focus, sparked a flicker of unease in Chelsia.

"Morning," Caleb muttered, keeping his attention on his task as she approached.

"Morning," she replied, hefting a smaller bale and falling into step beside him. "You're up early."

"Gotta keep the boss happy," he said with a dry chuckle, nodding toward the farmhouse without turning around. When Chelsia glanced back again, Bellamy had already vanished inside.

"Did you two argue?" she asked quietly, even though the distance made it unlikely anyone could hear.

"I don't think anyone argues with Bellamy," Caleb said under his breath. "Not even Bennett. She gives orders; you follow."

The morning unfolded in silence, broken only by the sounds of animals and the occasional clatter of tools. Caleb worked methodically, his movements tight and controlled. Chelsia spotted him leaning against the fence, staring out at the fields.

She approached carefully. "You okay?" she asked, brushing bits of hay from her gloves. "Still upset about the plaza?"

He shrugged, his eyes fixed on the horizon. "I'm just tired."

Chelsia hesitated, choosing her words carefully. "Bellamy was watching earlier. She mentioned during breakfast that she's noticed you and me talking more."

Caleb turned slightly, his posture stiffening. "And?"

"No and," she said. "But she kind of implied I shouldn't count on you."

His jaw tightened. "Figures. She's expecting me to screw up—go back to being the guy who couldn't hold it together."

"I'm not so sure," Chelsia said quietly, her brow knitting in thought.

He turned fully then, his face lined with doubt. "What do you mean?"

"At first, I thought she was going to start in on you, like before," she explained. "But then she said there were... bigger things in store for you."

Caleb let out a humorless laugh. "Bigger things?"

"Yeah," she said softly, "and that she wouldn't be surprised if you left the farm. Do you think what happened at the plaza was a misunderstanding?"

He considered her question. "I know what she said, and there wasn't any gray area about it. As for what she told you about 'bigger things'..." He paused, shaking his head. "Let's hope she's right."

Before she could respond, Bellamy's voice rang out from the farmhouse, calling them in for lunch. Caleb sighed, pushing off the fence with a weary motion. Neither spoke as they walked back toward the house, the air between them thick with unanswered questions.

Caleb sat at the rustic dining table, idly fiddling with his napkin as Chelsia settled into the chair across from him. The aroma of freshly baked bread mingled with the savory scent of roasted vegetables and herbs. Despite the inviting meal, the atmosphere carried a noticeable weight.

Bellamy approached with a dish of vegetables, placing it on the table with an exaggerated flourish.

"There," she said brightly. "A proper meal to keep us all going."

Caleb offered a brief smile, though the stiffness in his posture remained. Across from them, Bellamy served herself a modest portion, her green eyes drifting between them as she settled into her seat at the head of the table.

"You know," she began conversationally, "I've been thinking about how much the world has changed since I was a girl. Back then, we understood the value of hard work and tradition. Not like now, with everyone chasing the next big thing, willing to sell their souls for quick money." She paused, spearing a carrot with her fork. "It's a shame, really."

Caleb looked up; his brow furrowed. "Guess that's why you've held on to the farm the way you have."

Bellamy's smile stretched wider as she chewed thoughtfully, then gestured with her fork.

"Exactly! The Porter name, our award-winning sausage, the reputation we've built... it all stands for something real. You wouldn't believe how many offers I've had to sell it all off to some faceless corporation. They'd churn out a product that couldn't begin to compare with the original."

She set down her fork with precision. "There's a reason Porter Sausage is beloved. It's unique. No one can duplicate it, no matter how hard they try."

Caleb's chuckle lacked warmth. "Because you're the only one who knows the recipe, right?"

Bellamy's posture remained composed, but her smile thinned slightly. "You bet I am. It's older than all of us at this table combined. My grandfather's grandfather created it during hard times, and it's been our family's treasure ever since. I'd rather take it to my grave than hand it over to someone who wouldn't understand its value."

Chelsia shifted in her seat, unsettled by the steel beneath Bellamy's words. Pride radiated from her, but something colder coiled around it. She caught Caleb's glance, his face carved with something she couldn't quite decipher.

"I guess that's why I've never had any," he said, voice casual but carrying a bitter undercurrent. "Being such a big secret and all."

Bellamy's laugh rang out, smooth yet hollow. "Oh, Caleb, look around you! Porter Sausage is in everything we do: the work, the time..." She swept a hand across the table. "The food... the people. You'll have your chance, don't you worry."

Caleb forced a smile, stabbing a roasted potato with unnecessary force. "I'll hold you to that."

Bellamy turned her attention to Chelsia. "And you, dear? Do you miss the simpler times? I'd imagine life hasn't been all that easy for you before now."

The question hovered in the air, wrapped in false sweetness.

"I think we all miss something," Chelsia said carefully, her eyes dropping briefly to her plate as she navigated the audacity of the question. "We find a way to make do."

"Wise words," Bellamy replied, rising from her chair with an air of practiced confidence. "Well, you two enjoy. I've got some calls to make."

As she disappeared down the hallway, the charged silence eased slightly. Caleb let out a breath, his fork resting on the edge of his plate.

"You ever get the feeling she's playing some kind of game?" he muttered.

Chelsia hesitated before answering. "I think she takes pride in what she's built. Maybe a little too much."

Caleb let out a short laugh, rubbing the back of his neck. "A little? That woman could write a book about how great she thinks she is." He paused, his shoulders sagging. "Sorry. I didn't mean to dump that on you."

"It's fine," Chelsia said gently. "I get it."

Caleb offered her a faint smile, gratitude flickering briefly in his eyes. Without another word, he stood, leaving his plate behind as he stepped outside.

Alone at the table, Chelsia stared at the half-eaten food in front of her. Bellamy's words echoed in her thoughts: pride, legacy, refusal to let go. The ideals that had brought her to Portland weren't so different from Bellamy's.

But to become like her, to be trapped in a loop of the past, preserved in amber and unable to move forward, was a fate Chelsia couldn't stomach.

CHAPTER THIRTY-FOUR

Chelsia adjusted her tool belt as she approached Caleb, her boots sinking slightly into the softened morning earth. Nearby, the sounds of axes felling trees reverberated through the air.

Caleb crouched near the fence, hammering a loose rail into place with a focus that bordered on frustration. His movements carried an edge, every strike landing with measured force. Chelsia stopped a few steps away, observing him briefly before speaking.

"You've been quiet today."

Caleb didn't look up. He wiped his brow with the back of his glove and reached for another nail.

"Guess I don't have much to say," he muttered.

Chelsia shifted her weight, hooking her thumbs under the straps of her gloves. "Is this still about Bellamy?"

Caleb froze for a fraction of a second, his hand hovering mid-reach. "Why would it be?"

"Why wouldn't it be?" she countered gently. "I mean, who else gives you that sour puss?"

Her attempt at humor earned a faint smirk, but it faded quickly. Caleb resumed hammering, each strike punctuating the silence like an exclamation point.

"She seemed... intense yesterday," Chelsia ventured. "The way she talked about the farm, the sausage... you."

Caleb let out a humorless laugh. Tossing the hammer onto the grass, he rose to his feet and dusted his gloves against his jeans. His shoulders squared and his posture stiffened as he faced her fully.

"Yeah, well, Bellamy's got her priorities, doesn't she?"

Chelsia frowned slightly. "Meaning?"

"Meaning I've finally figured it out." Caleb's words carried a clarity that cut through the stillness of the morning. "I was wrong about her. She doesn't care about people, Chelsia. Not really. Not unless they're useful to her."

"That's not fair," she said. "She's helped you, hasn't she? You've said so yourself."

"Yeah, she helped," Caleb admitted, his tone cooling. "She gave me a place to stay, helped me get clean, made me think I could start over." He shook his head, frustration flickering across his face. "But it was never about me. Not about me, you, or anyone else she's taken in. It's about her. Her farm. Her legacy."

Chelsia started to respond, but Caleb raised a gloved hand, stopping her.

"Listen, I'm grateful. I really am. Just... don't fool yourself into thinking she's doing all this out of kindness. Look at how her opinion of me hasn't changed, even after months of doing everything right. She's got a plan, and we're just pieces on her board."

His words hung between them, raw and unflinching.

"So, what are you going to do?" Chelsia asked softly.

Caleb rested his hand on the fence rail, fingers tracing the wood grain absently.

"I don't know," he said after a pause. "But I can't keep doing this. Apparently, I got too comfortable, and that was my mistake."

As Bellamy's voice called out from the porch, Caleb's jaw tensed. Without another word, he turned and walked toward the house.

Chelsia stood motionless, watching him leave. Bellamy's unseen presence felt heavy and intrusive, as if her call was deliberately timed to disrupt something crucial. The sensation was suffocating; her influence palpable even at a distance.

With a sigh, Chelsia shifted her tool belt into place and pulled her phone from her pocket. The weather app loaded slowly, revealing rain in the forecast for the next few days, followed by an abrupt drop in temperatures as another cold front moved in. The thought of leaving now, with conditions worsening, felt out of reach.

Not now. Not yet.

Still, the idea gnawed at her. If not now, when? And where would she go? She had no answers, only a vague frustration with the unseen force that seemed to tether her here. Oregon felt like a trap, even as it called her to stay.

Shaking off the thoughts, she slipped the phone back into her pocket and turned toward her next task. Her boots sank slightly with every step, the weight of Caleb's words and her own uncertainty clinging to her like the damp morning air.

The day dragged on, each task blending into the next. Feed the chickens. Gather the eggs. Check the water troughs.

Caleb's earlier words echoed in Chelsia's mind: *She's got a plan, and we're just pieces on her board.*

The overcast sky dimmed the landscape, muting the usual buzz of activity across the farm. The cold felt sharper today, biting through her coat and gloves as she worked. Even the animals moved sluggishly, their routine interrupted by an intangible weight in the air.

Mid-morning found her leaning against the barn, her phone in hand. She scrolled absently to Bennett's last text: *"Doing okay? Let me know."* His protectiveness felt like a tether, something solid in a place that increasingly felt like shifting ground.

His protectiveness offered a strange comfort, though it carried complications of its own. Bellamy's behavior during their trip to Portland had been off-kilter—her laughter too loud, her smile brittle. Bennett had glanced at her during the ride back to the farm, his concern clear despite his silence. Something had shifted between him and Bellamy, though neither had addressed it.

The low rumble of Bellamy's truck broke the silence. Chelsia straightened, slipping her phone into her pocket as the vehicle rolled into view. Bellamy stepped out, her coat hanging loosely over her shoulders. On the passenger side, another figure emerged: a young man with an uncertain energy, his hands shoved deep into the pockets of a worn jacket.

"Chelsia!" Bellamy called, her voice bright, her smile even brighter. "Come meet our new helper."

Chelsia hesitated, brushing dirt from her gloves before walking over. Bellamy placed a firm hand on the newcomer's shoulder, appearing oddly possessive.

"This is Evan," Bellamy said. "He'll be helping around here for a while. I'll have Caleb show him the ropes, just like Sam did when Caleb first arrived."

At the mention of Sam, the yard seemed to contract. Near the barn, Caleb appeared, his shoulders squared, and his stare fixed on the scene before him. His silence betrayed his mood as he kept his distance.

Chelsia forced a polite smile and extended her hand. "Nice to meet you, Evan."

Evan took her hand quickly, his grip loose and clammy. "Nice to meet you too," he muttered.

Bellamy's smile stayed fixed as her eyes darted toward Caleb, a silent challenge sparking in their depths.

"I've got a feeling you're going to fit right in," she said with casual certainty. "Let's get you settled. There are showers in one of the barns, and I'll show you where you'll be staying."

Chelsia stepped aside as Bellamy and Evan walked past her. Caleb hadn't moved an inch. He stood as though anchored to the spot, his eyes following them until they disappeared behind one of the smaller barns.

"Caleb?" Chelsia's voice was quiet as she approached. "What is it?"

Gripping a shovel propped against the barn wall, Caleb muttered, "Nothing."

"Doesn't seem like nothing."

He let out a short, humorless laugh, resting the shovel over his shoulder. "Sam was the one who showed me how to do everything when I got here," he said. "Then one day, he was gone."

Chelsia frowned. "Do you know why?"

"No. I got up one day to work on tasks as usual. By the time lunch rolled around and I still hadn't seen him, I asked Bellamy, and she said he left... needed a change and wanted to move on before the weather turned. Seemed off to me."

"Off how?"

"Bellamy pulls people in off the street, off the floor of a café..." he paused, chuckling dryly. "Gives them a place, a purpose. It's always temporary. Sam liked it here, though. He said it was the most honest work he'd done in years. He talked about sticking around, making this more than just a stopover." His tone dropped as he hesitated. "Sam was smart, Chelsia. He was good at this life and didn't seem like someone who'd just up and leave. I wondered if he thought I was replacing him. Maybe that's why he didn't say goodbye."

Chelsia crossed her arms, trying to piece together the fragments he was offering her.

"Is that what's bugging you? You think she's already planning to replace you with Evan?"

Caleb gave her a look, one sharp with both resignation and clarity.

"Isn't it obvious? She doesn't trust me. Not after everything I've done, everything I've given. And you know what? Maybe that's on me. I let myself get too comfortable here. I forgot the rules."

"You said you're ready to leave," Chelsia said softly. "Maybe this is the push you need."

For a moment, Caleb didn't respond. His shoulders sagged slightly, as though the weight of his own thoughts pressed down on him. Then he nodded, a faint glimmer of determination sparking in his hazel eyes.

"You're absolutely right."

The rest of the day passed in a haze. Chelsia moved through her afternoon chores on autopilot, her hands busy while her mind churned. The farm, once a place of predictable routine, now felt unnervingly orchestrated. Its rhythms were too precise, as if guided by an unseen plan.

She spotted Caleb and Evan several times throughout the day. Bellamy had wasted no time putting Evan to work, pairing him with Caleb to learn the ropes. Caleb's demeanor remained closed off, his posture unusually rigid. At one point, Chelsia caught sight of him showing how to mend a fence, his tone clipped as Evan hovered awkwardly nearby, nodding too quickly at every instruction. The entire interaction felt like a performance for an audience neither of them could see.

Bellamy's presence was everywhere, even when she wasn't. Chelsia's eyes drifted to the farmhouse more than usual, half-expecting to see Bellamy framed in a window or standing on the porch, observing with her signature unshakable calm.

By late afternoon, Chelsia leaned against the barn wall, her arms aching from hauling feed. The cold had crept back in, her breath visible in thin puffs of mist. A faint buzz broke the quiet, and she reached for her phone.

A text from Bennett: *"Planning to stop by tomorrow. Let me know if there's anything you need."*

Her thumb hovered over the reply button. She could tell him about Caleb, about Evan, about the invisible threads Bellamy seemed to pull tighter every day. But what could she say without sounding paranoid? She had no proof, just a growing sense of unease.

Finally, she typed, *"All good here. See you then."*

Sliding the phone back into her pocket, she felt the familiar sting of leaving too much unsaid. Bennett's visits were a lifeline, but their brevity always left her more aware of the isolation when he was gone. And lately, his presence carried its own weight. The unspoken tension between him and Bellamy hung heavily over every exchange.

The crackle of gravel underfoot broke her thoughts. Caleb approached, a bucket of tools swinging in one hand and a frown etched into his face. He stopped a few feet away and set the bucket down harder than necessary.

"How's Evan holding up?" Chelsia asked, attempting levity.

Caleb snorted. "About how you'd expect. He's green as hell with no clue about what he's walked into."

"You mean the work?"

Caleb shook his head, scrubbing his hands against the thighs of his jeans.

"Work's the easy part. It's everything else. Bellamy's already pulling him in, telling him this place will change his life, that it's a fresh start." He paused, his voice hardening. "Same speech she gave me."

"Do you think he'll stay?" she asked, though she felt like she already knew the answer.

Caleb shrugged, his voice losing some of its edge. "I think he'll mean to."

Grabbing the bucket, Caleb turned and walked away, his shoulders tense. Chelsia watched him go, uneasiness prickling at her thoughts. The pieces of the puzzle still didn't fit together, but the edges were becoming clearer. Bellamy's charm, a calculated tool, wasn't merely persuasive; it kept people close until she had used them.

As dusk crept across the sky, Chelsia trudged toward the farmhouse. The thought of stepping inside filled her with unshakable reluctance, but the chill in the air pushed her forward. She crossed the threshold into the golden glow of the kitchen, where Bellamy stood at the stove, stirring the contents of a pot. The rich aroma of something savory filled the space, wrapping itself around Chelsia in false comfort.

"Everything going okay out there?" Bellamy asked without turning around.

Chelsia hesitated. "Yeah. Just wrapping up for the day."

Bellamy glanced over her shoulder, her smile poised and unyielding.

"Good. Dinner'll be ready soon. I've got something special planned for tonight."

The way she said it made Chelsia's skin prickle. She nodded and retreated upstairs, closing the door and bracing herself against it as her mind raced. *Something special.*

Pulling out her phone, she opened the weather app again, staring at the forecast. Rain, followed by dropping temperatures. Travel would only get harder.

If not now, when?

Chelsia emerged from her room as the scent of dinner wafted through the farmhouse, rich and inviting, causing her stomach to twist in hunger as she made her way to the dining room. Bellamy was already there, setting the table with her usual efficiency. At the far end, Evan sat stiffly, his fingers fidgeting with the edge of the tablecloth.

"Hey, roomie!" Bellamy greeted brightly, glancing up as Chelsia took her usual seat. "Right on time. Dinner's ready."

Chelsia managed a small smile, sliding into her chair. Caleb entered moments later; his face carefully neutral as he sank into the chair across from her. Bellamy disappeared briefly into the kitchen before returning with a steaming casserole dish. Its golden crust bubbled around the edges, filling the air with a thick aroma of roasted meat and herbs.

"I hope you're all hungry," Bellamy said, her voice carrying a theatrical lilt as she placed the dish in the center of the table. "This recipe is perfect for a night like this."

Evan perked up, the nervous edge to his posture softening. "It smells incredible," he said quietly.

Bellamy's smile widened. "Thank you! It's an old family favorite. Everyone, dig in."

Before serving herself, Chelsia paused, glancing at Caleb. He had already helped himself to a modest portion. She did the same, despite the room's unsettling atmosphere affecting her desire to eat.

The first bite was rich and comforting, a fleeting escape from her apprehension. For a moment, the clink of utensils broke the silence at the table. Bellamy let them eat in peace before turning her attention to Evan.

"So, Evan," Bellamy said, her tone casual as she spooned a helping onto her plate, "how are you settling in?"

Evan paused, his fork hovering over his plate. "Good. It's a lot of work, but... it's nice to feel useful, you know?"

Bellamy nodded slowly, her eyes holding his with an intensity that felt like a net being cast.

"That's what I like to hear. Purpose is everything. Isn't that right, Caleb?"

Caleb froze briefly, his fork halting mid-air before clinking against his plate.

"Sure."

Chelsia's stomach twisted as she shifted her focus between them. Bellamy didn't acknowledge Caleb's tone, turning her attention back to Evan, her voice syrupy smooth.

"You remind me so much of Caleb when he first came here," she said. "So eager to learn, so full of potential. I'm sure you'll do just as well. I mean, people either learn their place or they have to be taught it, right?"

Caleb's shoulders stiffened as he remained silent. Chelsia lowered her fork, her appetite fading. She nodded politely, though her appetite soured. Bellamy's words clung to her, like the chill of a shadow passing too close. She wasn't sure if it was the patronizing tone or the chilling certainty in her voice, but she didn't forget them.

As if on cue, Bellamy turned to Chelsia, her smile curving gently. "And you, dear? You've been awfully quiet tonight."

Chelsia forced a smile. "Just tired. It's been a long day."

Bellamy nodded sympathetically. "Of course. Hard work is good for the soul, yet even the hardest workers need to recharge." She gestured toward the casserole dish. "Have a little more. You'll feel better."

Chelsia shook her head. "I'm fine, thank you."

Bellamy eventually rose from her seat to clear the plates. When she reached Evan, she paused briefly; her smile lingering as she took his plate, even though a few bites remained.

The air shifted slightly with her absence, and Caleb leaned closer across the table, his voice low and firm.

"Told you. She's working on him already."

Chelsia glanced at Evan, who stared at the empty spot where his plate once lay with a blank intensity.

"It's just dinner," she whispered.

"It's never *just* dinner."

Later, Caleb disappeared without a word, leaving Chelsia and Evan to do the dishes before tidying up the dining room. As they finished, Bellamy appeared, a plate of cookies in her hands and her smile as radiant as ever.

"Dessert, anyone?" she asked, setting the plate on the table. The cookies looked perfect, with golden edges and soft, chocolate-speckled centers.

Evan reached for one immediately. "Thanks," he mumbled as he took a bite.

Chelsia shook her head. "Not for me," she said. The casserole remained a heavy, rich burden in her stomach.

Bellamy's smile was unwavering. "Are you sure? They're fresh out of the oven."

"Maybe later," Chelsia replied, offering a small smile before excusing herself. She stepped outside, the cool air prickling against her skin. The damp earth carried the musk of wood smoke drifting from somewhere beyond the farm.

She rested against the porch railing, her eyes scanning the dark horizon. The events of the evening weighed heavily on her. Bellamy's talk of purpose, the pointed remarks directed at Evan, and the way she'd glanced at Caleb with undisguised intensity replayed in her mind.

The sound of footsteps in the grass pulled her from her thoughts. Without looking, she knew it was Caleb.

"She's laying it on thick, isn't she?" he muttered as he joined her at the railing.

Chelsia glanced at him. "Evan seems to like it."

"That's the point," Caleb said flatly, his eyes fixed on the distance. "She's making him feel like he belongs. Like this is where he's meant to be."

Chelsia hesitated. "And you think that's a bad thing?"

"I think it's how she gets people to stop asking questions."

Chelsia suppressed a shiver that had nothing to do with the cold. Caleb was voicing the thoughts she'd been trying to push aside, giving them form and weight. She no longer felt paranoid. She felt seen.

"You knew something was off when you got here," he continued, his voice low. "You tried to say something back when we were at the fence line, and I brushed it off. I shouldn't have. I'm sorry."

"Don't be," Chelsia said quickly. "I didn't exactly come across like someone you could trust. I showed up asking questions about the person who'd helped you. Of course, you'd defend her."

The farm's quiet enveloped them as they stood together in shared silence. Finally, Caleb pushed off the railing.

"I'm heading to bed," he said. "See you tomorrow."

Chelsia nodded, watching him disappear into the darkness toward the barn. She remained on the porch a little longer, her thoughts spiraling. Tonight, the stillness felt suffocating and as delicate as a thin sheet of ice.

Eventually, she turned and went back inside. The warmth of the farmhouse felt oppressive after the crisp clarity of the air outside. She paused in the hallway, glancing toward the kitchen. Bellamy was still there, humming softly as she worked. For a moment, Chelsia considered stepping in and breaking the quiet. Something stopped her. It felt staged, like a performance not meant to be interrupted.

Instead, Chelsia retreated to her room, closing the door firmly behind her. The mug of tea waiting on her nightstand didn't surprise her. It was always there. She sat on the edge of the bed, her phone in hand, staring at the weather forecast. Rain tomorrow, followed by freezing temperatures. Travel would become harder, yet the thought of leaving gnawed at her. If not now, when?

Scrolling through her phone, she skimmed headlines, her mind wandering to Bennett's upcoming visit. His text echoed in her thoughts: *"Let me know if you need anything."* Would she tell him what she'd been holding back? Or would she stick to her pattern of vague reassurances and polite smiles?

Chelsia sighed, setting the phone aside and lying back on the bed. The room was too quiet, the farmhouse unnervingly still. She knew that she'd have to get up again soon, to continue the routine: bath, tea, sleep. As she stared up at the ceiling, a tune reached her ears: Bellamy's humming from the kitchen. It carried softly through the walls, an almost melodic thread weaving into the silence like a lullaby.

Chelsia felt anything but soothed.

CHAPTER THIRTY-FIVE

The soft rumble of an engine broke the stillness before the sun fully rose. Chelsia stood on the porch, the early morning chill biting through her sweater as she waited. A light drizzle misted the air, slicking the ground and deepening the gray of the horizon. She had told herself she wouldn't wait outside, that she wouldn't make it obvious how much she needed to see him. Yet here she was, drawn by a quiet anticipation she couldn't ignore.

The headlights of Bennett's car cut through the fog as he pulled into the driveway. He stepped out, his broad shoulders silhouetted against the muted sky. Grabbing a bag from the passenger seat, he made his way toward her.

"Morning," he greeted, his voice low. "Didn't think you'd be waiting out here in this weather."

Chelsia shrugged, offering a small smile. "Didn't think you'd be on time."

Bennett smirked, holding up the bag. "Well, I figured coffee and breakfast might keep me in your good graces."

Her smile softened as she took the bag. The smell of fresh coffee drifted through the damp air, warming her in a way the sweater couldn't.

"Thanks."

They stepped inside, the warmth of the farmhouse enveloping them. Bellamy's absence was notable. There was no sign of her since the tea materialized on Chelsia's nightstand the night before. Though quieter, the house felt just as heavy without her presence. The feeling never left, even when Bellamy wasn't there to reinforce it.

Bennett leaned against the edge of the kitchen counter, watching her as she poured the coffee into a mug.

"How's it going here?"

Chelsia hesitated, stirring the coffee as she considered her answer. "The same, I guess."

"Same as what?"

"Same as always." She turned to face him, her fingers curling around the mug. "Caleb's been... distant since the plaza trip. And there's a new guy—Evan. Bellamy's already got him convinced this place is some kind of fresh start."

Bennett frowned. "Don't you think it is?"

Chelsia huffed softly, shaking her head. "I think it's exhausting."

His blue eyes softened. "You do look tired."

"I'm fine," she said quickly, taking a sip of coffee. "It's just the weather."

The rain tapped softly against the windows, filling the silence. Sensing her unspoken hesitation, Bennett didn't push. Instead, he reached into his coat pocket and pulled out a small envelope.

"I know you didn't ask for anything," he said, setting it on the counter. "I figured it couldn't hurt to be prepared. Just in case."

Chelsia's brow furrowed. "What is it?"

"Cash," Bennett said simply. "You never know when you'll need a little extra. Even though Bell already paid you, I know having to get a new phone was unexpected."

Her stomach twisted, and she frowned. "Bennett, I—"

"Don't," he interrupted gently. "It's not charity, Chelsia. Just a precaution. Humor me."

She looked away, her grip tightening on the mug.

"Thanks," she murmured.

Bennett nodded, shifting his attention to the window. "Where's Bellamy? She usually makes her presence known by now."

"I don't know," Chelsia said, setting her mug down. "She hasn't come down yet. She could be busy or slept in for once."

Bennett's jaw tightened slightly. Chelsia noticed the faint crease in his brow. He wasn't the type to give much away, but today, his stiffness was hard to miss.

The sound of footsteps on the stairs made them both turn. Bellamy appeared moments later.

"Detective Bennett," she greeted smoothly, deliberately formal. "What a pleasant surprise."

Bennett's posture straightened, his look remaining guarded. "Morning, Bellamy."

Her attention shifted to Chelsia. "I hope our guest is treating you well."

"He brought coffee," Chelsia replied casually.

"How thoughtful," Bellamy replied, stepping further into the room. "I'd hate for you to think we don't take care of our own here."

The air thickened, every word laced with unspoken meaning. Bellamy's smile widened as her gaze flicked briefly to the envelope on the counter.

"Such a considerate detective," she said lightly, her voice carrying an edge Chelsia couldn't quite name. "Always looking out for others."

Chelsia swallowed hard, the coffee cooling in her hands. She glanced between them, the tension as sharp as ever. Would leaving the farm ease it, or confirm her theory that she was part of the problem?

The rain intensified by mid-morning, drumming steadily against the windows as Bennett and Chelsia sat at the dining table. Bellamy offered tea, and Bennett responded with a polite shake of his head. Chelsia mirrored him, her barely touched coffee still warming her hands. Flitting through the kitchen, Bellamy filled the resulting silence with soft humming.

"So," Bennett said a short while later, "how's the new guy working out?"

Chelsia hesitated, glancing toward the kitchen. Bellamy stood with her back to them, her posture rigidly straight. She was obviously listening.

"He's... enthusiastic," Chelsia said, choosing her words carefully.

Bennett raised an eyebrow. "Enthusiastic?"

"It's a polite way of saying he has no idea what he's doing," Caleb interjected as he entered the room, carrying a small toolbox in one hand and a damp towel in the other. "But don't worry. Bellamy's got him convinced he'll be running the place in no time."

Bellamy's tune stopped abruptly. Her hand stilled mid-motion as she wiped the counter.

"Caleb," she said smoothly, "I hope you're not discouraging Evan. Everyone deserves a fresh start."

Caleb shrugged, his voice flat. "Just calling it like it is."

Bellamy turned, her smile unwavering. "And I'm just reminding you to be kind. We were all new once, weren't we?"

Caleb muttered something under his breath and shook his head, turning for the door.

"Shower's fixed, by the way," he said, pausing for a moment before stepping into the rain

Bennett frowned, watching Caleb leave. "He seems... tense."

"He's adjusting," Bellamy replied smoothly, brushing an invisible strand of hair from her face. "Change is never easy."

Nibbling her lip, Chelsia looked from one to the other. Every word resonated with a significance neither was ready to delve into. Bennett shifted in his seat, his hands resting loosely on the table.

"You seem to be handling the changes pretty well, Bellamy," he said evenly. "It's a lot to manage."

"Oh, it is," Bellamy said, her smile broadening. "I've always been good at balancing priorities. You remember that don't you, Ryan?"

Chelsia noted the cooling of Bennett's demeanor.

"I do," he said flatly. "It's just been a while since I've seen it firsthand."

Bellamy's laugh was light, almost melodic, yet tinged with an edge. "Well, it's not as though you've never been welcome here. Though I must say, you've been visiting quite a bit more often lately."

Chelsia's stomach twisted at the subtle barb; the way Bellamy's words curled around their shared history. She didn't need to know the details to feel the depth of it.

The sound of footsteps on the porch disrupted the moment. Evan appeared in the doorway, rain dripping from his hair. He hesitated, glancing between Bennett and Bellamy. "Sorry to interrupt," he said, his voice barely above a murmur. "Bellamy, I think some chickens got out. Caleb told me to check with you."

Bellamy's smile didn't waver. "Of course. I'll be right there." Turning to Bennett and Chelsia, she added, "You two stay and catch up. I won't be long."

Putting on her coat, she swept from the room with a grace that seemed almost rehearsed, Evan trailing after her. The door shut softly, leaving Chelsia and Bennett alone. With Bellamy gone, the room's tension lessened, yet a palpable silence remained.

Bennett sat back in his chair, exhaling a slow breath. "She's something else," he muttered.

Chelsia set her coffee down, kneading her hands together. "You could say that."

He studied her, blue eyes probing. "What's going on here, Chelsia? Really?"

She hesitated, her thoughts swirling. Chelsia wanted to spill everything: the control Bellamy seemed to exert, Caleb's growing frustration, the eerie predictability of Evan. She remained aware of Bennett's long history with Bellamy and wasn't sure she should, or even could, get in the middle of it. Why drag Bennett into an unnecessary mess when she was all-too-ready to bolt as soon as the opportunity presented itself?

"I don't know," she said finally, her voice barely above a whisper. "A lot."

Bennett's frown deepened. "What's a lot?"

Chelsia looked away, struggling to choose her words carefully. "I know you meant well by asking Bellamy to take me in." She looked back at him. "I appreciate it, I do."

"Is it the work? Is it too much for you?" He looked her over, as if searching for some sign of physical distress or injury. "If I need to talk to Bellamy..."

"No, you don't need to do that!" Chelsia answered quickly before sighing. "I mean, if I'm honest, it already feels like my being here has done enough to your... friendship... with her, right?"

"That's not for you to worry about," he said. "Your sole concern should be using this opportunity to get back on your feet." He sighed. "That's what I want for you, Chelsia. Me and Bell... aren't your problem."

Bennett observed her. After a long moment, he leaned back, his hands resting on his thighs.

"You're sure there's nothing else I can do?" he added.

Unable to look at him, Chelsia nodded. Doubt choked her, preventing the words she longed to speak from escaping.

"I'm sure."

The silence stretched between them, broken only by the rain tapping against the windows. For now, it was all she could offer.

Chelsia stood on the porch, watching Bennett's car disappear down the long, rain-slicked drive. The engine's rumble faded, leaving behind a stillness that seemed to seep into her bones. She remained there briefly, arms crossed to shield herself from the cool, damp air.

The house felt different without him there: quieter, emptier, as though his presence had briefly lifted something substantial she hadn't realized she was carrying. Now, with him gone, the weight settled back, harder to ignore.

The door opened behind her, its hinges creaking softly. Chelsia turned to see Bellamy stepping out, opening a small umbrella. The misting rain beaded along its surface as Bellamy moved with her usual grace.

"You're going to catch cold standing out here," Bellamy said after several moments of silence.

Chelsia offered a small smile and stepped back inside. Bellamy followed, giving the umbrella a quick shake before propping it against the wall.

"He's a good man," Bellamy said. "Ryan, I mean… always looking out for others."

The envelope in Chelsia's pocket felt massive as she nodded, unsure what to say. Rather than meet Bellamy's eyes, she studied the mud Caleb tracked in near the doorway.

"I hope you're not filling his head with unnecessary worries," Bellamy continued, her voice as steady as her footsteps. "Ryan's got enough on his plate without adding our little farm to his burdens."

Chelsia's head snapped up. "I'm not," she said quickly. "He just wanted to check in."

Bellamy's smile widened, though it stopped short of her eyes. "Good. I'd hate for him to get the wrong impression."

A heavy silence, full of unspoken words, settled between them. Chelsia nodded again, mumbling an excuse before retreating to her room. She closed the door softly behind her, leaning against it as she exhaled.

The room felt smaller today, the walls closer than usual. Pulling her phone from her pocket, she moved to the bed. The burden of planning her departure made her ideas seem weaker. Where would she go? Questions repeated endlessly, a cycle of doubt and frustration she couldn't escape.

A soft knock at the door startled her. She stood quickly, heart pounding, and opened it to find Caleb in the hallway. His stance was rigid.

"Got a minute?" he asked. Chelsia stepped aside, letting him in. He briefly glanced around the room, his arms crossed. "What did he say?"

"Who?" Chelsia frowned.

"Bennett," Caleb clarified. "What did he say about Bellamy?"

Chelsia hesitated, weighing her response. "Nothing, really. He just... wanted to make sure everything was okay."

Caleb snorted, shaking his head. "And you told him it was?"

"What else was I supposed to say?" Chelsia shot back, frustration creeping into her tone. "That Bellamy is acting like a weirdo, and you're pissed off about it?"

His jaw tensed as he stared at the floor, dark curls falling into his face as his shoulders sagged.

"I'm done," he said finally, his voice barely above a whisper.

She blinked, the words sinking in slowly. "What?"

"I've had enough," he said when he looked up at her. "Of this place and of Bellamy. I was going to stick it out, help Evan get the hang of things, but I can't do it anymore."

"Where will you go?" Chelsia asked softly.

"I don't know yet," he admitted. "Anywhere is better than here."

"Now?"

"Soon as the rain stops. I think the day or two after that will be more than enough for me to get far enough before things freeze up again."

Chelsia couldn't help thinking how similar this was to her own thoughts.

"You'll tell me first?" she asked. "You won't just go?"

Caleb studied her, his hazel eyes closing briefly before meeting hers again, carrying more than words could hold.

"Of course I'll tell you, I promise. You're the best thing about even being here. I'd probably have left already if not for you."

The sound of Bellamy's melodic warbling drifted through the hallway, interrupting Chelsia's response. Caleb's shoulders squared, and he straightened abruptly, brushing past her without another word.

She stood in the doorway, her eyes fixed on his retreating figure until the sound of his boots against the wooden floor faded into silence, leaving her alone in the stillness.

INFERNO

CHAPTER THIRTY-SIX

The rain hadn't let up. It drummed steadily against the farmhouse roof, a rhythmic backdrop to the morning. Chelsia woke to the dim, gray light filtering through her window, the chill seeping in before her feet touched the floor. After showering, she secured her hair into flat twists, wrapping it carefully before getting dressed as her mind wandered.

Downstairs, the kitchen was quiet save for the soft clatter of dishes being stacked in the drying rack. Bellamy glanced over her shoulder with a warm smile.

"Hey, roomie!" she said brightly.

Chelsia murmured a greeting, bypassing the tea in favor of filling a mug with coffee. The rain tapping against the windows seemed amplified in the silence between them. Through the glass, her eyes wandered toward the barn. The wide doors were slightly ajar, swaying lazily in the breeze, as if inviting her curiosity.

She stayed by the window, sipping her coffee. Caleb's words from the night before echoed in her mind: he'd planned to wait for a break in the weather, timing his departure to avoid the cold front moving in over the next few days. His certainty had been unshakable, leaving her with no reason to doubt him. And yet, a quiet part of her wished he'd reconsider, or that she could figure out why she wasn't following suit.

Pulling on her coat, Chelsia stepped outside into the rain. Her boots squelched in the mud as she made her way to the barn, the cold droplets needling her skin through the fabric. The animals stirred in their pens; their movements gentle in the dreary morning.

Inside the barn, everything was in its place. Neat. Tidy. The faint smell of damp wood hung in the air, unbroken by signs of activity.

"Caleb?" she called, her voice carrying in the stillness.

Her voice dissolved into the quiet. She paused, scanning the dim corners for any sign of him. There was nothing: no half-finished projects, no tools left carelessly behind. It was as though he hadn't even started his morning routine.

Chelsia's brow furrowed as she turned back toward the rain. Maybe Caleb was working elsewhere on the farm. Or perhaps he was with Evan. Shoving her hands into her coat pockets, she trudged back toward the farmhouse. She told herself she'd find him later. And maybe, while unraveling his plans to leave, she could start piecing together her own.

The rain hadn't eased by lunchtime, its steady rhythm masking the scrape of forks against plates. Chelsia sat absently picking at her food. Across from her, Evan wolfed down his meal, his energy almost frenetic as though he were trying to keep himself busy.

Bellamy, seated at the head of the table, moved with her usual grace, slicing into her portion of the casserole. The sound of the knife against the plate rang out in the otherwise quiet room. It wasn't until Evan reached for seconds that Bellamy spoke.

"Well," she said, setting her fork down with care. "I suppose I should mention... Caleb's gone."

The words landed like a stone in the pit of Chelsia's stomach. Her fork froze halfway to her mouth as she stared at Bellamy, unsure if she'd heard correctly.

"Gone?" she repeated, her voice louder than she intended.

Bellamy nodded, her smile unchanged. "He decided it was time to move on. Said he needed a change and wanted to leave before the weather turned and the frost set in."

The rain pounded harder against the windows, matching the quickening pace of Chelsia's thoughts. *Needed a change... Wanted to leave before the weather turned...* Caleb's words from the night before replayed in her mind, blending uneasily with what he'd said about Sam's sudden departure.

"He said this to you?" Chelsia asked.

Bellamy's smile faltered for the briefest moment, though she recovered quickly.

"Yes, mm-hmm."

"Did he... say goodbye?" Chelsia pressed.

Bellamy's eyes showed sympathy, and her tone softened.

"Well, not precisely. His intentions were obvious. I don't think he wanted to make a fuss. You know Caleb... always keeping things close to the vest. I couldn't convince him otherwise and... had to let him go."

Across the table, Evan frowned, his brow furrowing deeply.

"He was supposed to help me with the fence line this afternoon," he said, his uncertainty laced with frustration. "I don't know what to look for on my own."

"Evan," Bellamy said gently, her voice taking on the familiar maternal cadence that Chelsia recognized, "you'll manage just fine. And if you need help, I'll be here." She sighed, her expression smoothing back into calm authority. "Caleb has certainly placed us in a bind, but... I'll figure something out. I always do."

Evan nodded reluctantly, though his shoulders slumped as he returned his focus to his plate. Bellamy reached out, patting his hand with a reassuring smile, before returning to her meal. Chelsia, however, couldn't force herself to move.

Caleb wouldn't have left without telling her. He'd promised. It had been one of the few things he'd said with absolute certainty, and she'd believed him. Bellamy's explanation seemed too slick, her words too perfect. Chelsia knew that some of it was recycled.

The rain continued to tap insistently against the windows as Chelsia pushed the food around her plate, her appetite gone. Bellamy didn't seem to notice, or perhaps she didn't care. The conversation drifted to Evan's upcoming tasks, Bellamy's tone reassuring, though Chelsia wasn't paying attention to the details.

Once the dishes were cleared, Chelsia quickly exited, giving a flimsy excuse regarding the chicken coop. She needed to get outside, to clear her head, to find something, anything, that would make sense of Caleb's sudden absence.

The rain soaked through her coat as she crossed the yard, the damp chill biting at her skin. She stopped by the coop, her hands moving mechanically as she collected eggs and refilled the water. Her thoughts churned with every step, puzzle pieces clicking together with unsettling clarity as she considered the parallels between Caleb and Sam.

"And who knows who else?" Chelsia whispered, her breath forming delicate puffs in the cold air.

She tipped her face toward the sky, dots of rain splashing against her skin as a single thought circled her mind.

He'd said he wouldn't leave until the rain stopped.

As the afternoon wore on, Chelsia remained by the barn, the ceaseless rain falling around her. The sky hung low and gray, a pressing weight over the farm. She finished her chores, finding herself reluctant to go back inside. The air felt freer outside, less oppressive than in the farmhouse, where Bellamy's serene yet stifling presence seemed to fill every shadowed corner.

Across the yard, Evan wrestled with a tarp that had slipped loose from one of the hay bales. He fumbled with the edges, muttering under his breath as the rain slicked his hands and turned the tarp into a slippery, uncooperative mess. Chelsia watched him for a moment, debating whether to step in or let him sort it out alone. She finally stepped forward just as Evan threw the tarp down in obvious frustration.

He glanced around, his eyes briefly meeting hers before darting away. Without a word, he strode toward one of the smaller outbuildings—a squat structure tucked near the edge of the property. Chelsia frowned. She remembered Bellamy mentioning it when she first arrived, vaguely promising to explain its purpose later. Later had never come.

Evan didn't hesitate. He grabbed the handle and yanked the door open without so much as a glance over his shoulder. As the door opened, revealing a dark interior, Chelsia felt a knot form in her stomach. Something about the scene set her on edge.

"Evan!" Bellamy's voice rang out, harshly cutting through the rain.

Chelsia turned to see Bellamy striding across the yard, her coat flaring behind her. Her face was colder than Chelsia had ever seen, her usual warmth replaced by a hard, unyielding edge.

Evan froze, his hand still on the door's handle. "I—I was just..."

"What do you think you're doing?" Bellamy's tone was low and icy. She stopped a few feet from him, authority radiating from her slight frame. "That is off limits."

"I didn't know," Evan stammered, stepping back from the doorway. "I mean, I thought..."

"You thought what?" she interrupted softly. "That you could wander wherever you pleased? There are rules here, Evan, and they exist for a reason."

The gleam in her eyes betrayed the softness of her tone. Evan ducked his head, mumbling an apology.

"I know you're still learning," she continued, her tone softening as she stepped closer, placing a hand on his shoulder. "Let's avoid this mistake in the future. You go nowhere unless I specifically tell you to. Do you understand?"

"Yes, ma'am," Evan muttered.

Bellamy's smile returned, startling in its suddenness. "Good. Now, let's get you back to your chores."

Chelsia briefly caught her eye as she turned. For a fleeting moment, she thought she caught a flicker of calculation in Bellamy's eyes, but it vanished as quickly as it came as Evan was guided back toward the yard.

Remaining by the barn, Chelsia's thoughts churned. Ever since Bellamy had announced Caleb's sudden departure at lunch, she'd been trying to piece things together: fragments of Bellamy's words, her peculiar way of steering conversations, and the unspoken rules that governed the farm. Now, there was the way Bellamy had handled Evan, the shift in her tone, and his stumbling explanation as it replayed in Chelsia's mind: *I didn't know. I thought...*

Her attention shifted to the building Evan had tried to enter. The door stood slightly open, revealing only shadowy darkness. Chelsia hesitated, curiosity tugging her forward just as Bellamy's voice carried back to her, stopping her in her tracks.

"Never mind about that, I'll close it up later! Go inside the house before you catch your death!"

The chance to investigate was gone. Chelsia forced a nod, her heart pounding as she turned toward the farmhouse.

Chelsia stood by the kitchen sink, staring through the rain-speckled window. Rain blurred the yard, the gray sky heavy over the farm. Bellamy's voice drifted from another room, her cheerful lilt weaving through the air as she spoke on the phone, clashing with Chelsia's growing anxiety. The kitchen's warmth felt stifling, the walls closer, the air stale.

Bellamy's practiced words about Caleb, Evan's blunder, and her sharp criticism replayed in Chelsia's mind, mingling with the day's events. Yet the heart of the puzzle remained elusive.

Chelsia's fingers tightened on the counter as she remembered Caleb, resolute, in her room.

Of course I'll tell you. I promise.

He wouldn't have left like this. It felt unnatural, him not being there, as was the quiet hanging over the farmhouse.

The front door banged open suddenly, snapping her out of her thoughts. Chelsia turned quickly, her breath catching. Evan stumbled inside, rain plastering his hair to his forehead and soaking his clothes. His hunched shoulders and wide eyes made him look younger, stripped of the bravado he'd worn at lunch.

"Hey," he said tentatively, standing near the door and avoiding her eyes. "I, uh... just wanted to say sorry. For earlier. If I, you know, made things weird."

Chelsia blinked, momentarily disoriented. "You didn't make things weird."

Evan shifted on his feet, looking nervously toward the hallway where Bellamy's voice still carried.

"It's just... I didn't think it'd be a big deal, going in there. I mean, what's the worst that could happen? It's just a building, right?"

Chelsia paused, choosing her words carefully. "Bellamy takes her rules seriously," she said. "I've never had much reason to check those places out, so..."

Evan gave a weak snort, shaking his head. "Guess I shouldn't have, either. I was only hoping to find something to help with that stupid tarp." He ran a hand through his wet hair, sending droplets to the floor. "Anyway, I'll, uh, let you get back to whatever. Just wanted to say sorry."

Chelsia watched as he shuffled back out, his shoulders hunched against the rain. For a moment, she stood frozen, her thoughts churning. She and Caleb had never discussed the restricted areas much. She'd dismissed them early on, figuring they weren't worth questioning. Now Bellamy's insistence on their importance, and the way she'd reacted to Evan, made them impossible to ignore.

Her grip on the counter tightened, causing her knuckles to ache as her anxiety grew. She didn't have enough answers, just fragments of suspicion and doubt that refused to align. One thing was certain: Caleb's departure made no sense.

Her focus returned to the window, to the endless gray expanse of the farm. The rain continued to fall, echoing the weight pressing on her thoughts. Whatever Bellamy was hiding, Caleb's absence was only the beginning.

The forecast remained unchanged, offering no sign of relief. Chelsia turned her attention to the window, where the rain blurred the view of the lawn outside. Beyond the barn, the smaller building drew her focus. Something shiny caught her attention near the handle. A lock? The possibility sent a wave of discomfort through her, twisting her stomach.

Why had Bellamy reacted so strongly when Evan tried to go inside? And why lock it now, after all this time?

She didn't know the answers, and the questions were enough to make her skin crawl.

A creak in the hallway broke Chelsia's train of thought. She froze, her breath catching in her throat. The low hum of Bellamy's voice drifted through the silence, melodic and unsettling. Chelsia's pulse quickened as she stood slowly, tiptoeing to the door and pressing her ear against it.

The hum grew louder, accompanied by footsteps that stopped just outside. A soft, purposeful knock followed.

"Couldn't sleep?" Bellamy's almost playful voice came from the other side.

Chelsia swallowed hard before cracking the door open. Bellamy stood in the dim hallway, the interplay of light and shadow making her appear taller and more imposing.

"Oh, hey, Bellamy," Chelsia said, forcing a small smile. "I'm just... restless, I guess."

Bellamy tilted her head, her smile deepening. Her green eyes glimmered with an intensity that sent a chill down Chelsia's spine.

"That's understandable. People tend to be unsettled by change."

Chelsia's breath hitched. "Change?"

Bellamy stepped closer, filling the narrow hallway. "Of course. The change that's inevitable when someone leaves."

The air between them thickened with unspoken implications. Chelsia nodded mutely, unable to find her voice. Bellamy reached out, brushing a hand against her shoulder.

"Don't forget your tea," she said softly. "You'll need your rest for tomorrow."

Chelsia nodded again, her skin prickling where Bellamy had touched her. She stayed motionless until Bellamy turned and walked away, her footsteps fading down the stairs. The humming resumed, retreating into the distance.

Leaning against the door, Chelsia exhaled shakily. Her pulse pounded in her ears as the exchange replayed in her mind, each word laced with growing dread.

Caleb's promise echoed in her mind; his voice as vivid as if he were standing in front of her: *Of course I'll tell you. I promise.*

Her hands curled into fists. Caleb wouldn't have broken that promise, not willingly. Whatever had happened, whatever Bellamy was concealing, was likely tied to that building, the one that now seemed locked. The certainty settled deep within her, undeniable and unshakable.

The farm seemed different now, its secrets looming like the weight of an approaching storm. She didn't know when or how, but one thing was clear.

She wasn't leaving. Not until she uncovered the truth.

CHAPTER THIRTY-SEVEN

The front door creaked open, and Bellamy stepped inside, shaking droplets from her coat. Despite the weather, her hair remained perfectly gathered at the nape, untouched by the storm.

"Another day, another deluge," Bellamy said brightly, hanging her coat on the nearest hook. "You'd think the sky would've run out of rain by now. You and Evan have had it easy. This weather has practically handed you a reprieve."

Chelsia didn't respond, her fingers tightening around the mug. Bellamy studied her a bit too long before her smile widened, radiating cheer.

"Ryan's stopping by this afternoon," Bellamy added. "Thought you'd want to know."

The mention of Bennett pulled Chelsia from her thoughts. She set the mug down on the counter, the soft clink diverting her focus from the downpour.

"Did he say why?"

"Just his usual check-in," Bellamy replied with an easy shrug. "He seems unusually invested in those lately, doesn't he?"

Chelsia turned back toward the window, watching raindrops snake down the glass. Behind her, Bellamy moved to the counter, and the clink of shifting plates filled the room.

"Have you thought more about our conversation from yesterday?" Bellamy asked, her voice carrying a hint of insistence that made Chelsia's shoulders stiffen.

"About Caleb?"

"Of course," Bellamy said smoothly. "It's hard when someone leaves, especially when they mean as much to you as Caleb did."

Chelsia struggled to keep a straight face. "What's there to think about? It's not like anything can change now."

Bellamy sighed softly, the sound tinged with what could have been sympathy, or something less sincere.

"People leave for many reasons," she said. "Sometimes it's timing. Sometimes it's opportunity. And sometimes..." She paused, her tone shifting almost imperceptibly. "Sometimes they just don't have the strength to stay."

"Do you really believe that?" Chelsia asked, probing.

Bellamy looked up, her smile unwavering. "Oh, I do. What other reasons could there be?"

Before Chelsia could respond, the sound of tires rolling over wet gravel drew Bellamy's attention. A smile touched her lips as she looked towards the window.

"That'll be Ryan," she said.

Chelsia stayed where she was, watching as Bellamy retrieved her coat and stepped onto the porch. Her voice rose above the rain, warmly greeting Bennett as he climbed out of his car. Against the sodden expanse of the farm, even his broad frame seemed diminished. He looked directly at the house, spotting Chelsia through the window. The look held until Bellamy beckoned him inside.

"Well, you're a sight," Bellamy said as she shook rain from her coat and hung it again. "Miserable driving in this weather, isn't it?"

"You get used to it," Bennett replied, his tone clipped. "How's everything?"

"Oh, you know," Bellamy said. "We're adjusting. Losing Caleb has been a challenge we'll just have to manage."

Bennett frowned. "Losing Caleb? What do you mean?"

"He left," Bellamy explained evenly. "Said he needed a fresh start."

"And I'm just now hearing about this?"

Bellamy shrugged. "What was there to say?"

Bennett crossed his arms, his tone hardening. "Do you think he's gone for good? Or is this temporary?"

Bellamy paused, considering. "I don't think we'll be seeing him again," she said. "He was restless. After the trip to Eastport, it was clear he wasn't... stable. Sometimes, Ryan, people aren't meant to be saved."

Chelsia caught Bennett's flicker of doubt as his eyes sought hers for confirmation. She kept her face carefully neutral, turning instead to the rain-streaked window.

A soft knock on the door broke the moment. Bellamy opened it to reveal Evan, drenched and shivering.

"Sorry to bother you," he stammered. "There's water coming into the north barn. A lot."

Bellamy's expression softened into her familiar blend of patience and authority.

"Did you try the tarp?"

Evan nodded. "It's not holding. I think it's worse than we thought."

Bellamy sighed, slipping her coat back on. "I'll handle it," she said firmly. A smile, held a beat too long, played on her lips as her eyes flickered between Chelsia and Bennett. "Wouldn't want to disturb your little reunion."

The door clicked shut behind her, leaving Bennett and Chelsia alone in the kitchen. He slowly turned to examine her.

"Does she always look at you like that?"

Chelsia frowned. "Like what?"

"Like she's trying to figure out what you're thinking."

A smirk curved Chelsia's lips. "Maybe I'm trying to figure out what *she's* thinking."

He chuckled briefly before arching a brow. "Why didn't you text me about Caleb leaving?"

Chelsia shrugged; her tone distant. "People come and go around here. At least, that's how Bellamy makes it sound."

"So, you're not bothered by it?" he asked.

Chelsia let the words settle before shrugging. "What would you like me to do? Fall apart?"

"No, of course not, Chelsia. I just thought you'd feel some type of way about it. You two seemed... close."

She let out a dry chuckle. "Close enough to know he wouldn't just disappear like that."

The statement landed heavily, forcing Bennett to pause. Stepping closer, he tensed, his blue eyes narrowing.

"What's that supposed to mean?" he asked, his voice lowered.

Chelsia moved toward the window, her fingers grazing the counter, searching for support.

"Just that Caleb wasn't the type to vanish without a word. It doesn't sit right with me, that's all."

"People do unexpected things all the time. Doesn't mean there's something more to it."

"Maybe," Chelsia murmured. "Are you going to look for him?"

Bennett exhaled through his nose, a shrug rolling through his shoulders.

"Doesn't seem like Bellamy thinks it's worth pursuing, and maybe she's right. He's not a kid, after all. How much sense would it make to spend department resources on a twenty-four-year-old who clearly wanted to be on his merry way without so much as a hi, boo, or kiss my ass?"

"Officially, there's not much to go on. Caleb was only supposed to be here as part of a deal. If that's something he no longer wanted to honor..." His voice trailed off.

"Maybe Bellamy knows something you don't," she said.

"Yeah, maybe they fought... and she kicked him out," Bennett replied, tapping the edge of the table as his tone softened. "It's not like she'd tell me, I guess." He eyed her. "I suppose it's no big secret that she and I have been at odds lately."

"It's not a secret," Chelsia said, turning to face him. "Just... strange, since you two are so close."

Bennett let out a short, humorless laugh. "We *were*," he admitted. "Not so much anymore, even though she was... very important to me once. You already know about that."

Chelsia tilted her head, crossing her arms. "Bellamy was it for you, then?"

The smile vanished. Bennett's posture shifted, stiffening as he considered her question.

"As far as long-term involvement... yeah."

"Does being a detective mean you've got a good read on people?" she asked, her tone intentionally casual.

"I'd like to think so," Bennett said. "Why?"

Chelsia leaned back slightly, her voice low. "Because Bellamy's been a loose end for a long time, and you still don't know why."

Bennett's lips thinned, though he didn't look away. "Being able to read people doesn't make me magic, Chelsia. Bellamy... she's an enigma sometimes. It's part of her charm."

Chelsia studied him briefly. "You don't like loose ends, yet you're surrounded by them. Look at me. Look at Bellamy. This entire place is a loose end."

Bennett blinked, his brow furrowing as her words landed. "What are you saying?" He shook his head slightly. "Are you telling me that I should look for Caleb?"

Unwavering, Chelsia met his eyes. "I don't think you'd find him if you did."

Her words hung heavier than the rain pounding against the roof. As Bennett processed her response, she offered no further explanation. The relentlessness of the storm filled the silence, underscoring the budding friction between them. Bennett stared at Chelsia, barely concealing his curiosity. She remained still, her arms loosely crossed as though shielding herself from further questions. Finally, he straightened, his boots scuffing against the wooden floor.

She studied him for a beat longer, catching the flicker of doubt in his eyes, but didn't press further. Bennett still wasn't ready—not yet.

Noticing movement outside, Chelsia glanced toward the window. Bellamy was on her way back, her coat flaring in the breeze, the rain doing little to slow her purposeful strides. Chelsia tensed, instinctively bracing for whatever was coming next.

Moments later, the door opened and Bellamy stepped inside, her presence filling the room as if she'd never left. Her eyes darted between Chelsia and Bennett, briefly resting on him before finally settling on her.

"I hope I'm not interrupting anything," she said coolly. She hung her coat on the nearest hook, smoothing her sleeves before turning to face them fully.

"Just catching up," Bennett replied, his tone matching hers. He stepped back, creating a space between himself and Chelsia.

Bellamy's smile widened; her green eyes gleaming. "So, you keep saying."

Chelsia forced a smile, her hands slipping into her pockets.

"Everything good at the barn?" Bennett asked, shifting to a more conversational tone.

Bellamy nodded, brushing a damp strand of hair from her cheek. "Oh, yes. Evan was a big help, though I think he needs a bit more practice with a hammer. He'll get there." She looked at Chelsia, her smile softening. "And you, my dear? Have you given any more thought to what we discussed?"

Chelsia hesitated, her mind scrambling to pin down Bellamy's intent. "About Caleb?" she asked, buying time.

Bellamy's smile flickered momentarily.

"Of course. And about the way he left us. It's hard when someone leaves, isn't it? But, we move forward. That's what we do."

Chelsia nodded, her lips pressing together. She didn't trust herself to speak, not with Bennett's eyes still on her, quietly dissecting the interaction.

"Well," Bellamy said brightly, clapping her hands once as though concluding the matter, "I suppose we should all get back to it and just move on."

Chelsia muttered something agreeable, stepping away from the counter. She could feel Bellamy's eyes upon her, following her across the room.

"Well, I should get going," Bennett said, straightening. He glanced briefly at Chelsia, his expression carefully measured, before addressing Bellamy. "Thanks for the... update."

Bellamy's smile deepened, though her eyes gleamed. "Of course, Ryan. Always a pleasure to see you." She handed him his coat, her gesture smooth and unhurried. "Don't be a stranger."

"I'll try not to be," Bennett replied, slipping on his coat. He hesitated at the door, his hand resting on the knob. "Take care, Chelsia."

Chelsia nodded, offering the faintest smile. "You too."

The door closed softly behind him; the sound muffled by the relentless rain. Bellamy stared at the door as if willing it to stay shut. Then, with a bright smile, she turned back to Chelsia.

"Well," she said, brushing her hands together as though ridding them of dust. "I suppose it's back to the usual, isn't it?"

Chelsia didn't answer, her thoughts already spiraling elsewhere. Bellamy's forced cheer and the suffocating warmth of the kitchen only added to the pressure building in her chest. As Bellamy moved toward the counter, her humming soft and lilting, Chelsia slipped out of the room, her boots silent against the floorboards.

The damp air outside hit her like a reprieve. On the porch, she leaned against the railing, watching the taillights of Bennett's car fade into the distance. The rain blurred the edges of everything: the barn, the house, the yard. Even the locked building seemed less solid, its silhouette dissolving into the mist.

Her thoughts churned like the storm clouds overhead. Caleb's sudden departure, Bellamy's unsettling calm, and Bennett's uncertain navigation through a web of loose ends, coalesced into a murky knot she couldn't untangle.

Chelsia exhaled slowly, her breath curling in the cold air. Whatever answers she was looking for wouldn't come easily—not here, not with Bellamy's eyes on her every move. The storm pressed on, relentless; the rain hammering the porch roof in uneven rhythms. She took a moment to quiet her mind before going back inside.

Whatever came next, she'd have to tread carefully.

And, she realized with a sinking certainty, she'd have to do it without Bennett.

CHAPTER THIRTY-EIGHT

By morning, the rain had eased to a fine drizzle, leaving the farm cloaked in a mist that softened the edges of the landscape. The air carried the damp scent of wet earth, mingling with the aroma of hay and the tang of metal tools left scattered by the barn.

Chelsia stepped onto the porch, pulling her coat tight against the chill. In the yard, Evan crouched by the chicken coop, his brow furrowed as he wrestled with a feed trough that had shifted during the night. The coop sagged slightly on one side, the mud beneath churned into a thick, slippery mess. He grunted as he maneuvered the trough, feed spilling unevenly from the bag in his hands.

"You're going to scare them off," Chelsia called dryly. The chickens clucked and flapped their wings, darting erratically around the commotion.

Evan looked up; his face flushed with frustration. "I'm not trying to," he said through gritted teeth. "They keep moving every time I get close. It's like they know I'm new."

"They probably do." Chelsia smirked, stepping off the porch. She remembered her own early days on the farm when the chickens seemed just as determined to outsmart her. "They're smarter than you think."

She reached Evan just as Bellamy's voice floated through the mist. "Good morning, dears!" Bellamy emerged from the side of the barn, her coat trailing behind her, the edges dampened by the drizzle. She carried a small pail, likely filled with scraps for the pigs.

"Evan, you're doing a fine job," Bellamy said warmly, though her brow creased gently at the sight of the spilled feed. "Perhaps we should refine your technique. We wouldn't want the chickens to miss their breakfast, now would we?"

Evan straightened, his shoulders sagging. "Sorry, Bellamy. I'm just... not used to all this yet."

Bellamy's smile softened, though her voice carried a firmer note. "Of course! These things take time. But we'll need to keep up the pace, won't we?" For a moment, her smile faltered as she glanced at Chelsia. "The farm can't run itself."

Chelsia raised an eyebrow but said nothing, Bellamy's unspoken expectations thick in the air. Setting the pail on a nearby crate, Bellamy crouched beside Evan as she adjusted the feed with ease.

"It's a learning process," Bellamy said as she guided him. "We'll get there."

Evan nodded, carefully mimicking her motions. Chelsia stayed nearby, her arms crossed, watching in silence. Rising, Bellamy smoothed her coat, her eyes falling on the pigpen.

"Maybe it's time to bring in another set of hands. Things should run smoother with more of a balance." She turned back to Evan, her smile gentle. "Don't worry, dear. You're doing just fine."

Chelsia tilted her head as Bellamy's words echoed in her mind. Another set of hands. Was Bellamy hinting at replacing Evan? Or was she already considering someone new to fill Caleb's place? The thought gnawed at her, but she kept it buried.

Bellamy moved toward the pigpen, humming softly, the tune drifting in the damp air. With her gone, Evan's shoulders relaxed, and he sighed. He didn't notice the shadow of doubt crossing Chelsia's face or how her gaze fixed upon Bellamy's retreating form.

The mist lifted, revealing the familiar contours of the farm. It did little to clear the haze of questions clouding Chelsia's mind. She turned back toward the house, her boots squelching in the mud.

Chelsia worked quietly in the storage shed, her hands sifting through sacks of grain while her thoughts roamed. The shed's stillness contrasted with the chaos in her mind. Bellamy's meticulous touch was everywhere, even in the precise arrangement of tools and supplies. Yet, the small inconsistencies gnawed at her: empty hooks where feed sacks should have hung, tools she'd seen only days ago now mysteriously missing.

In the corner, a stack of unmarked crates caught her eye. They hadn't been there before. The lids, made of rough and weathered, yet solid wood, were securely nailed shut. She approached cautiously, brushing her fingers along the coarse edges. As she leaned closer, a metallic bitterness clung to the air, a scent that turned her stomach.

Her chest tightened, memories rushing in unbidden: the delivery weeks ago, larger crates unloaded near the barn. She'd watched as Caleb joked about their heaviness, speculating about their contents. *Just some replacements for worn-out equipment,* Bellamy had explained, her tone effortlessly casual. Too casual. Chelsia remembered the dark stain seeping into one crate's corner, the ventilation holes drilled into its sides, and the way Bellamy's smile seemed brittle, never quite reaching her eyes.

Now, these.

Chelsia stepped back, glancing quickly toward the shed door as if expecting Bellamy to appear. The thought sent a shiver up her spine even as she crouched beside the crates, fingers tracing the edge of the nearest lid. These were smaller than the ones Caleb had unloaded, but the similarities were undeniable. The wood carried the same scent of damp metal, sharp and clinging.

Her fingers hovered near the lid, her instincts colliding with her growing need for answers. The wood was secured with deeply hammered nails too deep for removal without tools. Straightening, she wiped her hands on her jeans, her pulse thrumming in her ears.

What were these?

The tap of boots on gravel snapped her attention to the doorway. Evan appeared, his damp hair plastered to his forehead, a sheepish grin on his face.

"Bellamy sent me for a hammer," he said, gesturing toward the tools on the far wall. Curiosity flickered in his eyes as he glanced at the crates. "What're those?"

Chelsia kept her tone neutral. "No idea. They were here when I got in."

Evan grabbed a hammer, his interest fading as quickly as it came. Adjusting his grip on the handle, he muttered, "Weird," more to himself than to her, before turning and vanishing back into the mist.

With a slow breath, Chelsia looked back at the crates. Opening them wasn't an option—not without drawing attention—yet she had so many questions. Were they tied to the earlier delivery? To Caleb's sudden departure? Or was she simply reaching, her imagination filling in gaps Bellamy had intentionally left blank?

Now the crates looked larger, laden with untold mysteries. Grabbing a sack of grain, she slung it over her shoulder and headed for the door. Answers wouldn't come here. Not yet, but soon. She could feel it.

As she crossed the yard, mist clinging to her like a second skin, she glanced back toward the shed. The crates were out of sight now, swallowed by shadows, but their presence felt as real as ever. A new piece of the puzzle had surfaced, and Chelsia couldn't shake the feeling it was one she wouldn't be able to ignore for long.

Chelsia carried the sack of grain into the main barn, her body moving automatically while her thoughts circled back to the storage shed. Asking about the crates outright was pointless. Bellamy had already brushed her off once before. Chelsia couldn't risk tipping her hand, not when the stakes felt higher than ever.

Bellamy was waiting inside, leaning against a post with her arms crossed. Her alert green eyes tracked Chelsia's every move like a hawk watching prey.

"Took you long enough," she said, though her words carried an undertone that prickled Chelsia's nerves.

"Got sidetracked in the shed," she replied, keeping her tone neutral.

She set the sack down near the feed bins and crouched to untie the coarse string securing its opening. Grain spilled out in a slow cascade, and she used a scoop to transfer it into the bins as Bellamy watched.

"Hmm. Busy day, isn't it?"

Chelsia nodded as she gripped the scoop. She poured another measure of grain into the bin, the sound of kernels hitting wood filling the space between them. Each word from Bellamy felt like a test, every glance a silent probe she couldn't quite deflect.

"You've been a little distracted lately," Bellamy remarked after a pause. "Everything all right?"

Chelsia froze briefly, the scoop hovering above the sack before she resumed.

"I'm fine," she said evenly, brushing some spilled grain from the edge of the bin. Then, realizing the risk of sounding curt, she added, "The rain's been throwing everything off. Makes it harder to keep up."

Bellamy studied her for a long moment, the silence stretching taut. Finally, her features softened, and her voice took on a gentler edge.

"It weighs on you, doesn't it? I know this place isn't easy, but you're doing good work. I'm glad you're here."

The words sounded genuine, though they sat uneasily in Chelsia's chest.

"Thanks," she murmured, forcing a slight nod as she tied off the sack's opening and balanced it upright against the bins.

"I should have kept you paired with Caleb longer," Bellamy mused, almost absently. "Evan could use more guidance. He spends more time fixing his mistakes than getting things right the first time."

Chelsia felt the impact of Bellamy's words and the intensity of her stare. Unsure if silence implied defiance or wisdom, she remained quiet. After a beat, Bellamy straightened, her boots tapping softly as she strode out of the barn without another word. Chelsia slowly exhaled, her shoulders gradually relaxing.

There was always something unsettling about Bellamy's presence, but today it felt more pointed and intense. Chelsia busied herself with the grain, though her thoughts drifted to the shed again, to the crates and the unanswered questions they represented.

Caleb's voice echoed in her memory, his teasing lilt vivid: *You keep looking at these like they're about to sprout legs and walk away.* Even though his grin had been easy, and his tone playful, the thought of those crates had haunted her ever since. She wondered now, with a sinking feeling, if she'd missed her chance to notice what really mattered while it counted.

A sudden shout broke her reverie. Bellamy's voice cut across the yard, cross and commanding. Chelsia frowned as she left the barn, her boots sinking into the softened ground as she made her way toward the commotion.

Near the restricted outbuilding, Evan stared at an overturned barrel, his face ashen as dark, viscous liquid oozed across the ground in uneven rivulets. The biting, sour scent hit Chelsia as she approached—a cloying mix of chemicals and something organic, unsettling in its familiarity.

Bellamy stood a few feet away, her fingers curled into fists at her sides.

"Do you have any idea what you've done?" she barked, her voice cutting through the air like a whip.

"I—I was trying to help," Evan stammered, his hands hovering uselessly, as if he was unsure of where to place them. His dark hair clung damply to his forehead, and he seemed impossibly small under Bellamy's withering glare. "I didn't mean to—"

"You didn't mean to what?" Bellamy snapped, stepping forward. "Do you mean to do anything, Evan? That barrel was marked for a reason. Have you any idea how unsafe this is? If that had gotten on you, or near the animals…"

Her words faltered, trembling at the edges as though she were holding back something deeper. Evan flinched, his shoulders folding inward.

"I'm sorry! I didn't mean to—"

"Sorry doesn't fix this!" Bellamy's tone cracked, her fury spilling over in a way that felt severely unrestrained. "You could have ruined everything! Do you understand that? Everything!"

As Bellamy scolded Evan, Chelsia looked down at the puddle. A shard of something pale amid the spill caught her eye, and her stomach lurched.

Bellamy exhaled sharply, the sound more hiss than sigh, and lifted a trembling hand to her temple. Her chest rose and fell unevenly as she visibly pulled herself together. When she spoke again, her tone was quieter but no less taut.

"I'm sorry," she said, quickly smoothing the front of her flannel shirt. "I didn't mean to raise my voice. It's just… this could have been dangerous. One mistake could hurt you. I got scared."

Evan nodded hastily; his voice barely audible.

"I get it. I won't mess up again."

"I know you won't," Bellamy replied, her smile returning with an unsettling smoothness. She placed a hand on Evan's shoulder, the gesture steeped in control. "Just be more careful, okay?"

"Yes, ma'am," Evan murmured, staring at the ground.

A fleeting smile played on Bellamy's lips as she turned toward Chelsia.

"Help Evan clean this up," she said briskly. "Use shovels to mix it into the ground. I'll see to the rest of the barrels before anything else happens."

Without waiting for a reply, she grabbed the handle of the pallet jack, expertly steering the load into the restricted outbuilding, where the door creaked shut behind her. Chelsia turned back to Evan, who stood motionless, his hands fidgeting with the hem of his shirt.

"Wait here," she said evenly. "I'll grab the shovels we need."

She crossed to the nearby shed and opened the door. Tools hung neatly on their hooks, her thoughts fixed on the shard she'd glimpsed within the spillage. The sour smell of the liquid clung to her mind, mingling with the memory of the crates' rough, sealed wood. Shaking off her unease, she grabbed two shovels and returned to Evan.

"Here," she said, handing him one.

"Thanks," Evan muttered, gripping it loosely. His eyes remained fixed on the puddle, the look on his face flickering between frustration and defeat. He sighed, driving the shovel into the ground. "She probably hates me now."

Chelsia crouched at the spill's edge, examining it.

"What was in there?" she asked.

Evan shook his head, his voice quiet. "I don't know. Bellamy said it was for cleaning something in the barn and then sent me out to the fence line. I came back with a question and saw the barrels on the pallet jack. I thought... maybe if I moved it for her, she'd see I could handle more. Prove I'm not just some screw-up." His voice wavered, bitterness creeping in. He thrust the first load of dirt over the puddle with more force than necessary.

Taking advantage of Evan's distraction, Chelsia shifted, using her shovel to nudge the ivory fragment closer. Her breath caught as she recognized its unmistakable curve.

A tooth.

His voice cut through her thoughts. "You okay?"

She glanced up, brow furrowed. "Yeah," she said quickly, her voice steadier than she felt. She scooped dirt over the tooth, covering it before Evan could notice. "Just... thinking."

"About how mad Bellamy is?" Evan muttered, turning back to his task. "I don't get it. It's just some gross liquid. Why act like I burned the place down?"

Chelsia didn't answer immediately. She pushed the shovel deeper into the soil, marking the spot inconspicuously with a subtle line.

"She's protective of this place," she offered carefully. "Doesn't want anything going wrong."

Evan paused, leaning on his shovel. "Yeah, well, she sure made me feel like everything already did."

In the distance, Chelsia saw the looming shadow of the outbuilding. Despite Bellamy's disappearance, the residual intensity of her anger was persistent.

"She's been on edge lately," she whispered. "It's not about you."

Evan grunted, resuming his task without responding. The wet earth muffled the sound of their shovels. Tension hung between them, unspoken and thick. Chelsia focused on the task at hand, each scoop of dirt an attempt to bury the simmering discomfort. With the contents of the puddle mixed into the mud, Evan stood up, wiping his forehead.

"Thanks," he muttered, glancing at Chelsia with a flicker of gratitude. "I didn't mean to make things worse."

Chelsia rested her hands on the shovel, her eyes briefly sweeping the ground to ensure the line she marked remained visible.

"Just... be careful, Evan. Don't touch anything important looking without asking."

Evan nodded, his posture slumping. "Yeah... lesson learned." He glanced at Chelsia with a thoughtful look. "Is that why Caleb left in such a hurry, you think? Because of her? Because of the way she acts sometimes?"

Chelsia cast one last glance toward the barn, biting her lip as the questions in her mind refused to settle.

"Yeah," she said finally, her voice soft. "Something like that."

CHAPTER THIRTY-NINE

The cold bit at Chelsia's cheeks as she stepped outside, her breath clouding in front of her face before dissolving into the crisp morning air. The world around the farm was hushed, blanketed in the stillness that comes before a freeze. Her boots left faint imprints on the frost-dusted ground, and she tightened the collar of her jacket against the chill creeping in from the west.

She'd known this was coming; the weather app had warned of plunging temperatures and a return to icy conditions. The prediction hadn't felt real until now, standing in it. Her fingers itched to check the app again, as though confirming what she already knew would provide some strange comfort.

Chelsia exhaled slowly, watching the wispy plume of air drift away as her thoughts tugged her back to the day before. The spill. The tooth. The burden of it stuck in her thoughts, like an unreachable splinter.

She had slept little—couldn't, really—not with the image of that curved fragment haunting the edges of her thoughts. What was it doing there, mixed in with whatever sinister brew had spilled from the barrel? And why had Bellamy been so rattled, her brusque tone giving way to an unsettling softness by the end of her tirade?

Chelsia's fingers curled into fists, her nails biting into her palms through the fabric of her gloves. She couldn't stop thinking about the tooth buried just beneath the surface where she and Evan had shoveled. A part of her wanted to rush out there now, to dig it up and finally hold it in her hand, though she did not know what she'd do once she had it.

The rational part of her mind warned against it. What could she possibly prove? Bellamy's reaction, angry, then oddly tender, still left her questioning whether she was seeing too much in the situation. Bennett certainly wouldn't believe her, not without more to go on. A single tooth wasn't a smoking gun; it was debris, easily explained as an unfortunate, if macabre, workplace accident.

And yet, she couldn't shake the feeling that it meant something more.

Her eyes drifted toward the barn; its dark outline distinct against the pale morning sky. Somewhere in its shadow lay answers, or at least a clue, but she'd have to wait. Bellamy wasn't the kind of person you surprised without risking consequences.

Chelsia inhaled deeply, the icy air stinging her lungs. For now, she'd bide her time.

She had no choice.

The day unfolded slowly, dragging with the kind of monotony that made every sound and movement feel amplified. Inside the farmhouse, the wood floors groaned underfoot as Chelsia moved through her morning routine. The chill seeped into the house despite the vibration of the heater, and she wrapped her hands around a steaming mug of tea, savoring the warmth as she stared out the kitchen window.

Beyond the glass, the farm stretched in muted tones; the frost clinging stubbornly to the grass despite the weak sunlight filtering through a veil of clouds. Evan was out by the chicken coop, a smear of dark clothing against the landscape. His motions were jerky, almost frantic, as he tossed feed into the enclosure. She watched as a chicken flapped away from his heavy boots, its feathers scattering in a brief puff of motion before settling again.

Bellamy's voice broke the quiet from somewhere upstairs, calling instructions down to Chelsia.

"The barn needs sweeping," she said briskly. "And make sure the feed bins are topped off before we lose daylight."

Chelsia acknowledged with a nod she knew Bellamy wouldn't see, setting her mug down and pulling on her coat. The barn. Of course. Bellamy always seemed to find a reason to send her there lately, as if testing her patience or prodding her to notice something, or nothing.

Outside, the air clung to her skin, biting, as she trudged toward the barn. Walking along the frost-dusted path, she felt a prickle of awareness, as if the farmhouse's windows were watching her retreat. She shoved the thought aside, focusing instead on the pacing of her steps.

Evan was still near the coop as she passed. He straightened when he saw her, his brow furrowed beneath damp strands of hair.

"You get the barn today?" he asked, his tone carrying a note of sympathy, or perhaps relief that the chore wasn't his.

Chelsia shrugged, the motion stiffer than she intended. "Seems like it."

Evan's mouth twisted as though he wanted to say something else, but he thought better of it. Instead, he adjusted the collar of his jacket and gestured vaguely toward the shed.

"Bellamy's in one of her moods again. I think she's still upset about yesterday. You'd think the world was ending with how she's been pacing this morning."

Chelsia glanced toward the barn, her lips curving into something that wasn't quite a smile.

"Maybe it is," she said simply.

Evan blinked, surprised. Before he could respond, she was already walking away.

Inside the barn, the air was thick with the smell of hay and the earthy odor of animals. Chelsia took a moment to let her eyes adjust to the dim interior, the soft rustling of animals filling the space. The broom waited for her near the entrance, its handle worn smooth from use.

As she swept, her mind drifted, the repetitive motion doing little to quiet the churn of her thoughts. Bellamy's words from yesterday echoed in her memory, clipped and cold, then soft and calculated. She thought of the barrel, the spill, and the tooth buried beneath the surface.

Her hold on the broom handle tightened as she struggled with the uncooperative puzzle pieces.

As the afternoon waned, the farmhouse grew quieter, its stillness broken only by the occasional creak of floorboards or the muted thud of a door closing. The frost hadn't melted entirely, clinging stubbornly to shaded patches where the sun couldn't reach. By the time dinner was ready, the sky had shifted to an ashen hue, streaked with smudges of lavender and steel.

Chelsia set the table while Bellamy stirred a pot on the stove, the aroma of something savory filling the air. Evan shuffled into the room; his shoulders hunched as he rubbed his hands together for warmth.

"Cold out there," he muttered, glancing toward the windows as though expecting to see frost creeping up the panes.

"Supposed to drop more tonight," Bellamy said, her tone casual as she turned to face them, a ladle in hand. She glanced at Chelsia. "We'll need to make sure the animals are settled before it gets too bad. Maybe you and Evan can check the pens one last time after dinner."

Chelsia hesitated, catching the faintest shift in Bellamy's expression, a glimmer that was gone too quickly to name. She nodded, keeping her own countenance carefully neutral.

"Sure."

Evan grumbled something under his breath as he sank into a chair, his damp hair gently curled at the ends. Bellamy served the stew in generous portions, and for a moment, the three of them ate in silence, the scrape of spoons against bowls the only sound in the room.

"You've been quiet today," Bellamy said suddenly, her eyes settling on Chelsia. The words were smooth, almost conversational, though a note of warning made Chelsia's stomach lurch.

"Just tired," Chelsia replied evenly, forcing a small smile. "Didn't sleep well last night."

Bellamy acknowledged this with a soft hum before turning her attention back to her bowl.

"You should definitely rest tonight. Big day tomorrow."

Chelsia didn't ask what she meant.

After dinner, Evan excused himself quickly, muttering something about checking on the pigs before heading to bed. His footsteps echoed briefly through the yard before fading into the frosty night.

Bellamy moved with an unhurried grace as she cleared the table, her gestures almost hypnotic in their rhythm. Chelsia watched her carefully, searching for cracks in the mask Bellamy always wore so flawlessly. There were none, only the experienced calm of someone entirely in control.

"I'm going to shower and call it an early night," Bellamy said. "Don't stay up too late."

Chelsia nodded; her throat dry. She waited until the muffled sound of water running in Bellamy's ensuite bathroom reached her ears, then allowed herself to exhale.

The farmhouse settled into an uneasy stillness, the kind that pressed against the walls and left the air feeling heavier than it should. Chelsia moved to the window, peering out at the shadowed landscape beyond. Frost glittered under the weak moonlight, and the barn loomed dark and solid against the horizon.

Her pulse quickened as she thought of the tooth buried beneath the moist soil. She couldn't ignore it any longer.

Chelsia remained in the kitchen, the overhead light humming, listening for sounds emanating from Bellamy's room. She knew her plan carried a significant risk, like trying to outmaneuver a predator while already in its den. The muffled sound of running water from Bellamy's bathroom told her she had only a small window of time.

Pulling her coat tighter around herself, she stepped cautiously out of the door, the cold hitting her like a wave. The frost had thickened in the night air, crackling beneath her boots as she made her way to the shed. She paused, her breath slow and shallow, glancing back toward the farmhouse. A faint glow emanated from the windows, yet the interior remained still.

As she opened the shed door, its creak made her wince. The night remained still, offering no other response. Her fingers glided over the neatly hung tools until she found the shovel she'd used the day before. Its solid weight in her hand steadied her against the unease stirring in her chest.

She stepped back into the night, her pulse quickening as she moved toward the barn. The moonlight cast the yard in pale silver, illuminating the rutted dirt path she followed. Every sound seemed amplified: the distant rustle of animals, the dry snap of a twig underfoot. She kept her focus ahead; driven by a gnawing urgency she couldn't explain.

The spot near the outbuilding looked undisturbed at first glance, but Chelsia knew better. She approached cautiously, her eyes scanning the ground for the line she'd marked. It was gone, the soil now smooth and freshly turned, as though someone had been here ahead of her.

She gripped the shovel before crouching low, pressing her fingers into the dirt. The cold, loose earth shifted easily under her touch, confirming what she'd already suspected: someone had dug here, and recently.

Her breath caught as she continued searching for the tooth. Her heart thudded in her ears, each shovelful of dirt sending a jolt of expectation through her. There was nothing, only the unsettling emptiness of disturbed soil.

The tooth was gone.

Chelsia straightened slowly as her mind raced. Had Bellamy done this? Was she already onto her? The thought was enough to liquefy her bowels. She forced herself to stay calm.

Carefully, she returned the dirt to its place, smoothing it as best she could. She glanced back at the farmhouse, its windows still glowing. She couldn't stay any longer, or she'd risk being caught.

Chelsia replaced the shovel in the shed, her hands trembling only slightly as she latched the door behind her. She walked back toward the house with measured steps, forcing herself not to look over her shoulder.

The warmth of the farmhouse embraced her as she stepped inside, though it did little to calm the storm in her mind. She turned toward the hallway and started for the stairs to her room, pausing when a voice broke the stillness.

"Hey, roomie!"

Chelsia froze, her heart leaping into her throat. Bellamy stood in the kitchen, damp hair curling loosely around her face as she stirred a mug of tea. Despite the warmth of her wide smile, the glint in her eyes made Chelsia's stomach twist.

"Oh, hey, Bellamy," Chelsia said.

"Everything okay?"

"Yeah... fine. Evan already checked on the pigs, so... I took care of the rest..."

"Good," Bellamy said, her voice as light as the steam curling from the mug. She looked Chelsia over with quiet scrutiny. "You mentioned earlier that you didn't sleep well last night."

Chelsia swallowed hard, forcing a smile. "Something like that."

Bellamy took a slow sip.

"Well," she said, her tone wrapping around the words like velvet, "looks like we'll have to fix that... won't we?"

CHAPTER FORTY

The farmhouse felt warmer than usual, the air carrying the scent of freshly brewed coffee and the smell of wood smoke from the fireplace. Bellamy moved briskly through the kitchen, her smile brighter than the weak winter sunlight filtering through the windows.

"Big day," she said as she set a basket of croissants on the table, her tone almost celebratory. "I thought it'd be nice to do something special tonight. We've all been working so hard, and we deserve a little reward, don't you think?"

Chelsia nodded noncommittally, stirring a splash of milk into her tea. Bellamy's cheeriness felt off, especially after the strain of the past few days.

Evan perked up at the mention of a reward. "Special, huh? Like what?"

Bellamy's smile widened, her eyes gleaming. "Porter Sausage, of course. And a few other surprises."

The tooth, the disturbed soil, Bellamy's unsettling greeting from the night before all simmered at the back of Chelsia's mind. After the awkward greeting in the kitchen, she had half-expected Bellamy to demand what she'd been up to.

"Couldn't sleep either?" Bellamy had asked instead, before insisting that Chelsia join her for a cup of tea.

The tea Bellamy gave her smelled very similar to the usual evening blend, except for the hint of berries. Chelsia hadn't asked what was different, and the sip she took had been tentative as Bellamy explained with disarming casualness, "Just a little something extra. We've got to make sure you get a good night's sleep."

Evan didn't seem to notice anything unusual. "Finally," he said with a grin, slapping the table lightly. "I've been waiting for this sausage forever."

Bellamy laughed, a delicate, breezy sound. "Well, you won't have to wait much longer, will you?" She winked, her tone playful.

By the time dinner preparations began that afternoon, the farmhouse smelled of herbs and a hint of spice that grew stronger as the hours passed. Bellamy worked efficiently as she chopped vegetables and basted the sausage. The aroma differed from the stews and roasts Chelsia was used to. There was sweetness mingled with the savory, something that teased the edges of familiarity.

Candles flickered on the table by the time the meal was ready, their soft glow dancing against the polished wood. Bellamy had insisted on using the good china—heavy, cream-colored dishes with a delicate floral border.

Evan hovered near the table, practically vibrating with anticipation. He'd already peeked under the lid of the serving dish twice, his face lighting up at the sight of the sausage nestled among roasted vegetables.

"Porter Sausage," he said with a reverence that bordered on absurd. Chelsia found him a little too eager to forgive Bellamy's recent transgressions. "Man, I've really been wanting this."

With a tight smile, Chelsia kept her eyes on the dish. The sausage was golden brown, its casing glistening, though something about it was oddly off-putting.

Bellamy swept into the room, a glass of wine in hand and a triumphant smile on her lips.

"Dinner is served," she announced, her voice warm and inviting.

Chelsia's stomach gurgled as she took her seat, the flicker of candlelight casting delicate shadows across Bellamy's face.

Dinner was a tableau of warmth and apprehension, the golden glow of the candles contrasting with the knot in Chelsia's stomach. Bellamy served each plate with a flourish, placing the sausage and roasted vegetables front and center like a proud artist unveiling her masterpiece.

Evan didn't wait long to dig in, spearing a thick slice of sausage with his fork and popping it into his mouth.

"Oof," he said around the mouthful, his voice heavy with satisfaction. "This is so good."

Bellamy smiled, taking Evan in with something close to fondness. "I told you it'd be worth the wait," she said smoothly, taking her seat at the head of the table.

Chelsia picked at her vegetables, her fork moving methodically but rarely reaching her mouth. The sausage sat untouched on her plate, its glistening surface catching the candlelight in a way that made her stomach churn.

"You haven't made this since I got here," Evan said, glancing toward Bellamy. "What's the occasion?"

"It felt like the right time," she said before sipping her wine, her lips curving into a smile. "'Tis the season, after all."

The silence weighed heavily on Chelsia as she cleared her throat. "Is Bennett joining us?" she asked casually.

Bellamy paused mid-reach, her fork hovering just above her plate. The moment stretched a fraction too long before she responded.

"No," she said, setting her fork down gently. "I imagine this time of year keeps him busy. All those holiday calls, people needing help. You know how it is."

Evan nodded, already halfway through another bite. "Makes sense."

With a manufactured smile, Bellamy looked back at Chelsia.

"Don't worry," she added, her voice dropping just enough. "He'll likely want to check in again soon enough."

Chelsia's stomach twisted, her grip on the fork tightening at the implication. She forced a smile, nodding slightly as she returned her focus to her plate.

Bellamy paused before she took up her wineglass.

"Now, I think we should toast to all of us: our hard work, our resilience. It hasn't been easy, but we've done well."

Evan raised his glass enthusiastically. "Hear, hear!"

Chelsia mirrored the gesture, her glass cool and smooth in her hand. The wine, a sweet red, slid down easily, though it did little to loosen the knot in her chest.

Bellamy set her glass down, glancing between Evan and Chelsia. "You know," she said, her voice taking on a more wistful tone, "this is exactly the meal Caleb would've loved. He was quite persistent about wanting to experience my family's recipe... I suppose, in a way, he is. In spirit."

Evan hummed a note of agreement, clearly absorbed in his plate. Chelsia froze, the edges of her vision sharpening as her mind tried to process the comment.

Bellamy looked at Chelsia, her eyes gleaming with something inscrutable. "You haven't tried yours yet," she said, gesturing toward the untouched sausage on Chelsia's plate.

Chelsia forced a smile, her mind racing. "Oh, I will. I'm just savoring these vegetables first," she replied carefully. "They're amazing. You've outdone yourself, Bellamy."

The meal ended with Bellamy clearing the plates. She insisted Evan and Chelsia stay seated, gesturing for them to relax as she disappeared into the pantry.

Evan stretched in his chair, letting out a contented sigh. "That was incredible. I don't know how she does it."

Chelsia murmured an agreement, though her words felt hollow even as she said them. The lingering taste of the vegetables on her tongue was oddly cloying, and the thought of the untouched sausage made her stomach twist.

Bellamy returned moments later, holding two small boxes wrapped in plain brown paper tied with twine.

"I'm not one for big holiday gestures," she began, setting the boxes down in front of Evan and Chelsia. "However, I enjoy showing my appreciation for the people who make this place feel like home."

Evan grinned, tugging the twine loose with a childlike eagerness. Inside, he found a set of leather work gloves and a rugged utility knife.

"Whoa," he said, holding the knife up to the light. "This is... really nice. Thank you."

"You've earned it," Bellamy said, her smile deepening. "I know how hard you've been working."

Chelsia's fingers worked carefully as she untied the bow and peeled back the plain brown paper. Inside the box was a locket, its casing gleaming softly in the candlelight. She lifted it gingerly, the chain slipping through her fingers like silk.

The locket was delicate yet solid, a striking contrast of elegance and durability. Intricate engraved floral patterns adorned its surface, creating an aura of timeless beauty. As she turned it over, something about it felt... strange. The casing wasn't as smooth as it appeared; faint ridges interrupted the polish, barely noticeable, but undeniably there.

Its weight was disproportionate to its size, heavier than expected. As her thumb brushed the edge, she caught a slight irregularity, a shallow groove that didn't quite match the rest of the seamless design. She frowned, holding it closer to the light, and found the engravings a distraction, drawing her eye back to their elaborate detail.

"It's beautiful," she said carefully.

Bellamy leaned in, a strained smile on her face. "I thought it suited you. Understated. Classic. Mysterious."

Chelsia flipped the locket open, finding the interior empty save for the faintest impression of its material, a texture that seemed organic and almost porous. Her stomach instinctively turned.

"There's no photo in it yet," Bellamy continued. "One day, I'm sure you'll find someone worth adding."

Chelsia nodded absently, her mind snagging on the odd texture of the locket's surface. It felt familiar, though she couldn't place where she'd encountered it before.

"You work hard," Bellamy said suddenly, breaking the moment. Her tone was contemplative, almost probing. "I can't help wondering... is your heart really in it? Or is there something else driving you?"

Chelsia blinked, her mind stumbling over the question. "I—I don't know," she said, the words slipping out before she could stop them.

Bellamy tilted her head, her gaze unwavering. "You don't strike me as someone who works without purpose."

Her breath hitched as she swallowed hard. "Well, everyone's driven by something, I guess."

Bellamy kept smiling, her eyes drawn to the locket.

"Perhaps." She paused, her voice softening sweetly. "You've been such a help here, Chelsia. I know why Bennett brought you, why he thought this would be a good fit. Your work has been invaluable. I only hope you'll remember me, and the farm, fondly... when it's time to move on. People have a way of forgetting the little things... and the people they encounter along the way." She gestured toward the locket. "This will remind you... of who I am."

Her words hung in the air, both weighted and unspoken, as Chelsia nodded stiffly. She forced her fingers to relax around the chain before tucking the locket back into its box.

CHAPTER FORTY-ONE

Evan worked with a new vigor, the gleam of restored confidence practically radiating from him as he hefted a sack of feed onto his shoulder. His dark hair clung to his damp forehead, and a smile played on his lips as he crossed the yard toward the barn.

"Looking good, Evan!" Bellamy called from the porch, her voice as warm as the sunlight breaking through the scattered clouds. She leaned against the railing, her flannel shirt sleeves rolled up to her elbows. Her approving nod sent a flush of satisfaction across Evan's face.

"Thanks!" he called back, his grin widening as he disappeared into the barn.

Chelsia swept the farmhouse steps nearby. Though physically present, her mind was miles away, circling back to the tooth, the mysterious liquid, and the locket in her room upstairs.

Evan reappeared moments later, hauling a length of hose from the barn. Chelsia held his buoyant form in her scrutinizing gaze, marveling at how easily he'd been won over by a coil of Porter Sausage. He whistled softly as he carried the hose to the equipment shed, his focus singular and driven by the spark of Bellamy's restored approval.

He dragged the hose toward the water pump, connecting it with apparent ease. Water sputtered briefly before gushing through, its steady stream spilling into the trough with a rhythmic splash. Satisfied, Evan moved back toward the barn, humming softly under his breath as Bellamy turned to head back inside the farmhouse.

Lost in her sweeping, Chelsia's thoughts drifted as she contemplated her next step.

The early afternoon sun hung high in the sky, casting a dim light over the farm. Despite its position, the chill in the December air persisted, stinging Chelsia's cheeks as she carried a bucket of feed toward the storage shed. Her steps crunched softly against the frostbitten ground, the crisp air stinging her lungs.

She hadn't seen Evan or Bellamy for a while, the two of them busy on the other side of the property, working on part of the fence line. Fine by her. The brief solitude allowed her to breathe without Bellamy's calculating eyes on her or Evan's unrelenting chatter.

Her route took her past the outbuilding, its faded exterior and padlocked door like a deliberate mark on the landscape of the farm. Chelsia slowed her pace, the bucket's handle pressing into her gloved palm as she allowed herself a closer look.

The padlock gleamed, its surface pristine against the wooden door it secured. She stepped a little closer, feigning a need to adjust her grip on the bucket as she leaned forward. Though sturdy, the lock didn't appear impenetrable. She'd seen plenty that were tougher.

Chelsia lingered just long enough to commit the details to memory: the brass sheen of the lock, the scuff marks near its base, the latch that sat slightly askew, and the engraved brand name stamped just below the keyhole.

A distant shout from Evan startled her. She tensed, her heart skipping a beat, though his words were indistinct. She glanced back toward the fence line, where Bellamy and Evan were little more than silhouettes against the horizon. The rhythmic clatter of a hammer echoed, underscoring the surrounding silence.

Turning back to the shed, she hesitated. The lock caught the light as she shifted, and for a fleeting moment, she considered testing it just to see if it might give. She dismissed the thought almost as quickly as it came. Bellamy's wrath was a risk she wasn't willing to take. Not yet.

With a last glance at the door, she straightened, readjusting the bucket's weight in her grip. The chill of the air seemed crisper now, biting through her gloves as she resumed her path toward the storage shed. The lock could keep its secrets for just a little longer.

By the time the chores were done, the afternoon light had softened, the warmth of the sun dwindling against the crisp December air. Chelsia was halfway through washing her hands at the kitchen sink when Bellamy appeared in the doorway, a warm smile on her face and an unmistakable gleam of excitement in her eyes.

"I thought we could take a little trip," Bellamy announced, her tone cheerful. "To Portland. It'll be nice to get out and do something... normal."

Chelsia turned off the faucet and grabbed a dish towel, her stomach flipping at the suggestion.

"Portland?"

Bellamy nodded. "I have a few errands to run, and I thought it might be nice for you and Evan to join me. Stretch your legs, pick up anything you need. And," she added with a playful tilt of her head, "it's payday."

That caught Evan's attention as he entered the kitchen, his face lighting up at the word.

"Payday? Seriously?"

Bellamy chuckled, reaching into her back pocket to pull out two envelopes. "Seriously. You've both earned it." She handed the first envelope to Evan, who opened it with enthusiasm usually reserved for Christmas morning.

"Cash?" he said, his tone both surprised and thrilled. "I've never been paid in cash before. Is that, like, normal here?"

Bellamy smirked, leaning against the counter. "Farm life differs from a regular nine-to-five. Simpler this way."

Evan held up a few of the crisp bills, a grin spreading across his face.

"No complaints here."

Chelsia accepted her envelope with a quiet nod, her fingers brushing the edges of the crisp paper. She tucked it into her jacket pocket without looking inside, her thoughts already spinning.

The drive into Portland was quiet at first, the hum of Bellamy's Ford F-250 filling the space between them. Chelsia sat in the middle seat, flanked by

Evan on her right and Bellamy on her left as she steered the truck. The cabin was warm, the vents blowing just enough heat to ward off the cold.

Evan's excitement bubbled over in intermittent chatter and idle observations about the passing scenery. Chelsia barely registered his words, her focus on the envelope in her pocket and the hostility that seemed to hum beneath Bellamy's otherwise sunny demeanor.

It was a relief when they pulled into the parking lot at Eastport Plaza, the bustling strip mall alive with shoppers bundled against the chill. Bellamy parked the truck, cutting the engine as she turned to them.

"All right," she said, her tone brisk. "Two hours. Meet back here when you're done."

Evan was out of the truck in seconds, his dark hair bouncing as he hit the pavement with an almost childlike eagerness. As she exited, Chelsia carefully adjusted her scarf for warmth.

"Have fun," Bellamy called over her shoulder as she disappeared into the crowd.

Chelsia's errands passed in a blur. She picked up what she needed with methodical efficiency, her thoughts only half on the task at hand. The allotted time passed more quickly than expected, and soon she was back at the truck, her hands shoved into her coat pockets as she waited for the others to return.

Her phone buzzed. She pulled it out, her brows knitting together as she read the message.

"I'm at the house. Where's everyone?"

A knot formed in her stomach. She quickly typed out a response.

"At Eastport. Leaving soon."

The minutes stretched as she waited, her mind racing with the implications of Bennett's unexpected visit.

The drive back to the farm was anything but quiet where Evan was concerned. He sat by the passenger door, his energy still bubbling over from the trip, periodically peeking into the shopping bag cradled in his lap.

"Look at this," he said, pulling out a neatly folded sweatshirt emblazoned with a bold graphic. "It's perfect, right? And the price? Absolute steal." He tucked it back into the bag with care, grinning at his own good fortune.

Chelsia sat in the middle seat, her bag wedged carefully between her feet. She kept one hand resting on its edge, subtly shielding it from view. She didn't want to invite questions, not from Evan, and especially not from Bellamy.

Bellamy drove with an air of contentment, her hands relaxed on the wheel as the truck rumbled steadily along the road.

"Such a good day," she remarked, her tone almost whimsical. "I think we all needed that."

"Yeah, definitely," Evan agreed, his voice brimming with enthusiasm. He peeked into his bag again, his smile stretching wider as he shuffled through his purchases.

While the distant farmhouse lights flickered, Chelsia remained silent, keeping her eyes locked on the horizon. The truck's heater hummed softly, though it did little to warm the knot forming in her chest.

Bennett's message occupied her thoughts. She hadn't told Bellamy about his unexpected visit, and she wouldn't. Letting Bennett's presence come as a surprise might throw Bellamy off her game, and Chelsia wanted to see how she'd react.

Her fingertips toyed with the handle of her bag as she stared out the windshield. The lights of the farmhouse grew brighter, the distance between them closing with every second.

Should she tell him? What could she even say without opening doors she wasn't ready to walk through? With her resolve to leave stronger than ever, why did it still matter?

CHAPTER FORTY-TWO

The porch light cast a soft glow over the farmhouse as Bellamy pulled the truck into the driveway. Evan was the first to notice the vehicle parked off to the side.

"Who's here?" he asked, craning his neck to get a better look.

Bellamy's brows furrowed as she eased the truck into its usual spot. Chelsia looked up, pulled from her thoughts. Her heart skipped a beat when she spotted the figure waiting near the porch steps.

"Ryan," Bellamy murmured, her tone more curious than annoyed.

They climbed out of the truck, the cold air biting at their skin as they made their way toward the house. Bennett greeted them with an amiable smile, clad in a thick coat that looked more suited to the city than the farm.

"Hope I'm not intruding," he said, his voice warm and unassuming.

Bellamy's lips curved into a smile. "Not intruding at all. Always a pleasure. Let's get inside before we catch our death."

The warmth inside the farmhouse was welcoming, the scent of wood smoke wrapping around them as they stepped through the door. Bennett stood near the kitchen table, his large frame seeming to take up more space than normal.

Bellamy set her keys on the counter, looking at him with a mix of curiosity and surprise.

"Didn't expect to see you tonight, Ryan," she said.

"Thought I'd stop by, see how things were going," he replied. He held up two small gift bags. "I brought presents."

Evan perked up instantly, shrugging off his coat and draping it over a chair.

"Seriously? That's awesome!"

Bennett handed Evan the first bag as they all took seats around the table. Inside, he found a box filled with decadent treats, each piece carefully arranged in gold foil.

"Chocolates?" Evan said, his excitement bubbling over. "Man, this is great. Thanks!"

Bennett nodded, his grin widening. "I wasn't sure what you liked, so I went with something safe."

"Safe and perfect," Evan said, already popping one into his mouth.

Bennett turned to Chelsia next, offering her the second bag. She accepted it, sliding the small box from within before carefully opening it. Her eyes swept over the delicate bracelet inside, its charm etched with a floral design.

"It's lovely," she breathed as her mind raced. "Thank you, Bennett."

Bellamy looked at the bracelet. Though she appeared composed, there was a flicker in her eyes, something Chelsia noted and didn't acknowledge.

"It goes beautifully with what Bellamy gave me," Chelsia added, glancing toward her.

Bennett sat back, a glimmer of curiosity crossing his face. "Bellamy gave you something like this?"

She nodded. "A locket. Let me grab it. It'll only take a moment."

Bellamy's posture shifted, and she spoke just as Chelsia rose from her seat, her bag of purchases from Eastport Plaza in hand.

"Oh, there's no need to trouble yourself! I'm sure Ryan gets the idea."

Chelsia looked at her for a heartbeat longer than necessary.

"It's no trouble," she replied evenly, heading toward the stairs.

The locket, in its box, remained untouched on the bedside table. She ignored it in favor of the shopping bag, reaching in to sift through its contents until her fingers closed around a smaller package nestled at the bottom. She withdrew it, tossing the larger bag onto the bed as her breath hitched.

Carefully, she unwrapped the package, revealing the lock she had purchased at Eastport Plaza. It was an identical match to the one securing the outbuilding's door. She turned it over in her hands, her eyes tracing the engraved brand and smooth, gleaming surface. The weight of it felt significant, though she couldn't decide whether that was because of its physical heft or what she intended to do with it.

Even if she picked the original cleanly, there was no guarantee Bellamy wouldn't notice the faintest sign of tampering. The replacement lock wasn't about covering her tracks forever, just long enough to ensure no one would question what had happened until she was long gone.

After a moment, she slipped the lock back into its bag and stowed it carefully in the bottom drawer of her dresser, tucking it beneath a folded scarf. With a last check to ensure it was hidden, she straightened and turned her attention to the locket.

Crossing to the bedside table, she lifted the box and flipped it open, the locket's polished surface gleaming under the dim light. Its intricate engravings were beautiful, almost disarming in their elegance, yet she couldn't shake the feeling of wrongness that clung to it. She hesitated, her thoughts churning, before finally heading back downstairs.

The murmur of conversation drifted up the stairs as she descended, the rustle of paper as Evan helped himself to more chocolates punctuating the quiet. When she stepped into the kitchen, Bennett glanced up, his smile returning as she approached. Casually leaning against the counter, Bellamy's observation of her felt pointedly restrained.

Chelsia set the locket box on the table and opened it carefully. "Here it is," she said. The locket caught the glow of the kitchen light, its engravings casting intricate shadows on the box's interior.

Bennett moved closer, his brow lifting as he studied the piece. "That's stunning," he said after a moment, his voice carrying an admiring note. He gestured toward the floral design etched into its surface.

"Beautiful craftsmanship. Unique, too." He paused briefly. "From Bellamy, you said?"

Chelsia's eyes briefly met Bellamy's. "Yep," she replied simply.

"You're right," he said as he straightened, nodding with approval. "They do make a nice pair."

For a moment, Chelsia felt a pang of disappointment, though she remained outwardly calm. She had observed him, hoping for some tell—a flash of recognition, the slightest shadow of discomfort. Instead, his reaction remained calm and untroubled.

Bellamy's voice broke the moment, smooth and lilting. "I thought it suited her," she said, pushing away from the counter. "Something timeless, like Chelsia herself."

Chelsia shifted her focus, closing the locket's box and tucking it under her arm. So much for that.

"So," Bellamy continued, her tone warming as she redirected the conversation, "are you staying for dinner, Bennett?"

He glanced between them, the corners of his mouth lifting. "If the invitation's open, I'd be happy to."

"Of course it's open," Bellamy replied smoothly. "We'd be delighted to have you."

In her room, Chelsia placed the bracelet onto her bedside table, its delicate charm catching the light momentarily. Pulling open the dresser drawer, she carefully lifted the scarf concealing the lock she'd purchased earlier and tucked the bracelet alongside it. Its presence felt oddly dissonant among the secrets she was collecting.

The locket, still in its box, joined the others in the drawer. She replaced the scarf, smoothing it over to ensure everything remained hidden before closing the drawer with a quiet click.

The shower was quick, the comforting warmth washing away the day's grit, but not the thoughts spinning in her mind. Afterward, she stood before the mirror, her damp coils falling loosely against her shoulders as she began shaping them into a series of carefully detangled and generously moisturized flat twists. The routine was almost meditative, though her thoughts stubbornly remained on Bennett and the locket.

She finished by securing the ends neatly in a crisscross with hairpins at her nape, dressing swiftly in clean clothes. Ensuring everything was in place, she left the room satisfied, her footsteps soft as she made her way downstairs.

The indistinct murmur of voices drifted upstairs, punctuated by the occasional clatter of cutlery. The sounds were calm and ordinary, though she knew better. Nothing was ever as it seemed.

Chelsia stepped into the dining room to find the table already set. Bennett stood at the far end, aligning the edge of a plate with meticulous care.

The fragile china seemed even more delicate in his large hands. At her arrival, he glanced up and offered a smile.

"Almost ready," he said, nodding toward the kitchen.

The aroma of roasted herbs and garlic hung in the air, warm and inviting. At the stove, Bellamy worked with her usual efficiency, her back to them as she scraped a spatula against a pan. The bubbling of a sauce mingled with the steady rhythm of her movements, a domestic symphony at odds with the anxiety Chelsia couldn't shake.

She slid into her seat, her thoughts distant. Her mind returned to the collected items upstairs. The bracelet. The lock. The locket. A disheartening feeling of disappointment returned. Bennett's lack of reaction still gnawed at her. He was a detective. How could he not see what she had?

The creak of the front door pulled her from her thoughts. Evan stepped inside, his hair still damp. With a grin illuminating his face, he approached with energetic, refreshed steps.

"Sorry I'm late," he said, his voice breaking through the quiet. "I couldn't decide which one to wear."

He smoothed his hands over the front of his shirt, obviously part of the Eastport Plaza haul: a deep red, soft fabric with a checkered texture and stitching in a lighter shade along the cuffs.

Chelsia glanced twice in quick succession. The shirt looked familiar.

At the stove, Bellamy turned abruptly. Her eyes found Evan. Her expression changed instantly. Her grip faltered. The serving platter tipped in her hands, and its contents, perfectly browned meat, steaming vegetables, and a glossy drizzle of sauce, crashed to the floor in a loud, wet clatter.

The room fell silent.

"Bellamy!" Bennett was the first to move, his chair scraping loudly against the floor as he rushed to her side. Evan followed, his earlier cheer replaced by concern. "Are you all right?"

Bellamy waved them off with one trembling hand. "I'm fine," she said, her voice thin. "The platter—it was too hot, and I wasn't paying attention."

Chelsia remained seated, watching. Bellamy crouched to gather the broken pieces of ceramic. The tremor in her hands was almost imperceptible, but she caught it. She looked from Evan to Bellamy.

"You look like you've seen a ghost, Bell," Bennett said softly, his brow furrowed with concern. "You sure you're all right?"

Bellamy straightened, brushing her hands against her apron as though shaking off the moment.

"I'm fine," she insisted, gently clearing her throat. "I just need to tidy up. Excuse me for a moment."

She turned and disappeared toward her room without waiting for a response. Bennett watched her retreat, his arms crossed, concern etched across his features. His lips parted, as if to speak. After briefly looking at Evan, he shook his head.

"Let's get this cleaned up," Bennett said finally, gesturing for Evan to help. "Maybe we should eat out tonight. I think Bellamy could use a break."

Chelsia nodded, biting her bottom lip as a fresh wave of realization washed over her, and she said nothing.

CHAPTER FORTY-THREE

The gravel crunched under the tires as they pulled back into the farm, the engine fading to stillness. Evan was the first to climb out, holding a bag of leftovers close to his chest like a prized treasure. He turned toward Bennett and Bellamy with a wide grin.

"Thanks again," he said sincerely, "for dinner and the chocolates. Tonight was... nice."

Bellamy's smile didn't quite reach her eyes.

"You're welcome, Evan. Sleep well."

He nodded and headed toward the barn. Chelsia watched him go, his silhouette disappearing into the shadows.

Bellamy sighed softly, raising a hand to her temple. "I think I'll turn in too," she murmured. "That headache is still bothering me."

Chelsia glanced at her, noting the stiffness in her shoulders and the way she avoided making eye contact. Bellamy didn't wait for a response, instead offering a quiet goodnight before retreating into the house.

Near the porch, Chelsia and Bennett remained, the night air crisp around them. The sky was a deep, endless black, punctuated by scattered stars as they sat on the porch steps, neither speaking at first. Bennett settled comfortably, resting his arms on his knees, while Chelsia wrapped her coat tighter around herself. The chill seeped into her bones, but it was nothing compared to the knot forming in her stomach.

Her thoughts churned, each one darker than the last. She cursed herself for even considering trying to tell Bennett anything earlier. What was she thinking? She'd done too much, seen too much, been through too much to risk getting caught for someone else's mistakes. She had to get away from the farm. From Portland. A snowstorm could rage on for days for all she cared. She'd find a way out.

In the dim porch light, her eyes fell upon Bennett's calm and composed profile. He didn't know. About Bellamy. About Caleb. About any of it. And why would he believe her if she said something?

Dinner replayed in her mind over and over, each moment looping, refusing to settle. Bellamy's too-loud laugh when Evan cracked a joke. The way her smile wavered ever so slightly when she thought no one was looking. How her eyes kept straying to Evan's shirt, just enough to be noticeable if someone was watching closely.

Chelsia pressed her lips together, her chest tightening. The puzzle pieces continued to shift into place. Instead of satisfaction, she felt only dread.

"I'm coming back tomorrow."

The words broke the silence, low and measured. She blinked and turned to Bennett. He stared at the horizon, his face giving nothing away.

She frowned, the unexpected statement throwing her thoughts into disarray.

"What time should I tell Bellamy you'll be by?"

He shook his head, a hint of a smile tugging at his lips. "I'm not coming to see Bellamy. I'm coming to see you." Before she could process the meaning behind his words, Bennett stood, brushing off his hands. "Good night, Chelsia."

She watched, still seated on the steps, as he made his way to his car. The engine roared to life, the headlights cutting through the darkness as he drove away.

Chelsia sat there for a long moment, the chill forgotten. Her thoughts swirled, confused and uneasy, as she replayed his words. Coming to see her? Why?

The quiet of the farm settled around her like a shroud, the stars above offering no answers.

Exiting the bathroom, Chelsia smoothed her nightshirt and switched off the light before entering the bedroom.

She stopped at the doorway.

The mug of tea was on the bedside table waiting for her. Its familiar shape and aroma seemed almost intrusive, like an uninvited guest. Chelsia stared at it for a long moment as she approached the bed. Her fingers brushed the edge of the mug, but the warmth beneath her touch felt wrong. She pulled her hand away. Bellamy had made this tea for her countless times before. Tonight, it felt different.

Tonight, the thought of drinking it turned her stomach.

She left the mug untouched and climbed into bed, pulling the blankets around her shoulders. The room was cloaked in an oppressive stillness that amplified her thoughts. Turning onto her side, Chelsia stared at the wall, her buried memories returning.

Cities and towns blurred together in her mind, each one a temporary refuge, a place to lie low until it was time to move again. Atlanta. Dallas. Santa Fe. Sacramento. Boise. Every stop along the way was the same—always looking over her shoulder, never staying long enough to plant roots.

Portland was supposed to be different. It wasn't, of course. It couldn't be.

Her thoughts drifted to Michael, and a crease formed in her brow. When had his face blurred in her memory? His handsome features, the way he laughed, even the warmth of his touch, was all fading and blending into the swirl of others left in her wake.

How much longer before she couldn't picture him at all?

Chelsia exhaled slowly, the weight of the past pressing down on her. There was no room for sentimentality now. Porter Farms was just another stop, nothing more. She had to leave, and soon. It wasn't a matter of if, but how. How to slip away without drawing attention, without letting things spiral beyond her control.

Her thoughts turned to Bennett. What could he possibly want with her? His words replayed in her mind: *I'm coming to see you.*

Chelsia frowned, her fingers twisting a loose thread on the blanket. Bennett didn't strike her as someone to waste words or time. His visit felt intentional. Too focused to be casual. What was going on?

Sleep pulled at her, loosening her thoughts into fragments. She teetered on the edge of unconsciousness when...

Her eyes snapped open.

Evan's shirt.

She sat up slowly, her pulse quickening as the realization hit. Other than the color, it was identical to the one Caleb bought during the last Eastport Plaza trip.

Her breath caught in her throat. It was clear now: the way Bellamy's face had paled; the platter falling from her hands. Bellamy had been more than startled. She was scared.

Chelsia shifted, pressing her back against the headboard as her mind raced.

Bellamy. Caleb.

The tooth.

Her thoughts focused on the small, solitary discovery. Had it belonged to Caleb? Sam? Or someone else Bellamy had "helped" along the way?

The thought sent a chill rippling down her spine, heavier than the night air pressing against the windowpane.

It was time to go.

CHAPTER FORTY-FOUR

Dawn broke with hazy light filtering through the window as Chelsia stepped out of her room, the mug of cold, untouched tea in hand. She descended the stairs quietly, each step muted against the smooth wood. The house was eerily silent. No clatter of pans or cheerful humming greeted her from the kitchen.

Bellamy wasn't there.

The absence felt strange, but not entirely unwelcome.

Chelsia moved to the sink, tipping the tea down the drain. The aroma briefly lingered before being washed away under the stream of water as she rinsed the cup. She turned to the coffeepot and poured herself a cup. As she slowly sipped, her eyes drifted toward the window. The farm stretched out in muted tones, the frost on the fields catching the first light of day.

Though still tired, she finished her coffee quickly and grabbed her coat. Outside, the air was bracing, though it did little to dispel the heaviness in her chest. Her routine took over as she moved across the farmyard, slipping into the routine of her chores.

The tasks were straightforward—checking on the animals, hauling feed, and clearing icy troughs—but her mind was elsewhere. She hadn't seen Bellamy or Evan yet, though she assumed they were somewhere on the property, each tending to their own duties. The thought didn't bother her. Solitude was preferable.

As she worked, her thoughts churned. When should she leave? It was no longer a question of *if*. She looked up at the gray sky and then back at the farmhouse. Her phone was in her pocket, and she pulled it out, fingers stiff from the cold as she tapped open the weather app. Snow was still in the forecast. Tomorrow, the next day, it didn't matter. She would leave.

Chelsia slipped the phone back into her pocket, her focus shifting to the outbuilding. She had passed the locked door countless times, always wondering what lay behind it. A sudden thought struck her: what if Bellamy's secrets could help her leave? Money. Resources. Anything to ensure her escape was swift and clean. Bellamy might be more useful than she'd realized.

The possibility was tantalizing. Bellamy wouldn't keep anything important in the house... but the outbuilding? That made sense.

Chelsia exhaled slowly, her breath clouding in the wintry morning air. Tonight. She would investigate tonight.

The gravity of her decision was palpable, but surprisingly soothing. The plan was falling into place. Porter Farms wouldn't hold her much longer.

By mid-morning, Chelsia was in the barn, brushing down one of the horses. The familiar motions of her hands moving over the animal's coat helped to quiet her thoughts, if only for a little while. The quiet sounds of the farm—birds singing, hay rustling, machinery whirring—were barely noticeable.

A shrill, blaring car horn broke the calm. Chelsia paused mid-stroke, her hand stilling on the horse's flank. She stepped back, setting the brush down on the edge of the stall before walking to the barn door.

Bennett was climbing out of his vehicle, tension in his broad frame. He looked flushed, and as Chelsia approached, she caught a flicker of something in his eyes: anger, maybe, though not directed at her.

"Morning," she said cautiously, her voice cutting through the crisp air.

Bennett nodded curtly. "Where's Bellamy?"

Chelsia frowned. "I haven't seen her yet. She must've gotten an early start somewhere on the farm."

His lips pressed into a line, and he turned toward the farmhouse without another word. Chelsia followed, curiosity prickling at the back of her mind.

Inside, the quiet of the house felt more intense with Bennett there, his presence charged like a storm cloud. He turned to her abruptly, reaching into his pocket and pulling out a thick envelope. He held it out to her.

"You already got me a gift," she said, eyeing the envelope warily.

"This is different," he replied, his voice low. "That's why I'm giving it to you with no one else around."

Chelsia hesitated before taking it. The envelope was heavier than she'd expected, and when she opened it, her breath caught. It was filled with cash.

"Bennett... what?" she began, but he cut her off with a casual wave of his hand, brushing aside her question.

"The weather's not going to be so bad in a few days," he said as their eyes met. "Text me. I don't care what time it is... but let me know when you're safely on the road." A tenseness appeared in his blue eyes. "You let me know soon. Understand?"

Chelsia's fingers tightened around the envelope as she met his eyes. In that moment, something shifted.

He knew.

He'd pieced it together, and now he wanted her out, away from this place, so he could face Bellamy without distractions.

Their shared gaze buzzed with the weight of unspoken words, and her thoughts fractured and collided. She'd underestimated him, his perceptiveness, and his resolve.

Before she could respond, a piercing, nearly primal scream tore through the air.

Both of them froze, the sound echoing through the walls of the farmhouse.

Bellamy.

The scream, raw and furious, chilled Chelsia to the bone.

Bennett's eyes darted to the door.

"Stay here," he ordered, his tone clipped, before striding outside.

Chelsia tucked the envelope deeply into her coat pocket as the shouting outside grew louder. Bellamy's voice carried across the yard, a torrent of rage and obscenities. Somewhere in the tirade, Evan's name surfaced repeatedly.

Chelsia heard his shaky, defensive responses, trying and failing to stem the tide of Bellamy's rage.

Bennett had told her to stay put, but the escalating chaos gnawed at her instincts. Chelsia hesitated only for a moment before stepping toward the door, her curiosity and unease driving her to investigate despite his warning.

When Chelsia rounded the corner of the barn, the chaos unfolded before her. Bellamy stood rigid near the hay baler, her face flushed and her gestures wild. Water pooled beneath the machine, spreading toward the equipment shed in muddy rivulets.

"What were you thinking?" Bellamy's voice cracked, her arms flailing toward the baler as though rage alone could undo the damage. "Do you have any idea what this costs? What you've destroyed?"

Evan stood a few paces away, his head bowed and his hands wringing together.

"I—I'm sorry. I didn't mean—"

"Sorry doesn't fix this!" Bellamy snapped, her words slicing through the cold air. "You've ruined it! This wasn't just some cheap piece of junk! It's worth more than you could ever imagine, and now it's wrecked because of your negligence!"

Chelsia glanced over at the nearby water pump. The hose Evan had connected the other day still lay stretched between the pump and the shed, its slack trailing through the mud like a careless afterthought.

He hadn't shut it off.

Bennett, standing a few steps away, looked visibly shaken. The calm he usually carried was gone, replaced by quiet disbelief.

"Bellamy, calm down," he said firmly. "I'm pretty sure Evan didn't mean—"

"Calm down?" Bellamy rounded on him, her eyes blazing. "I want this little punk arrested!"

"For what?" Bennett demanded, his voice rising for the first time.

"He destroyed a valuable piece of my property! I can't fix this!" Bellamy's voice climbed with each word, her fury nearly spilling over. "Neglect! Malice! Whatever you want to call it, it was his fault!"

"Bell," Bennett said, his tone softening. "Come on. Evan would never—"

"If you can't do your job, Ryan Bennett," she spat, her voice dripping venom, "I'll find someone who will!"

Chelsia froze where she stood, her eyes flickering between them. Bennett's jaw clenched, though he said nothing in response to the jab. He redirected his attention to a distraught Evan, visibly affected by Bellamy's rage.

"I just... I didn't think... I was only trying to help."

Bellamy sneered, her voice dropping to an acidic growl.

"Help? You've done enough. You're not even worth the meat on your bones, much less the trouble you've caused."

Her words echoed in the ensuing silence, harsh and final.

"Enough!" Bennett snapped, stepping forward. His tone carried an authority that silenced Bellamy's tirade. He turned to Evan, his voice softening. "Come on. Let's go."

Evan blinked, his voice cracking as he asked, "Go? Where?"

Bennett's lips thinned. He placed a hand on Evan's shoulder, gently guiding him toward the car. As they passed Chelsia, his tone was low.

"Let's give her time to cool off," he murmured. "We'll figure out what to do next."

Evan sniffled, his head hanging as he climbed into the passenger seat. Bennett hesitated, glancing back at Chelsia. Their eyes met, and in that moment, she saw the unspoken message:

Get ready to leave.

She nodded, her hand brushing against the envelope in her pocket.

As the car pulled away, the silence returned, broken only by the sound of Bellamy angrily kicking the hose, muttering curses under her breath. She straightened, her eyes locking onto Chelsia with an intensity that made her stomach twist.

They stared at each other across the yard, neither moving, neither speaking. The icy wind whipped between them, carrying with it any remaining reasons for Chelsia to stay.

CHAPTER FORTY-FIVE

The afternoon dragged, the hours bleeding into one another in a haze of halfhearted activities. Chelsia went through the motions of her chores, though her focus had shifted entirely. The weight of the envelope from Bennett was a tangible reminder of her to-do list.

Bellamy was absent for most of the day, her whereabouts unknown. Perhaps she needed a breather after what happened with Evan. The farmhouse, the barn, and the surrounding fields felt unnervingly quiet, like a held breath. Even the animals seemed subdued.

Chelsia's mind churned as she worked, the stillness amplifying her thoughts. She replayed Bennett's earlier words:

"... let me know when you're safely on the road... You let me know soon. Understand?"

She understood.

As the shadows lengthened and the sky deepened to a muted gray, Chelsia realized it would soon be time for dinner. She made her way back to the farmhouse, noting the unsettling stillness of the air.

Bellamy had reappeared, working in the kitchen with her usual fastidiousness, though she didn't hum, didn't speak, and her energy felt frayed at the edges. Chelsia eyed her. Bennett's warning echoed in her mind, and the unusual heaviness in the air felt like it was about more than the circumstances of Evan's departure.

After dinner—a silent, mechanical affair—Chelsia cleared the table without a word. Bellamy lingered, staring at nothing, her hands folded neatly in her lap. Chelsia hesitated before speaking.

"Thanks for dinner," she said calmly. "How about I make us both some tea? You keep it in the pantry, right?"

Bellamy's eyes met hers as she looked up, blinking. For a moment, it seemed she might refuse.

"That's sweet of you, Chelsia," she said, the corners of her mouth twitching upward to manufacture a smile. "Yes, thank you."

Chelsia nodded and went to the pantry. Her eyes quickly found the small, intricately labeled tin, but they shifted to the one beside it. She grabbed the latter, opened the lid, and inhaled. Berries. This was the one. A short while later, she returned to the table with two mugs, setting Bellamy's down first before taking a seat with her own.

"I appreciate this," Bellamy said, her tone distant. She lifted the mug to her lips, taking a slow sip. Her eyes remained on Chelsia, unblinking.

Chelsia smiled. "It's the least I could do."

Bellamy didn't respond. With a steady gaze, she continued to sip her tea.

Once in her room, Chelsia closed the door behind her and set the untouched mug on the bedside table. She worked quickly, folding each item of clothing and packing them into her bag along with personal items from the bathroom, as well as the locket and bracelet from the drawer. The duplicate lock remained in place, ready for use.

Soft creaks echoed through the farmhouse, the wind rattling the windows as night settled fully over the farm. She waited, ears tuned for the familiar creak of Bellamy's bedroom door closing. For over an hour, she forced herself to remain still, waiting until the house fell silent.

Finally, she slipped into her coat, slung the bag across her body with the strap settling diagonally over her chest, and tucked the lock into her pocket. Taking a breath, she was careful when opening the door to avoid any noise. She left it slightly ajar to suggest she might still be inside.

The hallway outside her room was dark, the shadows stretching toward the stairs. Chelsia tiptoed toward the staircase. Each board underfoot felt louder than it should, the quiet of the farmhouse amplifying even the smallest sound. Her pulse quickened when she reached the landing.

At the base of the stairs, she paused, glancing toward the closed door of Bellamy's bedroom. The faint hum of wind outside seemed to mask her movements as she eased toward the front door. Chelsia turned the knob, opening it just enough to slip outside. The chilled air wrapped around her, bringing a welcome clarity to her racing thoughts as she donned her gloves.

Under the moonlight, the yard stretched before her, vast and carrying a daunting stillness. On her way to the outbuilding, she paused at the equipment shed and eased the door open. Her gaze swept over the shelves, catching on a slim, tapered tool resting near the edge. She grabbed it, the cold metal reassuring in her grip, before also taking a flashlight from the top shelf as her breath puffed in visible clouds.

The lock on the door of the outbuilding gleamed in the moonlight, and she crouched down, studying it for a moment. Tamper-resistant, sure. But she'd dealt with worse and she came prepared. Sliding the tool into position, she began working it with slow, controlled movements. The tension stretched with each passing second; her gloved fingers tightening as the mechanism resisted. Finally, a soft click broke the silence, and the lock popped open. She replaced it with the duplicate, leaving it ajar as a reminder to close it again once she was done.

As she eased the door open, a wave of pungent, cold air with a metallic tang hit her, causing her stomach to clench. Chelsia hesitated for just a moment, her breath fogging in the chill, before stepping inside.

The air within was heavier, that same coppery smell mingling with the musty scent of dust and old wood. She swung the flashlight in a wide arc, its beam cutting through the darkness to reveal a cluttered, cavernous space.

Her first impression was how ordinary it seemed: shelves stacked with tools, jars of screws and nails, and various pieces of farming equipment. As the beam swept farther, the details became stranger.

On the far wall, a series of large diagrams caught her attention. She moved closer, footsteps cautious against the creaking floorboards. The first diagram was of livestock, pigs and cattle, sketched with clean lines and precision. Next to it, pinned like an afterthought, was something with a label that froze her in place: human anatomy.

The lines on this diagram were different, more specific. Arrows on handwritten notes, marked with words such as "yield" and "prime cuts," pointed to various sections of the body.

Her stomach turned as she forced herself to move on.

The light landed on a nearby table, its surface shimmering in the beam. Cleavers, bone saws, and hooks were arranged in neat rows. Though meticulously cleaned, they felt strangely out of place. She swallowed hard, bile rising in her throat as her fingers tightened around the flashlight.

The far corner of the room drew Chelsia next, where a small pile of folded clothing sat on a wooden crate. She approached it slowly, her heart pounding in her ears. On top of the pile was a dark blue shirt with a checkered texture and stitching along the cuffs.

It was Caleb's, just as she remembered it. And she recalled Bellamy's reaction to seeing Evan wearing a shirt so much like it.

Her breath caught, and for a moment, the room seemed to tilt. She stumbled back a step, the flashlight shaking in her hand. Caleb hadn't left the farm. He hadn't just disappeared, nor had he broken his promise to her.

At one point, he was inside the outbuilding.

The realization struck her with sickening clarity, the remaining puzzle pieces snapping into place. She forced herself to breathe, her pulse racing as she turned back toward the center of the room.

A small lockbox sat on a lower shelf, its lid slightly ajar. Chelsia walked over to it and crouched, her hands trembling as she opened it. Pay envelopes filled the space inside, their edges crumpled and some stained with rust-colored smears that could only be blood.

Names were scrawled across some of the envelopes: *Lenora. Paul. Sam. Caleb.*

Chelsia stared at them, her vision swimming. The envelopes, still containing cash, were heavy; their weight symbolizing more than just money.

Her flashlight swept the room one last time as she shoved the envelopes into her crossbody bag. The light captured another diagram, this one marked with intricate notations and measurements. Her mind refused to dwell on the details, the horror of it all overwhelming her senses as she made her way through the room, her breaths shaky as she neared the exit.

"That tea was a nice touch."

Chelsia froze, her blood running cold as she stopped in her tracks. Bellamy stood in the doorway, silhouetted by moonlight, a calm smile curving her lips.

"You had to know, though," Bellamy continued, her tone almost amused as she stepped inside, the door creaking shut behind her. "I've been drinking it for years. It has no effect on me."

Chelsia's flashlight beam landed on Bellamy's face. The smile she wore didn't reach her eyes, which glinted with something threatening.

"I knew you were clever," Bellamy said as she stepped closer. "This, though? This little caper of yours; meant, I assume, as a departing show of thanks for my stellar hospitality? I must admit, I'm impressed."

Bellamy's smile widened as she moved deeper into the outbuilding. "You've seen too much now, haven't you?" she said, her voice like venom-laced honey. "I suppose that means we're at the end of our little arrangement."

Chelsia's flashlight trembled in her hand, though she held her ground.

"I want nothing to do with this," she said firmly. "I just want to leave."

Bellamy's laugh was bitter, cutting through the suffocating air.

"Oh, Chelsia, you're so naïve. With everything you've seen, how can I possibly let you do that?"

Chelsia swallowed hard, her pulse pounding in her ears.

"If you think I can just disappear like the others, you're wrong. Bennett will know something's off and he'll come after you!"

Bellamy's smile didn't falter. "No, he won't," she said, her voice calm and unnervingly certain.

The words hit Chelsia like a blow. There was no time to process them as Bellamy lunged.

Chelsia twisted, the flashlight spinning out of her grasp and clattering to the floor. The beam flickered wildly, throwing chaotic shadows across the walls as Bellamy closed the distance with startling speed.

The impact knocked Chelsia backward into the table, where her fingers scrambled for anything she could use. Something solid and cold brushed her hand—a cleaver. She seized it instinctively, swinging it upward.

Bellamy was faster. Her hand shot out, gripping Chelsia's wrist and twisting hard. The cleaver slipped from her grasp, clattering to the floor between them. Chelsia hissed in pain, her other hand striking out in desperation.

Her fist connected with Bellamy's jaw, the blow forcing her to stagger back a step. As they separated, Chelsia had a brief window to escape, which Bellamy swiftly countered by grabbing a wrench from the table.

Chelsia narrowly avoided the wrench whistling viciously through the air as she ducked. The hefty tool slammed into the wall behind her, splintering the wood and shaking the shelves. She spun away, her heart racing as her eyes darted around the room for another weapon.

Bellamy didn't give her much time. She advanced with the wrench raised high, relentless. Chelsia's back hit the wall, and she ducked just as Bellamy swung again. The wrench grazed her shoulder, the force enough to send a jolt of pain through her arm.

Chelsia dropped into a crouch, her hand fumbling against a nearby shelf. Her fingers closed around a small hook, its curve biting into her palm.

She lashed out; the hook catching Bellamy's forearm with a sickening tear. Bellamy roared in pain, the wrench slipping from her grasp as she yanked the hook free. Blood smeared her arm, dripping to the floor. A wild look contorted her features.

"You're not getting out of here alive!" Bellamy screamed.

Chelsia didn't answer. Her eyes darted to the hay hook near the doorway. She bolted toward it, narrowly avoiding Bellamy's outstretched hand. The cold steel felt solid and reassuring in her grasp as she spun, swinging the hook in a wide arc.

The curved tip tore through Bellamy's shoulder, and she cried out, staggering back into the table. Chelsia pressed her advantage, slamming her weight into Bellamy and driving her into the scattered tools.

Bellamy's hand shot out, catching Chelsia in the ribs with a forceful shove. The breath rushed out of her lungs, leaving her gasping as Bellamy scrambled upright.

Blood dripped from Bellamy's arm and shoulder, staining her shirt and the floor beneath her, as the fire in her eyes burned hotter than ever.

"You're going to wish you'd run the moment you got here," she said, her voice trembling with fury.

Chelsia gripped the hay hook, her chest heaving as she raised it again. She swung, catching Bellamy across the thigh. The blade tore through fabric and flesh, and Bellamy's leg buckled beneath her.

Bellamy hit the floor with a grunt, her blood pooling beneath her as she clawed at the table for support. Her lips curled into a snarl as she struggled to rise, her injured leg trembling under the strain.

"You think this changes anything?" she spat. "You think you'll make it out of here?"

Chelsia didn't answer. Despite the pain in her lungs and muscles, she pushed on as she advanced. Bellamy's hand darted toward a pair of shears lying among the scattered tools. The blades gleamed in the flickering flashlight beam as Bellamy lunged, swinging with an accuracy born of fury.

Chelsia barely dodged in time, the shears slicing through the air inches from her throat. She retaliated with the hook, aiming low and catching Bellamy in the side. The hook bit deep, and Bellamy let out a guttural scream, the sound reverberating through the outbuilding. Chelsia yanked the hook free, blood spraying across the floor. Bellamy staggered before she swung wildly; the blades catching the edge of Chelsia's coat and tearing through the fabric.

Chelsia drove her shoulder into Bellamy's chest, slamming her into the wall. The impact rattled the tools on the shelves, several clattering to the ground. Bellamy's head struck the wood with a sickening crack, but she didn't stop.

The two women grappled, their clash frantic and brutal. Bellamy's fingers found Chelsia's throat, squeezing with relentless force. Chelsia clawed at Bellamy's hands, her vision blurring as her lungs screamed for air.

Her hand found the cleaver again, the cold metal a lifeline in her grasp. With the last of her strength, she swung inward; the blade carving a vicious path into Bellamy's side. The force of the blow sent Bellamy stumbling back, her grip loosening as blood poured from the wound.

Bellamy fell to one knee, her breaths ragged and uneven. She tried to rise, her body trembling with the effort. Chelsia was faster. As she raised the cleaver again, its weight felt significant in her grasp. She hesitated briefly, the moment hanging suspended, taut with expectation and finality.

"No!" Bellamy rasped, her voice barely audible.

Chelsia brought the cleaver down, the blade slicing through Bellamy's neck with a wet, sickening crunch. Blood sprayed in a gruesome arc, painting the walls and splattering across Chelsia's face. Bellamy's body crumpled to the floor, her head lolling at an unnatural angle. The room fell silent, the only sound the ragged rhythm of Chelsia's breathing.

Chelsia stepped back, her chest heaving as she stared down at Bellamy's lifeless form. The cleaver slipped from her trembling hand, clattering to the blood-soaked floor. The air was thick with the coppery smell of blood, overlaid by the impact of what had happened. She wiped her face with a trembling hand.

There was no time for delay. The chilled air hit her like a slap, stinging against her skin. Chelsia didn't look back as she disappeared into the shadows, leaving Bellamy and the horrors of Porter Farms behind.

CHAPTER FORTY-SIX

The road stretched ahead, shrouded in shadows cast by the sparse overhead lights. Slowed by the weight of recent events, Chelsia moved with an uneven gait. The wind bit at her skin, its chill barely registering against the burn of adrenaline coursing through her veins.

Staying near the roadside brush, she tried unsuccessfully to remain hidden from the streetlights. Her steps were cautious, her gaze shifting nervously between the shadows and the glow of the lights ahead. She had to keep moving. She had to get away.

Chelsia's breath hitched as she looked at her gloved hand, a dark smear of blood streaked across the palm. Blood dried on her skin, her jacket was torn, and her clothes were disheveled. The thought occurred to her that she should have stayed at the farm long enough to get cleaned up, but it wasn't worth the risk.

Her heart pounded as she shoved her hand into her pocket, her mind racing.

I can't text Bennett. Not now. Maybe never.

The thought came unbidden, twisting in her chest like a blade. She forced herself to keep walking, the idea of stopping unbearable. She needed as many miles as possible between herself and the farm before anyone could see her.

Before anyone could stop her—again.

The words barely settled in her mind when the soft purr of an engine broke through the stillness. Chelsia's breath caught, and she pressed herself deeper into the shadows. The beam of headlights swept over the road, their harsh glow a spotlight on her retreating figure.

The vehicle slowed.

A sleek, black SUV, newer and expensive, came up behind her, idling to a stop. Chelsia's body tensed, her instincts screaming at her to run, but her legs refused to obey. She edged further into the brush, her pulse hammering as she silently prayed for the driver to pass.

A voice, smooth and unmistakably amused, shattered her hope.

"I can see you."

Chelsia froze, her breath catching in her throat. The words were casual, almost playful, but their impact was immense. Slowly, she turned, her mind racing through her options. Continuing alone and vulnerable on foot felt overwhelmingly bleak and unrealistic. Her eyes fell upon the SUV, and a wave of nausea washed over her. The passenger-side window was down, and a man leaned toward it, his bright smile a startling contrast to the dark night.

His face was angular, wide at the forehead, with chiseled cheekbones tapering to a delicate, squared jawline. Clean-shaven, his thick black hair was neatly styled, and his sculpted eyebrows framed brilliant blue eyes that studied her with unsettling calm. A single dimple studded his right cheek, softening the lines of his face.

"Wow," he said, his tone smooth, "you must have had a wild evening."

Pausing, his smile broadened as he took in her tousled appearance.

"Looks like I found you just in time."

EPILOGUE

Revelation

The suite was a sanctuary of modern luxury. A king-sized bed, made with crisp white linens, was the centerpiece of the room. Textured walls in muted grays and taupes complemented the space. The furniture exuded quiet luxury; every piece prioritized both comfort and style. Floor-to-ceiling windows on one side offered a stunning view of the city's skyline, softened by the pale morning light. Extending just beyond the windows was a balcony, its glass railings gleaming subtly under the dim sky.

In one corner, a grand piano stood like a silent sentinel, its polished surface reflecting the soft glow of the minimalist chandelier above. The suite's sophisticated design included a sleek TV mounted opposite the dining table.

The air carried a clean scent, a stark contrast to the tang of blood still clinging to Chelsia's senses. Her body ached as she stirred, a vivid reminder of the night before. The crisp sheets beneath her felt alien as she stared at the ceiling, her breaths steady while her mind worked to catch up with reality.

Bruised and sore, she gingerly sat up, her muscles protesting with every movement. The room was quiet, save for the distant murmur of the city beyond the glass. The pristine bedroom felt worlds away from the blood-soaked horrors she had left behind.

She forced herself to stay present, anchoring within the surreal safety of this place. Swinging her legs over the side of the bed, her bare feet met the plush carpet. The ache in her limbs carried the weight of every frantic moment, every desperate swing of the cleaver, every instinct that had brought her here.

The bathroom was a sanctuary of marble and glass, its design echoing the understated elegance of the suite. Steam rose as she turned on the shower, the water's warmth beckoning her like a reprieve.

She stepped under the spray, letting it cascade over her bruised skin, the heat chasing away the persistent chill in her bones. The night's events remained stubbornly etched in her memory: flashes of Bellamy's rage, the confirmation of what became of Sam, Caleb, and others, and the visceral stains that seemed to cling to her even now.

Chelsia tilted her head back, letting the water stream over her face and hair, as if it could wash away the memories as easily as it did the grime and gore. But the weight of what she'd done lingered, heavy and unyielding—a silent companion she knew would follow her wherever she went.

She stayed under the water longer than she intended, her fingers tracing the scratches and bruises that dotted her arms. The scalding heat turned lukewarm, and she finally stepped out, wrapping herself in one of the thick robes hanging nearby. She was securing her wet hair in a microfiber towel when something stopped her in her tracks: a soft series of notes.

She emerged from the bedroom of the suite to find a man sitting at the piano, his fingers moving across the keys. The melody was exploratory, as though he were testing the instrument rather than performing.

He glanced up, his dimpled smile bright against the chiseled lines of his angular face.

"Good morning," he said, his tone cheerful and unhurried. "I hope you're feeling rested."

He exuded an air of effortless composure, his dark hair neatly styled, his blue eyes alight, and his pointed features softened by the warmth of his smile. Nothing seemed to faze him—not even when he'd come upon Chelsia scurrying away from Porter Farms, clearly having committed an unforgivable sin. He had welcomed her warmly into his vehicle, blood-splattered as she was, and made sure her face and hands were clean enough to escape scrutiny before securimg her lodgings for the night.

"What an evening you've had," he added, as if they were discussing the weather.

Her throat tightened, and she swallowed hard.

"Listen, I—" Chelsia began, her voice barely above a whisper.

The man rose gracefully from the bench, stopping her with a gesture, his tailored suit fitting him perfectly as he crossed the room toward her.

"You don't have to say anything," he said gently. "Not yet, anyway. Breakfast first."

He gestured toward the table, stepping aside as if giving her space to move at her own pace. Chelsia paused, glancing at the tray on the table by the window. The smell of something delicious escaped from beneath the covered dishes, and the unmistakable aroma of coffee wafted through the air.

She looked between him and the inviting spread before drifting to the table, lowering herself into one of the upholstered chairs. The man remained standing, his posture relaxed yet attentive, as though watching her was as effortless as breathing.

Chelsia lifted the silver dome from one of the dishes, revealing Eggs Florentine, thick-cut bacon, and slices of buttery croissant toast. The smell was rich, and her stomach twisted, part hunger, part unease.

The man reached for the carafe, pouring a cup of coffee and placing it in front of her.

"Were you able to sleep at all?" he asked casually.

"A little," she replied, wrapping her fingers around the cup.

"You look better than when I picked you up," he said, dimpling.

"Why'd you bring me here?" she asked.

"You needed to rest," he said simply.

"I could have rested just as easily in a motel."

He chuckled softly, the sound low and easy. "Why settle?" His eyes glinted with amusement as he studied her. "Have you decided what you're going to do next?"

Chelsia stiffened. "The only thing I've decided is that this city isn't the place for me," she said, her tone clipped.

He nodded slowly. "That's fair. I've felt the same way for months now." His eyes briefly rested on the window. "I've been here, trying to figure out my next move... waiting for something." His smile returned, the dimple in his cheek deepening. "Now I see I wasn't waiting for something, just someone."

Chelsia scoffed, letting out a short, incredulous laugh. "You don't even know me."

His smile didn't waver. "That's easily fixed," he said, extending a hand toward her. "The name's Gabriel."

She hesitated before taking his hand. Despite his powerful grip, his long, tapered fingers and soft skin seemed strangely delicate.

"I'll let you enjoy your breakfast," Gabriel said, releasing her hand. "While you eat, you should check the forecast. I think there's a hell of a storm brewing."

Chelsia frowned in confusion as he gestured toward the television on the wall. With seemingly all the time in the world, he moved languidly toward the piano.

She noticed the remote beside the breakfast tray. Her appetite faded, the food forgotten as she hesitated before picking it up. With a press of a button, the television flickered to life, the image of a somber news anchor filling the screen. The words scrolling across the bottom of the broadcast left her breathless:

BREAKING: GRISLY DISCOVERIES AT PORTER FARMS—POLICE INVESTIGATE LINKED DISAPPEARANCES

Reckoning

"We're continuing our coverage of a breaking story out of Canby. Porter Farms, a beloved staple of the area, is now the center of a grisly and unfolding investigation that's left its community in shock.

"Authorities swarmed the property early this morning after a mechanic, contacted yesterday about a broken hay baler, discovered what officials called a horrific scene.

"Initial reports confirm the presence of evidence suggesting the property was the site of a multi-year operation involving the use of human remains. Though details remain sparse, speculation has already begun regarding a connection between that operation and a signature product of the company, the award-winning Porter Sausage.

"51-year-old Bellamy Janine Porter, of the acclaimed Porter family, was discovered dead on the property. Known as a prominent figure in the Canby agricultural community and a celebrated humanitarian, Porter's death was confirmed to be the result of a confrontation on the premises. Investigators have not disclosed additional details.

"Also included in the investigation is Sergeant Ryan Bennett, a senior officer out of a precinct within the City of Portland. Bennett's vehicle was located on the outskirts of Porter Farms; however, he appears to be missing. Sources confirm that he was last seen yesterday afternoon at his precinct after processing the release of Evan Clarke, 22, on unrelated charges. Clarke has been ruled out as a person of interest in this case and has declined to comment for the purposes of this story.

"Bennett's presence at the property is questionable, since he wasn't known to be handling any cases in the Canby area. Officials continue to search for answers as the investigation unfolds.

"Meanwhile, the findings at Porter Farms have sent shockwaves through Canby, a community that once celebrated the Porter family as pillars of trust and tradition. Many are struggling to reconcile the image of a beloved local business with the horrifying allegations now emerging.

"This story is still developing, and we will provide updates as more information becomes available."

The room was silent as the television screen shifted to muted footage of the farm. Chelsia sat frozen, her breath shallow, her hands clenched in her lap.

The anchor's words echoed in her mind: *Bennett's vehicle was located... no sign of him... presence at the property is questionable.*

Chelsia's thoughts flashed to the fight in the outbuilding, to Bellamy's cold, calculated certainty when she'd insisted Bennett would go after Bellamy if she disappeared.

No, he won't, Bellamy had said, her voice calm, her smile chilling.

Chelsia exhaled shakily, her pulse loud in her ears. Bennett had gone back. She didn't need the report to fill in the gaps; the truth was obvious.

She looked down at her untouched breakfast, then back at the screen. Her breath caught, the enormity of everything crashing over her. Chelsia turned slowly to find Gabriel standing near the piano, watching her with an enigmatic smile.

"Some storm, huh?" he said.

Requiem

The winter sky had darkened by the time Chelsia reached Moira's house, the small porch light casting a feeble glow over the walkway. She hesitated on the steps, her breath clouding in the cold air as she glanced back toward the empty street. Finally, she rang the doorbell.

The door creaked open, and Moira's face appeared, her expression shifting from surprise to something guarded.

"Chelsia?" Moira asked, her tone a mixture of confusion and suspicion. "What are you doing here?"

Chelsia looked down, her shoulders hunched against the chill. "I—I didn't know where else to go," she murmured.

Moira's eyes, now slightly narrowed, reflected her curiosity.

"Where have you been?" she asked, stepping partially into the doorway. "Gillian tried calling a few times, and your number was disconnected. She hasn't shut up about it for weeks."

Chelsia swallowed hard, her eyes glistening as she looked up. "I've been... trying to figure things out," she whispered. "I thought I could, and now..." Her voice broke, and she shook her head. "I don't know what I'm doing anymore."

Moira's posture relaxed just enough, her suspicion giving way to a guarded sympathy. "You look like hell," she said bluntly, though her tone lacked malice. "I suppose you'd better come in before you freeze to death."

Chelsia stepped inside, her arms folded across her chest as Moira closed the door and leaned against it. "So?" Moira said, folding her arms. "What's this all about?"

Hesitantly, Chelsia looked down at the floor. "I don't even know where to start," she admitted, her voice barely above a whisper.

Moira gestured toward the living room, her tone brusque. "Well, sit down or something. You're making me nervous just standing there."

Chelsia nodded and moved toward the worn couch, lowering herself onto the edge of the cushion. She clasped her hands in her lap, her shoulders still hunched.

From the armchair opposite, Moira watched her intently. "I can't believe you've been gone this long without a word," she said, her voice carrying equal parts exasperation and curiosity. "What have you been doing?"

Chelsia's lips parted as though to answer, but she hesitated, her eyes darting to the floor.

"It's hard to explain," she said finally. "I thought... maybe if I left, I could figure things out. It didn't work. I just ended up feeling more lost."

With a tilt of her head, Moira's expression softened. "You're not the only one who's been dealing with a mess, you know. Gillian's been in a mood ever since you left, and Becky... ugh, don't get me started."

Chelsia's brow furrowed as she looked up. "What about Becky?"

Moira rolled her eyes, leaning back in her chair. "She's been playing up to everyone like she's the best thing that ever happened to the apothecary. It's making me look bad, Chelsia. Me."

Chelsia stared at her blankly. "I didn't mean to make things harder for you," she mumbled.

Moira scoffed, waving a dismissive hand. "You didn't, really. I mean, you leaving was inconvenient, sure, but Gillian's been riding my ass ever since. Now Becky's got her all convinced she's some kind of prodigy." She paused, her voice taking on a speculative tone. "Maybe I could talk Gillian into figuring something out for you. Now that you've come to your senses."

Chelsia's jaw clenched as she lowered her head. "That's... kind of you," she murmured.

Moira leaned forward, her elbows on her knees, as she studied Chelsia more closely.

"What's really going on, Chelsia? Why'd you come back here?"

Chelsia's smile was distant. "I guess I missed having someone to talk to. I remembered how much... easier things were when I was here."

Moira, mollified, leaned back in her chair with a satisfied air. "Well, I can understand that. Things were good here when we lived together." She leaned forward. "That's all I was trying to get you to see after you decided to up and move out for... you know."

Chelsia nodded slowly. "Yes... I know." She glanced toward the hallway, her voice tentative. "Could I... use your bathroom?"

Moira waved a hand toward the hallway. "Sure. You know where it is."

Chelsia rose and went to the bathroom, quietly shutting the door behind her. She soon returned, her face calm as she re-entered the living room. Moira glanced up from her phone, her brow lifting expectantly.

"Feel better?" Moira asked.

"A little," Chelsia replied, offering a gentle smile as she moved toward the couch.

"You can take that coat off, you know."

"Yeah, of course I know," Chelsia agreed good-naturedly. "It's just that I still have something of a chill. Seems like I've been cold forever." With a pause, her eyes scanned the room until they rested on Moira. "Would it be okay if I made us something to drink? Tea, maybe?"

Moira blinked, clearly surprised by the gesture. "Tea?" she echoed, her lips twitching in a smirk. "Yeah, sure. Knock yourself out."

Chelsia nodded and disappeared into the kitchen. After a moment, the quiet gurgle of the kettle and a clink of mugs carried into the living room. Moira barely seemed to notice.

"You know, Gillian's been driving me insane since you left," Moira began, leaning back in her chair. "I swear, it's like she's forgotten everything I've done for that place. Becky this, Becky that—it's nauseating. You'd think she's the chick version of Jesse Boot or something."

She gave a sharp laugh, gesturing with her hands as she continued. "The other day, Becky suggested rearranging the displays, you remember how particular Gillian is about those and how she's always wanted that lived-in look. And you know what? Gillian actually agreed. Can you believe that?

"And don't even get me started on the staff meeting last week. You heard me—staff meeting! We never had those before, and now every Thursday we close for lunch to have one. Which means I'm working an extra hour every week."

The kettle clicked off in the kitchen, the soft clink of spoons against ceramic punctuating Moira's rant as she sighed, rubbing her temples.

"Whatever. Let Becky have her little moment. Gillian has to get tired of it eventually. I'm seriously regretting even suggesting Becky get hired."

Chelsia returned moments later with two steaming mugs, setting one on the coffee table in front of Moira before taking her seat on the couch with her own. Moira, still caught up in her tirade, reached for her mug, blowing gently at the steam before taking a sip.

"And you know what Becky said to me when I told her she was doing too much?" Moira continued. "She said, 'I think it's important to be open to a fresh perspective.' A fresh perspective. Can you believe the nerve?"

Chelsia chuckled softly, her gaze dropping to the rim of her mug. "Well, a fresh perspective can be nice... but only if the person suggesting it shares your goals."

Moira's shoulders relaxed slightly as she took another sip. "True," she said with a small nod, her tone almost approving. "I didn't ask, so she shouldn't have offered."

Chelsia lifted her mug, taking a slow sip before lowering it to her lap. Moira smirked, leaning back in her chair.

"So, what's the plan now?"

Chelsia shook her head thoughtfully. "I'm still deciding," she admitted. "I was in a rush at first... but it's no longer necessary."

Moira waved a hand dismissively. "Well, of course not. You're here now. That's what matters."

The two lapsed into a brief silence. As Chelsia sipped her drink, she looked at Moira's mug.

Moira cradled the mug in her hands, letting out a soft sigh. "I'll give Becky one thing, though—she's got energy. Probably all those ridiculous smoothies she drinks. You know the kind, with kale and flaxseed and whatever else health nuts think will make them invincible."

Chelsia smiled, her expression unreadable. Moira took another sip, her words faltering, as though she were organizing her thoughts. She shifted in her seat, a crease forming on her brow.

"Anyway," Moira resumed, her tone slower, "she can't keep this up. She has to burn out eventually, or get bored. Chicks like her use the apothecary for work experience before trying to get into an OHSU pharmacy or something."

Chelsia nodded absently as Moira rubbed her temple.

"I've been getting these headaches lately," Moira remarked, almost as an afterthought. "Probably from all the stress Gillian puts me under. I swear, sometimes I think—" She broke off, blinking rapidly as though trying to clear her vision. "Huh. That's weird."

"What is?" Chelsia asked, keeping her tone casual.

"I don't know. My head feels... off. Like it's swimming. And my arms feel—" She frowned deeply, her voice trailing as she flexed the fingers of her free hand. "They feel tingly. Kind of numb."

Chelsia set her mug down on the coffee table, leaning forward slightly. "You okay?"

Moira blinked, irritation flashing across her face. "Of course I'm okay!" she snapped, though her words slurred slightly. Her hand trembled, the mug wobbling precariously in her grip, the liquid inside rippling dangerously. "Damn it," she muttered as she set it on the table with an audible clink.

"Maybe you should lie down," Chelsia suggested, her voice calm.

Moira shook her head, though the motion was sluggish. "No, I don't need to lie down. I just need—" She stopped mid-sentence, staring down at her hands, her eyes unfocused as her fingers flexed weakly. "Why... why do my hands feel so weird?"

Her breathing quickened, her chest rising and falling erratically as she shifted in her chair, her movements growing jerky.

"Chelsia," Moira said, her voice trembling now. "Something's wrong. I feel... I feel..." Her words faded as her wide eyes locked on Chelsia, her dawning fear stark and unmissable. "What did you—"

Chelsia stared impassively at the mug on the table's edge. Moira's head lolled to the side, her body sinking deeper into the chair. Each breath rasped louder, shallower, against the silence of the room.

Chelsia reclined, hands folded, eyes locked on Moira. Her calm demeanor betrayed no urgency as the seconds ticked by. The only sound left was the whistle of the wind against the window, punctuating the stillness between them.

Moira's breathing had grown faint, her head lolling further as her body slumped into the chair. Chelsia watched her for a long moment before rising, her mug in hand.

"Now it's my turn to talk," Chelsia said coldly.

She moved to the kitchen, her steps unhurried as she rinsed the mug under the tap. She scrubbed the rim carefully, inspecting it before setting it on the drying rack.

"Do you know why I came back, Moira?" she asked, her voice carrying easily into the living room. "Not for closure, if that's what you're thinking. Closure is a fantasy for people who don't know how to let go."

Chelsia returned to the living room, standing just inside the doorway as she studied Moira's slackening features. "Now, you? You've been clinging to the past. Holding onto grudges. You just couldn't let it go, could you?"

She moved closer, her shadow falling over Moira as she leaned against the arm of the chair. "If you hadn't been so vindictive... so stupid and childish... so jealous of what I had with Michael," Chelsia hissed, "none of this would have happened."

Moira's lips twitched, as if trying to form words. Chelsia crouched beside her, her voice hardening.

"You couldn't handle the fact that I moved out of here to be with him. I had to deal with your snide comments and your bullshit for a year. And, what did you do? You intentionally called out sick on the morning of my anniversary, forcing me to go into work instead of being able to stay home with Michael. Petty, vindictive Moira, trying to make her point."

Chelsia's eyes darkened, her tone softening.

"Gillian thought she was doing me a favor. Can you believe that? She said I could scurry on home for an extended break and surprise Michael. Get a little extra time on the clock.

"Alan—the doorman—was nowhere to be found, probably off handling some meaningless delivery when I got home and went upstairs to surprise Michael."

Her lips curved into a bitter smile.

"I ended up with the surprise, though."

She rose and paced, each word landing sharper than the last.

"I walked in, and there he was—with Katherine Talbert. In the shower."

Chelsia paused, her voice hardening with barely restrained fury.

"Fucking."

She let the silence hang before continuing, her tone now eerily calm.

"They were way too busy to hear me, and I wasn't about to interrupt, so what else could I do? I needed to be quick, though. The windows were already shut tight because of the weather. All it took was turning off the pilot light in the fireplace before tampering with the valve just enough for gas to seep out."

Chelsia stared at the window, lost in the memory.

"Lucky for me, I slipped out of the building before Alan got back. Alan. I found out that he helped Michael smuggle Katherine into the building without a paper trail." She chuckled. "Just like he'd done for me since the first night Michael brought me to Marlowe House." She clicked her tongue. "It's surprising how something I thought set me apart would come full circle like that. No wonder they fired him.

"Anyway," she continued with a sigh, "I got back to work with Gillian being none the wiser. I guess that Michael and Katherine were so tired after their watery tryst that they went to bed and just... slept. Long enough. Deeply enough. Forever."

Her voice grew wistful. "It would have never happened if it weren't for you, Moira."

Chelsia crouched again, her tone turning colder. "Portland was supposed to be different. Michael was supposed to be different. Special. But, I lost him... just like I lost Jordan and Matthew and Shawn..." She trailed off, a smirk tugging at her lips. "And... oh gosh, what was his name again? Shit. Oh, well." Her eyes returned to Moira. "Michael was going to be my clean slate."

Chelsia reached into her pocket, pulling out the empty prescription bottle she had taken from the bathroom earlier. She examined it thoughtfully, turning it over and over in her hands.

"Gillian loves pushing pills, doesn't she?" she mused in a mocking tone. "I knew that if she was anywhere near as persistent with you as she was with me, there'd be something fun in your bathroom, and there was!" She shook the bottle. "Half a tablet is strong enough to knock someone out for hours, but you just had to take..." She glanced at the label, her smile widening. "... five. Poor little Moira."

She placed the bottle on the coffee table beside the empty mug, arranging them neatly.

"Distraught at being alone. Overlooked at work because of the new girl. Can't even get a pharmacy tech license because everyone knows you're a thief."

Chelsia straightened, her gaze cool and detached. "It must have all been too much. And Gillian, bless her heart, unwittingly gave you the means to end it all. She'll have some explaining to do to the Oregon Board of Pharmacy, won't she? I mean, especially when they find the other bottles you have with her handwriting on the labels."

Moira's chest rose and fell weakly, each breath shallower than the last as her head lolled to one side. Chelsia tilted her head, studying Moira's slackening form with something close to admiration. Everything was falling into place, just as it should. It always did when people learned their place—or were taught it.

Chelsia's lips curved into a smile as she chuckled. Imagine that. Bellamy's words. Amidst all her inane ramblings, Bellamy said something that stuck.

Her movements were careful, methodical. Chelsia wiped her own fingerprints from the bottle with the hem of her coat and adjusted it to an angle that would draw attention to the name on the label. Moira's mug remained untouched, the residue of tea clinging to its sides.

Chelsia stepped back, taking a moment to survey the scene. The scent of the tea still hung in the air, mingling with the warmth of the room. Everything was in place. With one last glance at Moira's lifeless form, she turned and walked to the door. The crisp night air greeted her as she stepped outside, the wind brushing against her face like a familiar companion.

The black SUV was silent as it pulled up in front of the house. Its headlights cut through the darkness, illuminating the path before her. As the passenger window descended, a familiar, dimpled smile came into view.

Chelsia grinned, each step toward the waiting vehicle bringing her closer to exactly where she belonged.

Their journey is far from over.
Chelsia and Gabriel will return.

AUTHOR'S NOTE

Every story begins as a whisper—an idea that tugs at the edges of my mind until it refuses to be ignored. This book was no different, but its journey was uniquely challenging.

This novel was planned as my second publication, following 2018's *Duality*. But while I was working on the manuscript, I realized the original premise too closely resembled the plot of a major motion picture that debuted during the writing process. Technically, I'd started my novel first—but who would believe that? Even I would've been skeptical if the roles were reversed.

So, I stepped away from the book entirely and shifted my focus to the project that took its place—*Vitae*, which became my second novel, published in 2020.

Still, the characters (and the mayhem I wanted to bring into their lives) never left me. I had no plans to use the original material, but *Duality* had set the stage, making it necessary to continue this narrative.

I can honestly say that this experience deepened my appreciation for the creative process. Starting over allowed me to build a stronger foundation—a new world, new plot, and new entanglements for Chelsia to navigate as she prepares to take her place.

To my readers: Thank you for stepping into this world and following me through its twists and shadows. Your enthusiasm and encouragement remind me of why I write—your curiosity and support breathe life into these stories. Whether you've been with me from the very beginning or are just discovering my work, I'm deeply grateful.

Finally, a quiet thank-you to the characters themselves. You've grown with me, stretched me, and—yes—kept me awake far too many nights. I can't wait to share the next step in your journey with readers who will love you (or fear you) just as much as I do.

Ametra

Discover where it all began with the prologue from...

DUALITY

She crouched as she forced her body deep inside the crowded closet. She wiped tears from her cheeks and shuddered as her fingertips grazed the clots of blood and flesh stuck to her skin. Gritting her teeth, she swallowed as bile rose in her throat.

An ear-splitting scream rang out. Guttural gurgles answered, twisting into something like laughter. She heard panting and the wet slap of bare feet scurrying down the hallway toward her. Her eyes flicked upward to the doorknob. She grasped the knob and held it in place with all her strength. As it rattled in her hands, she heard frustration and terror.

"Please!" a female voice cried. "I know you're in there! I heard you come this way. Let me in! Why is this happening?"

She closed her eyes, pressing her forehead against the cool wooden door as she tightened her grip. She did not know why this was happening. She should not have been there...

"PLEASE!" the voice on the other side of the door screamed. "You can't just stay in there and let this happen to me! Why won't you... NO!"

Pleas turned to choking.

Bones broke.

A high-pitched giggle followed, then the unmistakable sounds of flesh tearing and being devoured.

The victim's whimpering turned into a raspy keening... then nothing.

The stench of blood thickened in the closet. The sounds of sloppy consumption filled her ears while slippery blood crept beneath the crack of the closet door.

Minutes passed after the smacking ceased.

She caught a glimpse of a hulking shadow beneath the door.

She heard its purring as if content with the meal.

That was it. The others were gone.

She remained still, wondering how long she would have to wait, hoping her friend hadn't made it aware that someone was still left. Her grip on the doorknob trembled, but held fast.

A flickering shadow beneath the door locked her in place.

The door burst apart.

She screamed as it snatched her into the hallway.

www.ingramcontent.com/pod-product-compliance
Lightning Source LLC
Chambersburg PA
CBHW072349020726
47506CB00004B/1064